zen

and the
city of angels

also by elizabeth m. cosin

zen and the art of murder

zen

and the

city of angels

elizabeth m. cosin

st. martin's minotaur 🐟 new york

Library of Congress Cataloging-in-Publication Data
Cosin, Elizabeth M.
    Zen and the city of angels / Elizabeth M. Cosin. — 1st St.
  Martin's Minotaur ed.
      p.   cm.
    ISBN 0-312-20611-9
    I. Title.
  PS3553.0748Z34   1999
  813'.54 — dc21   99-15940
                                                            CIP

First Edition: October 1999

10   9   8   7   6   5   4   3   2   1

For Inaki,
who is in every word I write and *every breath I take,*
and
Dr. Patricia McCormack,
who put me back together again

acknowledgments

Thanks go out to my buddies in L.A. and elsewhere (including the real Father's Office) who prop me up when I need it. Too many to mention, but you know who you are. Also to Bob Crais, my friend, mentor and drinking buddy: thanks for being there to set me straight, pal.

A nod as well to Paul Sanchez for pushing me past my limits.

Nothing on the following pages would be possible without the love and support of my wonderful family: my sisters Anne and Susan, my brother-in-law David, and Jonathan, my brother the doctor, who, along with Dr. Jeff Abrahams, advises me on the medical stuff. Thanks, Jonathan and Jeff—if I got anything wrong, the mistakes are mine, not yours.

My parents, Toby and Allen, get a special thank you for putting up with my daily phone calls and years of raiding their reference library, historical memory, refrigerator and wallet when I've had no place else to go.

The real Martin Bergstein is my uncle and he was kind enough to lend me his name for a character who bears no resemblance to him, except where tennis is concerned.

Also to my cousin Emily Cosin, whose name I appropriated as well. Emily's not like the fictional Emily either—she's much cooler than that.

The writing, of course, is mine, but it wouldn't have become this book without the patient guidance of my editor Joe Veltre and the considerable assistance of Susie Putnam, copyeditor, consultant, advisor, friend and the wisest person I know.

Thanks also to Erika Fad at SMP for being there for me even if it was just to have someone to talk to.

Finally to my agent, Dino Carlaftes, for his undying faith in me and my work. The feeling is mutual.

While many of the places in this book are real, the author took liberties with the details. In other words, don't go searching the Santa Monica map for a pet cemetery. Along with other places and people within these pages, it doesn't exist anywhere but here.

PART ONE

one

Earthquakes scare the hell out of me. It's not so much the shaking. Or even the noise, which during significant quakes is like a steam engine bearing through every living room, breaking china, everywhere, all at once.

It's knowing that nothing, not even the ground you're standing on, is solid enough to keep from breaking apart at any moment. The revelation that there are greater forces at work every second of every day tearing down what you and every person who ever lived spent building up.

The funny thing is I never think about this while my world is shaking to bits, or even after it brings a whole damned city to its knees, making nervous wrecks out of even the most grounded among us. It only comes to me when I'm working a case, mired in the muck of some poor slob's personal trash heap, trying to make sense of why people who live such tenuous existences do such horrible things to each other.

And why knowing this doesn't make them try any harder to keep from falling between the cracks.

Some cases remind me of this more than others. Like this one. Here I was slumped low in the driver's seat of a nondescript rental car on the last legs of a September evening, mainlining Jamaica Mountain from a Thermos and listening to Albert King's blues, trying to remember what had led me here. I was on a stakeout, a stakeout for a fucking dog.

———

It all started with a favor. Come to think of it, everything bad in my life has started with a favor. Maybe it's the burden of being a private eye or maybe it's just because deep down I'm nothing like I pretend to be, a hard ass with gun.

Truth is when I let my guard down, I'm a sucker of mammoth proportions. It's a quality I hate even more than my eyes, two green-colored traitors, ready to betray my innermost feelings at the most inappropriate moment. Problem is I have no control over any of it.

I've always had jobs that trade on favors. When I was a sportswriter, it came in the form of swapping information and I find it's been good practice for my present profession. But there are all kinds of favors. Some carry more weight than others and require a greater investment of yourself. The kind you do because at the end of the day, you understand there is no choice. All you can do then is hope you survive it.

Two weeks ago, James Leroy Gray made such a request. The lesser part of me was still pissed I had said yes, and I didn't even know why.

two

The Santa Anas were blowing fierce that dull fall afternoon I drove to Century City to see Jim. It has been a relatively uneventful season. Summer came and went and except for the usual two weeks in August, it hadn't melted any asphalt. No riots, no big celebrity murder trials, no earthquakes and only a half dozen car chases. A mundane Los Angeles summer.

The Santa Anas don't come every year, but when they do, they churn up the sky like sharks to chum-infested waters. It's not the only thing they stir up.

September isn't the month most people would choose to be here. Some call it Indian Summer, those days that hang on in a desperate attempt to fend off fall, only it's like a gene is missing and the result is some mutant form of summer and fall, with a whole new heat of its own.

The Santa Anas have a lot to do with this, dragging thick, hot winds across the Southland with such ferocity, they seem to pick up every free particle that's not nailed down. It makes for some uncomfortable weather, the kind that gets up your nose, into your eyes and underneath your skin. There's a theory, too, that it makes people do crazy things. Like they needed any help.

We were heading for October with no sign of the Santa Anas and everyone was hoping they'd stay away this year. But I could hear the roar of the wind outside my open bedroom window just before sunrise and when I finally crawled out of bed, the back of my throat was raw and hoarse.

It seemed like a bad omen to me. I have this thing about omens and even as I made the short drive to Jim's high-rise office building, I felt a queasiness in the pit of my stomach.

I turned my radio up trying to drown out my inner voice with some Lucinda Williams country kick-ass, but it wasn't working. Even the scars on my chest from where they'd removed my cancerous lung eighteen months ago were starting to itch.

Jim's office was on the upper floors of a forty story building, a monument of glass and steel that reflected the daily Southern California sunshine as if it was trying to send it back to its source.

I parked the Alfa in the massive parking garage that covers three or four city blocks under Century City. It was built on what used to be a part of the Twentieth Century Fox lot back when studios owned movie stars and not vice versa. I hoped I'd be able to find it when I got back.

I strolled into the sterile lobby with the late-morning stragglers and visitors and seeing an open elevator door, quickened to beat it shut. I knew at least one person saw me hurry to make the elevator, because I locked eyes with him as the doors closed, leaving me alone in the massive lobby.

His shrug meant my feelings of dread were founded. Any other day, he would have held the door one more second. But the Santa Anas were back and like the moon and bad seafood, they made people turn on themselves. As if all the silt and debris they blew up were ominous harbingers of things to come, as if the very wind was a carrier of evil.

I was cursing them the whole thirty-nine floor ride up the next elevator to Jim's office suite.

———

The doors opened into the wood-paneled splendor that is home to J. L. Gray, Attorney-at-law. It's pretty fancy digs for a guy who represents people like me. But that's just one of Jim's many contradictions.

A former cop, Jim drinks with us at Father's Office, as comfortable belly-up to the bar as the neighborhood drunks and yet as a lawyer, he can tear apart a witness with the conscience of an office shredder.

Jim's a deeply private man who looks for answers inside himself and finds strength in the singularity of his own soul and the certainty it will get him through the night. I don't quite understand this in him, but I know I share some of the same qualities and while his mysterious nature irritates me, I still find it admirable.

Born in Minnesota and raised in Santa Monica, Jim is part Dakota Indian, a bloodline he can trace back to the Battle of Little Bighorn.

We've known each other for years. My friend and sometime partner Bobo introduced us back when we were all still living up in San Francisco. Jim was a cop, working the streets of San Francisco and going to night school.

He migrated south before we did and got a job with the LAPD while he was finishing up Law School at UCLA. He was the one who introduced me to Father's Office, my local pub. But times have changed and outside my occasional visits to his office, we don't see each other much anymore.

He's always been my lawyer but sooner or later many of my clients end up knocking on his door too. Particularly here in LA where despite popular opinion, people would rather the scandal of the moment be someone else's problem.

I walked the fifteen feet from the elevator to the main reception desk across a wood floor so well polished you could probably ice skate on it, staring at my disheveled reflection on the floor. Long kinky hair, baseball cap, blue jeans, boots and leather jacket—LA practiced casual. A few more years and I'd pass for a native.

I smiled at the receptionist, a woman named Betty who doesn't like me. I think it has a little to do with my appearance, but mostly she's like a lot of people who find my profession distasteful. Most days I don't disagree.

I walked up to her desk and started to speak, but she cut me off.

"One moment, Ms. Moses," she said, not even bothering to look up at me. I'd been snubbed. "If you'll just have a seat . . ."

"I'd rather stand," I said, immediately feeling like an idiot for being so petty. "I'm sure it won't be a long wait."

"Suit yourself," she said, and returned to her phone, computer, a pile of mail and her cup of coffee. Her own private dominion.

The wait was longer than expected. It was a good twenty minutes before his paralegal, a skinny kid in a blue suit and an earring named Myron, came out to take me back to see Jim.

The hallway opened up to a small divided office with two desks, one for his secretary and one for Myron, who left me at the open doorway to Jim's office.

He was on the phone, but he beckoned me inside. It was a big room, with a bookshelf on each side, a leather couch, a wet bar in the corner and a floor-to-ceiling window that offered a view that on those rare crystal days could reach halfway across the city. This wasn't one of them. The blue sky was more gray than blue, more cloudy than clear. The Santa Anas would change this. Tomorrow I was betting you could see Catalina, maybe even Japan from here.

Next to that window, Jim's desk was the most dominant object in the room. It's massive oak top was carved out of one big tree and was misshapen, almost angular. It was wider by a foot or more on one end, more narrow on the other.

It's not a lawyer's desk but it fits Jim perfectly. He doesn't look like a big-city lawyer, not in his soft denim shirt, bolo tie and smooth khaki slacks that have the sharpest crease I've ever seen. Like he'd used a steamroller for an iron.

His shirt sleeves were rolled up to just below his elbows, showing tanned, muscled arms. He wasn't very tall, six feet with shoes on, but he was solid, carrying his even 200 pounds as if every ounce had a perfect place on his body. His hair was blue black, cropped close to his head and styled with mousse — his only nod to current fashion — so it stood up in places.

"Sorry," he said again, wiping his face with both hands. "Pull up a chair, Zen. We need to talk."

There were two big leather chairs in front of his desk and it was only then I noticed someone was sitting in one of them. It was Bobo.

He nodded at me as I sat down.

Bobo's the kind of person whose presence can dominate a room or disappear into the walls. He was a good four or five inches taller than Jim, built like a mountain but with wide shoulders and legs like redwoods.

He's my mentor, my sometime partner, my savior, my soulmate, my friend and a hundred other things for which there are no names. Our relationship is complex, still being molded, yet never changing. Its base is as solid as Jim's desk. I like to think we keep honor and loyalty from going the way of the dinosaur.

There is no one, not even my beloved Uncle Sam, who I love more deeply or trust more completely. Most people think

Bobo shows very little emotion and the truth is that the burden of having spent his life in often violent worlds has turned him inside himself.

But to say he's unemotional is to not understand him. He speaks a very fluent, rich language that is specific to only him and in our years together, I have learned how to read it.

Of West Indies descent mainly, Bobo La Douceur is a part of more cultures than he'd been able to keep track of, among them French Canadian, Cajun and Italian. He has deep brown skin, a beautiful angular face and two mismatched eyes, one hazel which makes sense with the rest of him. The other is deep-sea blue that would have stood out even if it didn't have the tendency to wander when he was tired.

He was wearing all black. Cargo pants, knitted turtleneck, black leather jacket and, as usual somewhere expertly hidden from the casual observer, he was well armed.

"What the hell are you doing here?"

"Nice to see you, too," he said.

Jim was watching us, a hint of bemusement in his eyes, which I noticed looked tired. I looked at my watch. It was barely 10 a.m. Already he looked like he'd put in a 12-hour day.

"You look like hell," I said, ignoring Bobo. "It's not even lunchtime."

He laughed, suddenly. A big, booming sound that would have scared the shit out of me if I didn't know better. It was one of Jim's endearing idiosyncrasies, that crazy laugh that bursts out of him at the most inappropriate moments. Like a Texas rancher, leaning against a split rail fence, laughing his ass off at the joke he's told a hundred times to half as many people.

"What's so funny?"

"You," he said. "You never mince words, do you?"

I shook my head. "Nope. So what am I—are we—doing here anyway?"

He laughed again but this time, got control of it faster, rubbed his eyes and reached onto the floor for a pile of folders I hadn't noticed before. He sifted through them, found what he was looking for and tossed a manila envelope across his desk.

The three of us stared at it as if it was a deadly spider. I don't know why, but I didn't want to look inside.

"I need a favor," he said.

three

"I got a bad feeling about this," I said, feeling stupid for being so edgy. I blamed the Santa Anas. "I don't know why but I do. You sure you can't get someone else?"

"Damn, Zen," he said. "I haven't even told you what I need and already you're calling up your demons."

"Tell me I'm being stupid."

"You're being stupid."

He said it. We all heard him say it, but somehow his tone wasn't right. I can't tell you why or how, but deep down I knew he was keeping something from me.

Jim's got to be pushing fifty, but he looks ten to fifteen years younger than that. Today, he was showing every minute. I could see the lines around his mouth and the shadows under his eyes, deep enough to make me think he'd been spending his nights staring at the ceiling.

"What's going on, Jim? You look like you haven't slept in a week."

"You really know how to make a guy's day," he said and I watched his face, the set of his jaw, the deliberate breathing and for a moment, I got the feeling he was about to say something important, something he'd never told another soul. And I wanted to get out of there.

For a private detective, I don't handle inner confessions very well. I was the same way as a reporter, cringing even as my interview subjects were revealing things about themselves I wouldn't tell my own mother. It always made me nervous, as if I was giving up secrets, not them.

But then the moment passed. He leaned back in his big chair, took a deep breath and then smiled. It was an instant transformation that grin on his face, as if he had just shed ten years and even more worry. I wouldn't have believed it if I hadn't seen it for myself. Maybe I had made the whole thing up.

"Jesus," he said. "I'm getting melodramatic in my old age. I'm just in the middle of some tough cases and sometimes all this work just gets to me."

He pointed to the folder on his desk. "This client has been one royal pain in the ass and I want to close this out. It shouldn't take more than a couple of days. And don't worry about fees — he can handle it and then some."

"Okay," I said, not convinced. "What's the job?"

"Missing um, persons," he pointed to the envelope.

I picked it up, unlatched the metal clasp and pulled out the most amazing photo of a dog I'd ever seen. It wasn't just any snapshot. This was a perfectly posed, black and white Hollywood still. A traditional head shot, the kind that frame an actor's face in an ethereal glow as if a godly light follows him everywhere he goes.

The dog, some kind of terrier, was staring straight into the camera, its head slightly tilted, eyes glistening, nose moist. I couldn't help but smile.

"Do I look like Ace Ventura to you? I find missing people, not animals. Maybe Dr. Doolittle does house calls," I said, turning to Bobo. "You know about this?"

He shrugged, but didn't say anything. Bobo could go days

without saying more than three words and, depending on the situation, I either loved or hated him for it. Right now, I could use a verb.

"What if I told you that dog is worth more than your house?"

Jim got me there. "Okay, I'll bite."

He smirked at this. "You're staring at Noodles. Six time undefeated champion show dog," he said. "He belongs to one of my clients and he's been kidnapped."

"I think you mean dognapped."

He ignored me again and I thought I was being wonderfully witty. "The ransom note is inside the envelope."

I looked inside and pulled out a small, white card, the kind that people use for thank-you notes.

CHANGE OF PLANS.
DON'T MAKE US KILL THE DOG.

"Change of plans? What the hell does that mean?"

"We think it's the client's wife," he said.

"What? His wife kidnapped their dog?"

"Actually, they're in the middle of a pretty nasty divorce and we suspect she took the dog to up the ante on the settlement."

He was leaving something out. I knew it, he knew it. I was sure Bobo knew it too, but he had decided to sit back and listen. Probably the smartest thing to do.

"There's something else, right?"

Jim got up, walked over to his window to the world and turned toward the pale blue sky, the glare of the sun sending tendrils of bright light through the dense air and clouds. Like the movie version of God speaking from the heavens. He clasped his hands behind his head and I could see wet spots under his arms.

"What?" I said.

He turned back toward me, a grave look on his face.

"This isn't just any dog," he said.

"Yeah, you told me. It's a damned show dog. So?"

"Let me finish," he said. "This is difficult, a difficult thing for me to say, but the truth is I've got a mess on my hands. And you're the only two people I can trust."

His voice cracked and faded and for the first time since I'd known him his face revealed more about what was going on inside than out.

"This new client of mine has put me in a very, very awkward position," he said. "I never would have taken him on in the first place, but I had no choice. He found out something about my past, something that could destroy my career."

He let that sink in and my mind raced. I looked over at Bobo to see if he had known this was coming, but he had his head back and his eyes closed. His expression gave up nothing.

I looked back at Jim, my jaw down to my shoes. He has plenty of faults, but he's a good, kind, honest guy with the most solid heart I know. He doesn't act rashly and I've never seen him get really angry. My perception of my whole world was being shaken to the core. If Jim had skeletons then nobody was safe.

I started to say something but he held up his hand.

"The details aren't important," he said. "But I think I found a way out. I wish I could tell you more, but the silly thing is I'm bound by my professional ethics. I'm in a bind here and I'm flying by the seat of my pants."

"Technically I'm an employee," I said. "Doesn't that mean you can tell me?"

He shook his head.

"You probably could say that's true," he said. "But I'm not gonna tell you anyway. It's bad enough I got this shit on my conscience. No way I'm gonna get you involved too."

"I'm already in it," I said, waving the ransom note.

"And you're gonna be out of it as soon as you find that dog," he said. "I'm not looking for you to be the cavalry here. I can deal with my own problems, my own way. I need you to go along with me on this. The less you know, the better for both of us."

"How can I find this dog if you won't tell me anything about the case?"

"All the details you need are in that envelope," he said. "We've been able to determine the dog is here in Los Angeles, probably in plain view somewhere. We need someone to do the leg work is all."

I sat back in my chair. I didn't like what was happening here. For one, it was crazy, not to mention dangerous, to take on a case without knowing more about its background. You never knew what you were walking into. And for another, I was concerned about Jim. This wasn't like him and it was scaring me.

"Jim," I said quietly, evenly, making certain he understood the weight of the words. "How long have we been friends, you, me and Bobo? Whatever is going on you can tell me. You know that. I'd go to the wall for you. So would Bobo."

He plopped down in his chair, buried his face in his hands. For a minute, I thought he was going to cry.

"I need you to understand," he said finally. "Some things you have to handle yourself. I made some mistakes in my life and I knew someday I'd have to pay for them. I might go down in flames over this, but I'm not taking my friends with me."

I looked over at Bobo again. "You agree with this crap?"

Bobo nodded and I expected him to continue the silent treatment, but he didn't.

"He sounds like you," he said. "Let's go find the dog."

"I can't believe you two," I said. "Can't you at least tell me who your client is?"

Jim stared at me hard, determined, the look of a man who could survive the worst kind of torture and not give up his secrets.

"Believe me," he said, "you don't want to know."

four

This was one of those cases that had 'run like hell' written all over it. It's not that I don't like animals. Unlike people, I find animals wonderfully simple and direct and thoroughly uncomplicated.

But I don't like going blindly into the night, which is exactly what Jim was asking me to do. And I told him so. But while we raised our voices, I admit that my argument lacked the force of my own convictions.

There are some people you don't say no to. One, of course, is a paying client. The other is a friend. Frankly I don't have too many of those.

Whenever Jim needs an investigator he usually gives me a call, for which, most of the time, I am extremely grateful. It's usually small stuff like tracking down financial records or offshore bank accounts so he can make sure his clients get their legal share of the settlement. Occasionally he has asked me to locate someone and once he had me follow a cheating spouse but there was a good reason for doing it.

Jim is far too decent I think to be a lawyer but somehow he manages to make this trait work in his favor. One of the reasons I like him.

Jim has been there for me many times, helping me save more than one of my clients over the years and bailing my ass out of jail the times it has been necessary. I usually can't afford his fees and Jim never bothers to collect. But to him money isn't the only way to pay off a debt.

He has this code he attributes to his ancestors that says standing up for your friends is a thing you do. It comes out of duty, honor and loyalty, and not because one day that friend might return the kindness, even if in the end that's exactly what usually happens.

It is important to him in a way few things outside of my family and close friends are to me. Sure, I live by my own code that makes me feel like I am fighting the good fight in the right way, but for Jim things just run deeper. Maybe it's his Indian blood, the evolution of a people who even as they are threatened by extinction, walk this world with a strength that far outweighs their actual numbers. As if he carries every man, woman and child who lived and died and called themselves Dakota beneath his skin and throughout every capillary in his body.

Maybe it's that Jim's a believer and I'm not. Maybe it's as simple as that.

five

Jim was asking for a miracle, but I couldn't say no. Not to him. I figured two or three days work, hell maybe I'd get lucky. More likely I'd return empty handed. At least I'd feel better about myself for having tried.

My specialty is finding people, something I like to do and I am good at. Unfortunately, most of the jobs I actually get are divorce cases, though I've been trying my best to phase that out. Unfortunately, I have a mortgage.

Missing persons is tedious work, grueling and boring, often meaning I will have to talk to the same people and walk the same route dozens of times before I can even begin to put the pieces together.

But it's work that suits me because I can do it by myself at my own pace and in my own way.

Bobo is sometimes nearby like now, but his way of helping is usually to stay in the background, always a comforting thought.

So, while I was perusing pet stores, Bobo was doing the dirty work. He was looking into a good friend's past. It's not a decision that came lightly or even one either of us would ever feel good about, but it was the only way we knew how to help him.

I was just hoping Bobo would come up with something soon. I hated being in the dark like this.

Bobo was off God knew where digging into Jim's life, and I was knee deep in furry things.

Eight days later, after visiting every dog groomer, interviewing every vet and scouring every pet store, dog park and obedience school in LA, I finally hit on a break.

And its name was Susan Donnell.

I was parked a few doors down from Donnell's yellow- and gold-trimmed Spanish villa, on one of the narrow back streets in a section of Santa Monica the locals call North of Montana, in part for its proximity to the boulevard of the same name. This wasn't merely a geographical distinction; it was a social one. Most of the houses on this side of tony Montana weren't to be had for less than eight hundred G's and most of its denizens were wealthy and white. The only signs of the rest of the human rainbow were usually found pushing baby carriages or tending lawns the size of city parks.

A practiced eye could probably spot my rental from a mile away, but this was one of those neighborhoods where people don't think they have to lock their doors, even though they throw the double bolts every night just to make sure. Bad things happen to people in those other neighborhoods.

So for three nights running, I'd been parked under a large eucalyptus tree, watching and waiting, and so far not a soul seemed to notice.

It was a characteristic of this neighborhood that likely suited Donnell, who was the dog trainer to the stars, running hermulti-million-dollar business out of her multi-milliondollar villa in the middle of this quiet, residential neighborhood.

The massive house had two stories in the main structure and a separate recent add-on the size of a small barn that she used to board as many as twenty to fifty dogs during a six-week training period.

Donnell's expertise was in boarding, training and handling show dogs, particularly for people who were too rich to bother doing it themselves.

The word on the street was the wealthier the owner, the more likely the dog would find its way to Donnell. After two days of continual surveillance, I was able to get the routine down and find my mark.

He was one of the workers who took care of the dogs during the day. Donnell also has a small personal staff, an all-in-one assistant, live-in maid, two people who watch the animals at night and a driver/handyman.

Donnell is usually in the house most of the day, but she didn't seem to be around.

My target was a skinny guy with bad posture named Freddie Gallow, who spent his evenings at a cheesy bar on Wilshire, trying in vain to pick up women before returning to his rent controlled bachelor apartment over a dollar store on Pico.

After the third day, I followed him to the bar and got him to pour his pathetic heart out. He should have gotten suspicious, but he was too drunk and too hopeful of getting laid to realize what was happening to him. When I got what I needed, I excused myself, headed for the ladies room and then slipped out of the bar. I left the poor guy drunk and alone for what I suspect was not the first or last time in his unhappy life.

He was proud of his job working with the dogs, but he was more jazzed by his boss's clientele. I guess if you couldn't get to meet Demi Moore, the next best thing is picking up after her dog.

It was easy to get him to talk about the dogs and he told me about the new boarder: a Scottish Terrier that belonged, he said, to someone famous. It was a big secret and it irked him that he wasn't let in on it.

I tried to nurse my beer while we talked, but I had to keep

ordering so as not to make Freddie suspicious. By the end of the evening, I had a mild buzz on.

I called Jim at his office but he wasn't there. It was Saturday and he didn't usually keep long hours on weekends. I tried him at home, on his cell phone and finally paged him before I gave up and left word on his voice mail. Then I left a message for Bobo and settled in for the night.

Until I heard from Jim, I wasn't going to let this place out of my sight.

He called a half-hour later.

"You found Noodles? Amazing."

"You sound like you had no faith in me." I gave him the address and the pertinent information. "I'm going in."

"No you're not," he said. "Go home."

"What?"

"I'll take it from here."

"I thought I was the stubborn one," I said.

"You've helped me more than you know. Now get the fuck outta there and let me handle it. Please."

"What are you going to do?" I was wondering where Bobo was, wishing he was here.

"I don't know," he said. "But whatever it is, you're just going to have to let me do it myself. Please, Zen."

I wanted to argue with him but he was gone, leaving the static silence of my cell phone hanging in my ear and the thumping of my heart beating in my throat.

No sane person would have blamed me if I'd left that night. If I'd gone home, cracked open an Anchor Steam, put my feet up and watched the Lakers play an exhibition game.

I thought about doing just that. For all I knew, Jim was going to do the same thing. Maybe somebody else could live with that, but not me.

I quietly started the rental, pulled it down the street another half a block and slunk as low as I could in the driver's seat, turning off everything including Albert King.

And then I waited. Dusk had come and its shadows were distorting the partial darkness so that when the wind rattled the palms over my head, they shook like giants.

The Santa Anas were growing fiercer and a strong gust broke off a fragile palm frond. I watched it float silently, like a feather, to the empty street and didn't take my eyes off of it until it was too dark to see it anymore.

I didn't have to wait long for something to happen. It was maybe an hour later when Jim's big Mercedes cruised silently up the street and turned into Donnell's driveway, welcomed by her security gate which glided open and then shut again.

I watched through my night-vision binoculars as he got out and hurried to the door. Not long after Jim arrived, another car approached, gliding down the empty street. I ducked out of view again, waiting for it to pass, but the car, a late-model BMW, turned into Donnell's driveway instead.

Two men got out of the Beemer. The driver had his back to me, but it was the passenger who got my attention.

I focused the lens and craned my neck to make sure I was seeing it right. When he got to the door I was able to get a quick look at his face. It was more than enough.

I'd know that face anywhere. When you look evil in the eye, you never forget it. The Devil had just walked back into my life and his name was Eddie Cooke.

six

Edward Cooke is what I like to call a triple threat. A lawyer turned sports agent, he also owns a string of used car lots up and down the West Coast, from Tacoma, Washington down South to the California-Mexico border.

I made my sportswriting career in part on a story I wrote about Cooke secretly signing college athletes before they turned pro and paying the kids and their families to keep quiet. My story started a federal investigation and Cooke had to turn on his partner to avoid prison. Still, he got censured for five years and his firm went under.

He blamed me for his troubles and sued my paper. The suit had no merit. He was a public figure and I had done my homework; the story was solid. And the Feds further vindicated me. But newspapers aren't what they used to be and my publisher opted to quickly settle out of court. I ended up banished to the copy desk on a four-to-midnight shift. I got back to writing eventually, but by then the magic was gone. It wasn't long after that I had my legendary implosion and left the business for good.

The bad blood between Cooke and me has never faded. I'm not a vengeful person, but some days I dream about kicking his ass.

But then I'd have to get in line. He's among LA's new notorious. When it comes to sensational celebrity murderers in this town there is O. J., there is Edward Cooke and there is everybody else.

Cooke's alleged victim was his former partner, Bud Greeley, who the Feds claimed was about to make a deal that would implicate Cooke. Instead, he was found dead on his own billiard table, bludgeoned to death with a $3,000 teak and ivory pool cue.

Evidence was circumstantial but it all seemed to lead to Cooke. As the trial drew closer, the noose tightened around his neck. There was even talk of him cutting his own deal.

But mere days before the trial was scheduled to begin the bottom fell out. Santa Monica PD arrested John Dennis Moore, a phone company employee who confessed to a series of home-invasion murders, including the death of Bud Greeley.

Moore's story seemed unapproachable. All of his victims were in a five-mile radius of Greeley's Pacific Palisades home and all were killed by something found in their house. Suddenly, a whole lot of people owed Eddie Cooke an apology.

Everyone was saying he'd been wrongly accused, smeared by the media, unfairly tried in the court of public opinion and the victim of an overzealous police department.

But I was there the day they found Greeley on the pool table. I was there because my paper wanted me to interview him about the accusations against the firm. Not many people knew we had a meeting, but Cooke was one of them and I'd always wondered if he killed Greeley just so he could leave the body somewhere I'd find it. That was Eddie Cooke's kind of justice.

It was years before I became a private investigator, even more before I'd seen my first dead body. Bud Greeley's was the one I'd never forget.

Now Cooke is suing the city for millions and the man who

copped to his murder is already dead. Turns out Moore had terminal liver cancer and didn't even live long enough to be executed.

It was another fortuitous death for Eddie Cooke. And I didn't like the smell of any of it.

I had managed to keep Eddie Cooke out of my head for a long time and now he was back, walking into my case. Entering a house mere minutes after Jim had.

At least it settled the argument I was having in my own head. I was going inside.

I grabbed my black knapsack, stuffed a few items inside, tucked my Walther into a holster I had under my jacket and slipped quietly out of the rental.

There was a gate around the property with a modern security system. People who live in neighborhoods like these pay for their protection. But around back at the Donnell house the security was much more lax.

I went around to the side of the house where Donnell had built her new wing. There the yard was larger to give the dogs a place to run.

It was also a part of the house that didn't have motion sensors. If it did, the dogs would set them off all day and night—so my new friend Freddie had told me.

The fence was wrought iron with points at the top. It was about twelve feet high, though the first four feet or so was re-enforced with chain link to keep the smaller dogs from squeezing through to freedom. Still, I needed a spelunking hook and rope to scale it. I was up and over the fence and heading for the back door in less than five minutes.

The backdoor wasn't alarmed, but it was locked. It had a window at the top and a doggy door in the bottom panel. I peeked in through a sheer blue curtain into a dark storage room. In the dim light, I could see at least two big washers and matching dryers below shelves full of dog related stuff from rubber toys to big bags of dry food and Milk Bones.

It was easy enough to slip a wire through the doggy door and trip the dead bolt, which clicked loudly open. I waited.

Nothing. I was more worried about humans than animals, but just the same I waited a minute longer before going inside.

I had a hand-drawn map showing the layout of the house. It was amazing what a few bucks and a working knowledge of the county records office will get you. I used my light to get my bearings, took two steps into the room and suddenly got bum rushed by the biggest, furriest thing I've ever seen.

The force of the blow spun me sideways, knocking me backward so hard I broke the glass on the door with the side of my head. I don't think I screamed but even if I had it would have been muffled beneath the weight of 150 pounds of dog.

I slipped to the floor, grabbing the animal by the neck, wrestling it still. He thought it was a game and playfully yanked at one of my gloved hands as if the leather was a toy. He ripped one of the fingers, finally pulling the entire glove off, throwing it up with his mouth and catching it again. Then he jumped me again, mauling me on the face and neck with paws so big you could use them for catcher's mitts.

When I was a kid the only way to get the neighbor's retriever to stop wrestling was to play dead. So, I lay still. The weight of the dog was almost crushing me and he was having a hell of a good time at my expense, but I managed to outlast him. Finally, he backed off, licked my entire face with one swipe of his tongue and sat down as if he was the valedictorian of Donnell's Dog School.

I waited him out a few moments before sitting up and

checking the damage. The glove was in worse shape than me, the dog having claimed three of its four fingers. So much for not leaving any fingerprints.

There was a good amount of blood dripping down my neck, but it didn't feel too bad. I grabbed a towel from the floor and wiped the excess blood off, holding it to the cut to stem the bleeding.

The dog was a Newfoundland, an enormous breed that have thick, fluffy coats and big, broad heads. He was looking at me through two small, dark intelligent eyes. At least he wasn't a pit bull. Newfoundlands aren't supposed to be aggressive dogs, but quiet, sturdy and loyal. And playful, apparently.

He started to come at me again but I hissed at him to stay and by golly, he did. Maybe he was an "A" student after all. He whimpered a little and pawed the floor, but I kept a stern gaze at him, willing him to leave or shut up.

"Willie! Willie, come here boy. Willie!" the voice echoed through the house, muffled by the space in between it and me. It was coming closer.

"Shoo, Willie," I whispered to the dog and I swear he smiled at me. "Go home. Shoo. Get outta here. Go on, get!"

He looked over his shoulder and then at me and then back at the voice again. I could feel the gears in his mind working. The voice was getting closer. I felt for the Walther.

I looked around the room at the washers and dryers, the shelves, the piles of dirty towels in one corner—there weren't many places to hide. No time to dash back outside.

I could hear the footsteps getting louder. The voice attached to it was female, young, comforting. It was a voice that if I were a dog, I'd go running to in a nanosecond. But Willie didn't budge, sitting there staring at me like a watchdog.

I backed away from him and, thankfully, he stayed put. Quickly, I stuffed my bag into the large dryer and followed it inside, closing the door as a short, pudgy woman walked into the room and hit the light.

"Willie, there you are, boy," she said, patting the big dog on the head. "What's in here?"

She looked around the room and started pushing the pile of towels toward the washer. I said a little prayer she hadn't come here to do the laundry.

Willie wouldn't take his eyes off of me. He sat directly in front of the dryer, staring holes through the door. Then he reached one enormous paw up and pressed on the door latch. The door opened and swung ninety degrees on its hinge.

The woman was on the other side of the small room, bent over as if she'd lost a contact. She turned just as Willie unlatched the dryer door.

"Willie," she admonished. "You're so smart!"

I think my heart stopped as she walked over to the dryer. But the angels were smiling. She didn't even look inside as she slammed the door shut.

She finally found what she was looking for underneath the big sink in the corner. It was a red rubber toy shaped like a pinecone. Willie recognized it right away too.

The big dog took his eyes off of me and jumped up and down as soon as she held it up for him.

"C'mon, boy," she said and she clicked off the light and went back into the hallway.

Willie took one more look at me, turned and trotted out the door. I was getting claustrophobic and cramped and as soon as I watched his tail go around the corner, I pushed at the door of the dryer. It wouldn't open.

I tried it again, and again but it wouldn't budge. Great. Zen Moses, PI, locked in a damned dryer.

I tried to break the glass with the butt of my Walther but it was too confined a space for me to get much oomph behind my swings. I could shoot a hole through the door, but chances were the sound would wake the whole house or deafen me. Worse, the bullet could ricochet back and I'd meet my end that way.

I was considering my options and running out of air when Willie returned, threw his weight against the latch, freeing it. I swear he winked at me just before he trotted back out the door.

I scrambled out of the dryer. I had dog slobber all over my face. I was mad. To think all I was worried about was the dogs making noise. It didn't occur to me they would be free to run around the house and make a fool out of me.

I got to my feet, tucked the towel in my knapsack and crept to the doorway. The hallway was dark, quiet, and empty. I'd been in the house fifteen minutes.

I checked the map again and quietly headed to the main house. In the distance, somebody screamed. It was a horrible sound, not a cry for help, or in fear, but of agony.

Then everything was silent again until Willie came bounding back down the hallway.

He was alone, but there was nowhere to hide. I closed my eyes, put my hands over my head and braced myself for the same greeting he had given me five minutes ago. Nothing happened.

I looked up. Willie had come to rest about a foot from me, sitting quietly, his head cocked to one side the way dogs do sometimes to show their bewilderment with the world around them.

"I understand," I whispered, trying to figure a way around Willie.

Willie whimpered a bit and stuck his nose out at me, making me flinch backward. The darkness, the scream and possibly the fact that I was committing a felony were making me nervous.

He stuck his nose out again and this time, I could see he had something in his mouth. It gave me an idea. So I held my palm out to him and he obediently dropped the object into my open hand. I cracked the backdoor open and got ready to hurl it into the yard when something made me freeze.

I clicked on my flashlight and shined it on my hand. It was a man's right shoe, size twelve. A polished black wingtip from a store I know of but only dream of actually shopping in. It had hardly ever been worn and it was covered in blood. Warm blood.

seven

I checked Willie's mouth and white coat. There was no sign of injury, no cuts or abrasions, no recent surgical scars. But he had blood on his paws, his nose and around his mouth. A lot of blood. I had a feeling it wasn't from another dog.

My heart was in my stomach. Somewhere inside this house was my friend and for all I knew it was Jim whose blood was all over this dog.

I got up from the floor, grabbed some rope out of my bag and tied one end to Willie's collar and the other to the door knob. Then I climbed up on one of the washing machines and grabbed a box of dog biscuits. I tore it open and dumped the contents on the floor in front of Willie.

"Have a party," I said, patting him on his big head and leaving him to his banquet.

I didn't need Willie to lead me to where he'd gotten the shoe. He'd left a trail of red paw prints that ended at a sliding door, and led under a covered overhang and into the main house.

I had my Walther out as I crossed into Donnell's house through another door, which was wide open, and found myself in the kitchen. It was only then I heard the yelling.

Two or three voices, muffled in the distance, only one of which was distinct enough for me to make it out. I knew it well. It was Eddie Cooke's, a voice with no decibel level; it could be heard booming across a crowded freeway.

The kitchen was huge, all shiny aluminum and glittering white surfaces, now accented by the blood red paw prints on the floor.

I followed them into the empty dining room, through a wide living room and down a long hallway. With each step, the voices got louder. The hallway opened up into the main foyer of the house, which was lined with stones and brick and a black marble floor.

In the center was an enormous fireplace which had passageways on either side, leading into yet more rooms. I chose the one closest to me, crossing the wide foyer quickly, holding my breath as I peered around the corner.

It was dark save for a single light and I could barely make out a pool table, big-screen TV and a bunch of stereo equipment. In the corner, Eddie was standing over a man tied to a chair.

The light was coming from a spot Eddie was shining into the eyes of the man; it was Jim. A stream of blood was squirting from his left hand, where I noticed he was missing one of his fingers.

I felt my breath start to quicken and a smoldering rage began to build inside my gut.

Eddie was holding a hand gun to Jim's chin. I couldn't see enough to take a shot from where I was standing. Besides, I remembered there was another man with Eddie. He had to be around somewhere. I didn't want to take the chance he was hiding in the shadows.

I had to wait for an opportunity and it was killing me.

"Where the fuck is she?" Eddie was screaming at Jim who was trying his best to keep his head up.

"We had a deal," Eddie said, lowering his voice.

"We never had a deal," Jim said.

He was shaking with the pain and his shoulders were twitching, but his voice was strong and clear and this surprised me.

"The way I see it, you're in this as much as I am."

Jim said something but I couldn't make it out. Eddie just laughed at him.

"You're my lawyer, right? It's illegal for you to know of a crime beforehand and not report it. So that makes you an accomplice."

"Not if I beat you to the punch. As of right now, our lawyer-client relationship is terminated," Jim said, spitting at Eddie, who dodged the spray.

"You're bluffing. You don't have jack shit on me," said Eddie. But I could feel his mind racing, trying to figure another angle. That's what was so sleazy about him.

"Fuck you," said Jim.

"You could've walked away from this," said Eddie. "All you had to do is bring that pissant private detective here. It would've been so simple, so friggin' easy."

"I didn't want to see you get your ass kicked," Jim said and that's when I heard the cock of Eddie's pistol.

I stepped out of the shadows.

"Somebody looking for a pissant detective?"

Eddie and Jim both looked up at me though their expressions were completely opposite.

"Well, well, well," said Eddie. "Was wondering how long it was going to take you to get here."

"What are you talking about?" I said. Leveling the Walther in Eddie's direction.

"Payback," he said and I felt a sharp sting in my shoulder blade. I got weak suddenly, then nauseous and my legs started to go out from under me. My eyes blurred and I had to squint just to see Eddie. His eyes were wild and dark, a smile the size of Kansas plastered across his face.

That awful, evil, sinister grin was the last thing I remember before the lights went out. That and knowing his face with that look would be locked in my mind's eye forever.

eight

I awoke in a haze, lying on a freezing cement floor with the smell of blood in my nose and a wicked, bitter taste clinging to the walls of my mouth.

A tiny uneven swath of moonlight was trickling in through the room's only window. It was small and rectangular, not much bigger than a vent and was nearly as high as the ceiling. I tried to shake off the fog I was in, but all it did was make my head hurt more.

I reached to quell the throbbing and I saw for the first time my hands were covered in blood. Panic welled up inside me and I checked my body for any sign of a wound. That's when I saw it.

There was just enough light to see the body, lying on the floor in a mangled heap. I'd never seen so much blood.

It lay motionless, several feet across the room. Streaks of blood covered the space between us. There was an aluminum baseball bat on the floor near me, its handle slightly bent, and both ends looked like they'd been dipped in scarlet red paint. I knew better.

Not far from me I saw my Walther lying on the floor, its magazine missing. I reached for it. Like everything else, it was covered in blood. But when I smelled the business end, it didn't seem to have been used recently.

I suddenly felt woozy and coughed, then gagged and almost

threw up. But somehow the nausea settled and the spots in front of my eyes faded.

I started to hyperventilate as I sat there, staring at the body, unable to move, barely able to breathe.

I got to my feet, slowly, painfully, taking in my surroundings. I was in somebody's basement, me and the corpse.

I'm no good around dead bodies. It's one of the few times when I feel any relationship to God or religion or whatever spirits that in the light of day I swear don't exist. I felt the weight of death pressing in on me as if all the air in the room was being sucked into a vacuum.

It was a man and he'd been beaten to death. His clothes were soaked in blood. Not expensive duds; his jacket lay open revealing a local department store's house label.

I bent down to get a closer look and checked the man's pulse just to be sure. He didn't have one. I rifled through his pockets. Nothing. He'd been cleaned out.

I noticed he was holding something in his fist and I pried his fingers open. It was a matchbook advertising a technical school in the City of Industry, one of the many sorry-ass municipalities that make up the dreary Inland Empire, a stretch of territory east of LA out toward the Nevada border. I put the matchbook in my pocket.

The room was small, and in the low light I could see typical basement stuff: a wood-working bench covered in tools lined one wall, an old lawnmower rested against another, a water heater and a dirty sink in the corner. An unfinished wooden stairway was the only way out.

There was nothing familiar about this room, the man in the corner, the baseball bat. Not a thing.

The corpse wasn't giving me much. He was unrecognizable

from the neck up, his face bludgeoned beyond any identification. My girlfriend Leah says you can tell a lot about a man by his shoes. The corpse wore well-worn Rockports, which didn't say much except that he walked a lot. It seemed important somehow that he was wearing both shoes, but I couldn't remember why this occurred to me.

I couldn't remember much of anything, not in large pieces anyway. I remembered seeing Jim and a big dog named Willie, but little of it made any sense. The only clear thing in my head was Eddie Cooke grinning at me.

The thought filled me with something worse than hate and the feeling made me sick to my stomach again.

When I look at the body, I know I am not capable of such brutality. Yet these new emotions swirling in my gut are taking me to the places in my heart I didn't want to know were there, making me wonder.

A minute ago, I was certain this was a set up. Now I was questioning everything that was rational and decent inside me. They say everybody has a dark side. The question is, was I looking at mine?

nine

I didn't do anything for a while. I don't know how long I stood there looking into my own soul and trying to get a sign from the dead guy in the corner, but it felt like days.

I had to wipe blood off my watch to see the time. It was 2:30, I assumed in the middle of the night, but I couldn't say what day it was. It didn't matter. I couldn't stay here forever.

I went to the sink and, keeping the water to a trickle so it didn't make noise, washed as much blood off my hands and arms as possible. Pictures kept coming back to me in the form of vignettes as if I was watching a movie in the wrong order that had yet to be filmed. It only made my head hurt more.

I took off my Nikes, wiped the soles and headed for the stairs. I had to step over the aluminum bat on the way out, and when I saw it I stopped.

Whatever had happened here, whoever was responsible, there was a chance my fingerprints were all over that bat. I could have grabbed it out of the killer's hands, used it in self-defense, or worse.

I have skirted the law on many occasions, mostly to serve a purpose that at the time seemed justified. And always for the benefit of a client.

But this would be crossing a lot of lines. Tampering with the murder weapon wasn't just a slap on the wrist offense. Add to that my usual MO of leaving the scene of a crime and I could be looking at a situation even my friend Lieutenant Brooks would have trouble bailing me out of.

Yet when I looked at that corpse again I knew that whatever memories I couldn't get at, none could ever contain me bludgeoning a man to death with a baseball bat. Someone else was responsible for what had happened here and it wouldn't do me any good to be looking for the culprit from behind bars.

Somebody went to a lot of trouble to put me in this jackpot. The thought brought a sensation over me, unmistakable, solid, foreboding. It was an old feeling, one I hadn't had in a long time and, here inside this cold, generic room alone with a dead body and a sea of blood, it came rushing back with a vengeance.

I grabbed the bat from the floor and washed it clean of most of the blood and any remaining prints, that awful feeling growing inside me like a tidal wave.

I didn't even look at the body as I crossed the basement and quietly climbed the stairs. Instead, I was thinking of fear.

ten

The door at the top of the stairs was closed but not locked.
I waited at the top of the stairs for a few minutes, straining my
ears for any sign that there was someone on the other side.

Then I slowly turned the knob and pushed the door open
enough to get a look. I looked into a small, corner breakfast
nook, well appointed and surrounded on two sides by large
windows.

It was empty and I crept out from behind the door. The
nook opened up into a kitchen that seemed familiar. It was a
moment before I realized I'd been here before. It was Susan
Donnell's house.

Bits and pieces of my memory were sneaking out but it was
like trying to do a crossword with no clues. I suddenly remembered Willie and his paw prints but when I looked down at
the floor, they were gone.

Everything was clean and quiet. No signs that a dead man
was in the basement. Then I remembered Jim. I hurried
through the house, no longer worried about being discovered.

I didn't know why I knew he was here in this house but I
knew and I let my subconscious instincts take over. I rushed
through the kitchen, into the dining room, through the main
foyer and found myself in the den. Jim was there, on the floor
in the corner.

He didn't seem to be breathing.

When I got to him he still had a pulse, though it was faint

and labored. He was lying in a fetal position, cradling his left hand with his right, his face bruised and bloody.

But it was the hole just below his neck that was concerning me. The collar of his shirt had worked as a sort of tourniquet, but it was a losing battle. If I didn't get him help soon, he was going to die here.

There was a cordless phone nearby and I grabbed it but Jim's small, feeble, shaking voice stopped me.

I leaned closer.

"Don't worry, man," I said. "I'm gonna get you outta here."

"You . . . can't . . . stay," he said, each word a labor. "Frame . . . up . . . fault . . . mine."

"Stop talking," I said softly. I had one hand on his forehead and with the other, I was punching in 911 on the cordless. "Don't worry about me."

The operator answered and I realized I didn't know the exact address. I looked around and saw a TV Guide on the floor and read it off the mailing label. I covered the receiver so I could mask my voice as much as possible.

Then I left the phone off the hook and pressed it into Jim's good hand. He tried to say something else. His whole body shook with the effort, but he was losing consciousness.

"Stay with me, buddy," I whispered, my lips touching his ear. "Don't fucking die on me."

He shuddered again and closed his eyes. For a second, I thought he was gone, but he was just gathering his strength.

"Go . . . please," he said. "Set . . . up."

Then he drifted off, his breath coming in intervals that seemed days apart. I felt tears in my eyes and a burning sensation in my gut. Jim was right. I couldn't be here with him. Not with the dead body in the basement and no idea where I'd been or what I'd done.

I left him to get some towels and instead found a small First Aid kit in a closet off the kitchen. I went back and tried to stem Jim's bleeding. Then I kissed him on the forehead and found Donnell's office.

While I was using her fax phone to page Bobo, I saw her desk calendar and knew why her house was so quiet. She was in the middle of a two-week cruise.

I used our emergency code and it took Bobo less than a minute to call back. He'd never admit it but it was proof he was worried about me

"Nice to know someone cares," I said, my voice rough and cracking as if I was using it for the first time. I had to keep coughing to clear my throat.

"Where are you?"

"Trouble, Bobo," I said, explaining as much as I could. Sirens cut through the night, ruining the serenity of this quiet, affluent neighborhood. I'd run out of time. "Gotta go. Pick me up on Alta."

I scrambled through the house, found a back door and set off the alarm and the security lights as I scurried out the back, flinging myself over Donnell's back fence and into the alley behind her house.

Then with the sirens screaming in my ears and the rush of adrenaline in my gut, I slipped into the shadows of the night, keenly aware of only one thing.

The pain of my heart breaking.

Bobo was waiting for me, leaning against his Range Rover. He helped me climb into the passenger seat and when he got in, pulled out a small medical kit.

I was too wasted to argue. He shined a pen light into my eyes, made me say 'ah' and gave me a thermometer to check my temperature while he was using a blood pressure sleeve on my arm. I didn't need to look at the gauge to know my heart was beating way too fast.

It didn't slow any when I saw Bobo with a syringe.

"Whoa," I said. "No needles."

"Gotta find out what they gave you," he said, grabbing my arm, and wedging it under his so I couldn't move it. He wrapped a rubber band around my arm, found a vein and filled the syringe with my blood.

When he was done, I pulled my arm away.

"Obviously feeling better," he said, arranging his gadgets back into a box. "Probably a good idea for you to see a real doctor."

"All I wanna do is sleep," I said.

I told Bobo the rest of the story, sparing no detail. He listened as he always does, waiting for me to finish.

I leaned my head against the soft leather of the seat, closing my eyes, seeing Jim lying on the floor bleeding to death. I fought back tears.

"I should never have left him," I said.

"No other choice," he said. "Nothing you could do the EMT's can't do better."

"What are we gonna do now?"

"Find out what happened to you."

"I was drugged and set up," I said. "I wish I could remember more but I can't. It had to be Eddie. If I ever get to that son of a bitch . . . He's gonna be sorry he ever fucked with me."

Bobo didn't say anything, which was his way. Still, something about this particular silence was unsettling. More bad news?

"What?"

"Eddie Cooke," he said. "Nobody's seen him since Friday."

"Bullshit. I saw him in the flesh last night and that was Saturday, a day later."

"Not last Friday, the Friday before," he said, letting this sink in. "His wife reported him missing Monday."

"How the fuck do you know that?"

"It's on the grapevine. He's popular conversation downtown, you know," he said. "Sure it was him?"

"Of course," I said, but even I could hear the uncertainty in my own voice. The truth was I wasn't sure of anything.

We drove the rest of the way to my house in silence, his unspoken thoughts, like mine, were about Jim.

It was still dark when Bobo pulled into the alley behind my place on Euclid Street. He left to go get the rental car I had left parked near Donnell's house. If the cops found it first, they'd be at my door before sunrise.

I was glad he was up to it since I wasn't. Besides, I didn't really want company, even a friend who knows me better than I know myself.

I climbed up the back stairs and punched in the security code. I live at the end of a cul-de-sac that backs up to Santa Monica's lone pet cemetery. I like it for its combination of quiet and privacy, including the graveyard.

Cemeteries for people scare the hell out of me, but I was sure animals face eternity with a much healthier outlook. I doubt there are many dogs and cats walking through the after-world with heavy scores to settle.

There were no messages on my machine, nobody calling to tell me what had happened to me.

I took a hot shower, trying to wash off the rest of the dried blood. I threw my Nikes into the washing machine and tossed my clothes in the trash. Evidence be damned. No way I was gonna go down for something I didn't, couldn't do. That was my thinking anyway.

I crawled into bed and my cat Sassy sneaked underneath the covers with me. Willing the fatigue of the day to bring me a peaceful sleep, I shut my eyes, but the tighter I closed them the clearer I saw images of death.

As I slipped into a semi-sleep, I saw the body again, this time its head turned toward me, most of its features still intact.

My mind was unconsciously putting it together like a grisly jigsaw puzzle of flesh and bone. For the briefest of moments, I saw him staring back at me with that baneful grin. I knew it in a nanosecond and I didn't even know how or why. The body in Donnell's, the man with no face. It was Eddie Cooke.

eleven

I woke with a start with a new headache burrowing into my temples with the ferocity of a dog digging for a bone. I'd been asleep for less than an hour, but I wasn't tired anymore, just unbearably nervous, anxious. I wondered if this was from whatever had knocked me out and stolen my memory.

Whatever it was more sleep was impossible. I needed to do something.

I stepped outside onto my front porch, rubbing my eyes and the back of my neck and thinking about my predicament, wondering how long it would take for the cops to come knocking on my door.

Bobo called while I was asleep. He left a message that Jim was in the I.C.U., stable but in a coma. There was no telling if he'd ever come out of it. The man in the basement was as yet unidentified.

So far, the cops had no suspects.

Until last night, I hadn't seen Eddie Cooke up close in nearly six years. There was nothing about the body that said it was him, nothing that was left that is. There was only a matchbook in a dead man's hands, and my own insane musings.

I thought of calling Lieutenant Brooks but there was too much I didn't know. My story wouldn't be very convincing. Not if I barely believed it.

Brooks is becoming a good friend but he can't hide his skepticism. While he tries to be a hard ass, he's never been less than fair to me. This can't be said for a lot of Santa Monica cops.

I used to have a good relationship with many of them, but times have changed and my biggest ally is in New Mexico now, running a whole police force of his own. His replacement is a by-the-book blowhard named Watkins who has it in for me, though sometimes I think I see real human emotion behind his surly exterior.

I took in a breath of the warming air. After more than a week's worth of Santa Ana nonsense, here was a day even Steven Spielberg couldn't improve upon. The sky painfully blue and cheery, holding onto a bright, sunny day made for heaven by an intermittent breeze so delicate you would need a fine instrument of meteorology to measure it.

I was thinking of revenge, knowing in my heart Eddie had hurt my friend and that I wouldn't rest until I'd hurt him back. I didn't like feeling this way, but some situations demand it.

I dismissed my dream—that it was Eddie in the basement dead. That was just my imagination working without me.

I couldn't do anything about it today. So I made a cup of coffee, picked up the Sunday *New York Times* and went outside to the warmth of the sunshine. I lay back on the my Barcalounger, trying not to think of dead bodies and old enemies.

I drink in days like this, when Sundays are throwbacks to the time when everybody closed shop and spent the day at home or out searching for the perfect picnic spot or perhaps taking the new Chevrolet out for a spin around some as yet untouched countryside. Sentimental bullshit no doubt, but sometimes I am a sap.

But a darkness was hanging over everything I was doing and I just couldn't sit still long enough to enjoy the weather. I needed to clear my head.

I didn't want to think about my problems or my friend clinging to life with a bullet hole in his neck. I didn't want to think at all. I went back inside, left the paper on my kitchen table and changed into riding tights and a long-sleeve cycling shirt, filled a large bottle with cold water and grabbed my brand new mountain bike. I'd splurged on it from the money I'd made a few months back on a case involving a talk show host. It was dual suspension, ball-burnished aluminum, built a few miles down the Southern California coast by a former motorcycle engineer. And it was fun as hell.

Sometimes I load it on the back of my car and drive up to the mountains, but today I felt like suffering the hills the old-fashioned way. I rode down Euclid to Arizona and picked up Twenty-sixth Street going north. I followed it across San Vicente, than east on Sunset to Mandeville Canyon, where I veered off onto Westridge and up the steep climb toward the Sullivan Canyon Trail, one of many that crisscross the Santa Monica Mountains for miles up the coast and inland.

I paced myself the two-mile ride up toward the trailhead. It's a narrow, winding road crowded along each side by expensive houses with more expensive views. As I rode, the sun seemed to climb with me and all around the world was settling into a brilliant Sunday afternoon.

I made it up the hill in pretty good time, carried my bike over the bar at the entrance, then got back on for the four-mile ride up the rutted, dirt trail, nodding to a couple of riders who had driven up the road and were just getting their bikes going.

I exercise regularly, obsessively, mostly because of the cancer that took my right lung. Part of me wants to prove to the world that I haven't changed, the rest wants to prove this to myself.

But I am different. There are days when the simplest exertion saps my breath like a vacuum sucking out my insides. Colds kick my ass, getting even a light case of pneumonia can be life-threatening, and every autumn I'm supposed to line up with the babies and senior citizens for a flu shot.

Losing a lung is a life-changing experience in ways you can't fully explain to people who still have all their working parts. I wouldn't want to go through it again for anything and I'd change it in a second if I could, but living through it has taught me something about myself and my place in the world and what I am capable of under the worst of circumstances. And I'll never forget it.

It would be impossible. Every time I touch one of the three scars on my chest or look in the mirror each morning or feel a phantom pain on my side or get short of breath, I remember. Remember what it took to get here and what I had to give up to survive.

The sweat of my workout was dripping off my face and neck as I pedaled on toward the sky, pushing myself despite the fatigue, trying to expel whatever drugs had been injected into my body.

I stopped at the top of the big hill, by an overlook where you can get a spectacular view of Santa Monica spreading out toward Beverly Hills in one direction, Malibu in the other and the Pacific Ocean in between.

It was a stunning morning and the light breeze felt good on my face. I sat back on my bike, the sun gleaming off its silver sheen, and guzzled water until it was dripping down my chin. I stayed up there, facing the city I'd adopted for better and worse, wondering what made the evil in this world and how much of it was buried in our own hearts.

It had to be there, temporarily dormant, lying in wait for those moments when survival means doing the unthinkable. It was a constant battle in all of us, but was good stronger or just more resilient, and in the end which one would be left standing?

And at the moment of truth, would you be able to let the darkness take over and if you did could you ever go back? The truth was most of us don't know what we're capable of, not until we have no choice but to act. And even then, you can't always be sure.

These thoughts brought Eddie Cooke's name back to the forefront of my mind and I cursed myself for ruining a serenely beautiful moment.

I took a big gulp of water and spat it out, then turned my bike back where I'd come, gritted my teeth and started down-hill with the abandon of a landslide.

twelve

Life is simple when the only reason to kill yourself climbing up a hill is so you can joyride back down it. Bumping down the trail, bounding over ruts and fallen trees and rocks and around obstacles, was one thing, but once I hit the pavement, I really took flight.

Despite my tendencies, I'm usually a lot more cautious on those canyon roads that are barely wide enough with cars parked on both sides to get a small sedan through, but today was different.

With the wind roaring in my ears and my brand new cycle shoes clipped tightly into the pedals, I flew around corners as if it were my own private racetrack, only once just missing an SUV that was hogging the road.

By the time I got back to Euclid Street, it was coming up on noon and I felt like a new person, slathered in sweat and dirt, and feeding off the exhilaration like an addict.

The high lasted well into a long, hot shower and for a while there I even forgot about Eddie Cooke and the dead body.

The phone rang as I was making a turkey sandwich for lunch. I let the machine pick up. It was Brooks.

"Lane's. Tuesday night. Eight."

It was then that I remembered our date. Brooks has been trying to get me to go out with him since we met and I've been pretty good at fending him off. I finally agreed to go out with him mostly to shut him up and prove how incompatible we were. I was already sorry I'd said yes.

"Hello? Jonathan?" I said snatching up the phone.

"So you are there."

"Yeah, I'm here," I said. "It's Sunday. Where else would I be?"

"Down, girl," he said. "What's the matter? Can't figure out twenty-four across?"

"What?"

"C'mon I figured you'd be halfway through the Sunday crossword by now."

I was going to have to change my habits.

"Nothing personal, Jonathan, but I had a rough night. What's up?."

"Rough night? That sounds familiar."

"It's not what you think."

"Don't tell me," he said. "I don't want to know. Anyway, I was just calling to confirm our date. Tuesday night. Eight o'clock. Lane's."

Oh, that. "I almost forgot," I said. "Lane's? That's actually a nice place. I knew I was paying too much in taxes."

"I might make you pay considering the crap you put me through," he said.

"Happy to be of service," I said.

"By the way, I'm sorry about James Gray. He was your lawyer right?"

"Is," I said. "Is. He's not dead yet."

"Sorry," he said. "I didn't mean it that way. He got roughed up pretty good."

"Yeah, I know. You guys got anything?"

"Just bits and pieces," he said. "It's not my case. Watkins gave it to your old buddy Lennon. You know he made Detective three months ago. Anyway, he's keeping the investigation on the QT. We don't like to see people murdered North of Montana."

"But if it happens on this side of town . . ."

"You know what I mean," he said. "Santa Monica's well-do-to. Money talks. Bullshit talks louder."

"I guess," I said. "Listen, Jonathan . . ."

"Yeah?"

"Jim isn't just my lawyer. He's my friend. Me and Bobo, we've known him twenty years. He was a cop, you know."

"Yeah, I know. We're doing everything we can. Lennon's a son of a bitch, but he's a good cop. He gets convictions. But I know what you're saying. I'll keep my ear to the ground. Don't expect anything more than that. And don't think my saying this means I'm gonna do any favors for you."

"At least you can't say I don't have an interest."

"Yes I can," he said. "Pick you up Tuesday at seven-thirty. Try to stay out of trouble 'til then, okay?"

I hung up the phone wondering yet again if a date with Brooks was a good idea.

I dated a narcotics cop once and he spent more time with his therapist than me. Then when his ex-partner got in trouble, he backed him to the end, even when everybody knew he was dirty. Now his partner is serving 25-to-life for fraud and murder. My former boyfriend still thinks he's a saint who got nailed to the cross. Go figure.

Brooks showed me signs that he is different, that he knows how to separate the men from the bullshit. But cops are cops and when the blue line gets drawn, even the good guys have to have a damn good reason to cross it.

I grabbed the Sunday *New York Times* Magazine, a four-pack of Anchor Steam and settled back in my Barcalounger again, the quiet sounds of my cul-de-sac rippling though the afternoon like background noise in a home movie.

There was the faint smell of an outdoor grill wafting over the whitewashed wooden fence that separated my place from the rest of the world, and farther in the distance I could hear children playing. It was a sound that could drive anyone nuts on a regular basis, but sometimes it was music to me.

I set about trying to solve the Sunday crossword, a weekly obsession of mine at which I am woefully inept. My uncle Sam is a whiz and can go through the Sunday puzzle over breakfast. I rarely finish. When I do, it usually takes me a week and a good dictionary.

"Hey Zen! Girlfriend! What. Is. Up?" It was my neighbor Andrea, calling over the fence.

I don't know my neighbors well, which has nothing to do with the famous myth about LA having no real neighborhoods. As it happens, it has a lot more to do with me preferring my own company to just about everyone else but a few choice friends, my uncle Sam and my cat.

But that doesn't always keep them on their side of the dividing line. Especially Andrea who now dangled her well manicured fingers over my fence. Her scarlet nails looked like specks of blood against the recently painted wood.

Andrea is from New Jersey and has the big hair and never-pay-retail attitude to prove it. She is from that special breed of women for whom shopping is a vocation, gossiping a hobby and bubblegum a food group. While she still clings nobly to her Jersey accent, her few years in LA have garbled it, combining the "ya's" and "yo's" with "you knows," "likes" and "dudes" with a good sprinkling of "whatevers." A whole roomful of sociology experts would have a hard time pinning her to her native dialect.

I like Andrea but I know that's because I get her in very small doses. I work hard to keep it that way. She has two really irritating habits. One is her musical tastes, which tend toward vanilla pop icons like Michael Bolton, not the first or last of a breed of soul singers who have no soul to speak of. His version of Percy Faith's "When A Man Loves A Woman" should be outlawed.

The other is exactly the reason I avoid my neighbors whenever possible. If I didn't keep a cultivated distance, I would be inundated by Andrea's social calls. For her that means leaning over my fence, a mile-long Virginia Slim burning in one hand and a rapid-fire monologue pouring out of her mouth, threatening some lip-moving record.

Most of the time when she corners me and I don't have the energy or inclination to run away, she talks and talks and talks and I nod and pretend to be busy counting the blades of grass on my lawn, trying not to let her see me gritting my teeth. Today, I was too tired, too preoccupied with thoughts I didn't want to have, to care.

thirteen

"Hey," she said again.

"Hey yourself," I said back, looking up from the crossword that was kicking my ass anyway.

"Whatyadoin?" She speaks so fast sometimes it's as if she only uses one word. Why waste time on silence?

I pointed to my magazine. "The usual."

"Gimme one" She snapped her gum so loud it sounded like a car backfiring. Sassy, who'd been lounging on my lap, got scared so badly, she cleared the length of my good-sized yard in one leap. I knew where she was heading: her favorite hiding place through a small crawl space underneath my house. It formed a gap just wide enough for a small animal to scamper through. I kinda wanted to join her.

"One what?"

"Ya' know," she said. "Gimme a clue. I used to help my dad do them things."

"The puzzle?" I asked. "You sure?"

"C'mon." It was only one word, but the way she dragged it out like a child's plea made it seem like a whole paragraph.

"Alright," I scanned the squares for an easy one. There weren't many I hadn't already filled in. "Here's one: A kind of yoga, five letters, first letter, 'H.'"

She thought for a minute and I felt awful for taking part in her intellectual humiliation.

"Wait," she said suddenly. "I got it. Hatha. H-A-T-H-A. Does that work?"

I looked at Andrea, then back at the puzzle, then back at Andrea again. The word fit, but the picture I was seeing didn't.

"Toldya," she grinned, took an impossibly long drag from her Slim and blew a bubble through the smoke. Sophistication incarnate. "Gimme another."

I couldn't resist. "Silent actress Naldi, four letters, no clues."

She furrowed her brow, deep in thoughts I heretofore had figured on being extremely shallow. Maybe I ought to get to know my neighbors better.

"That'd be Nita. N-I-T-A. My dad always said I was a natch." Maybe I ought not.

"Natch" is short for natural, one of her newest colloquialisms. Another was using "with" to end a question, as in "Wanna go with?" or "Let's take it with." She told me she picked the expression up from her new roommate who had relatives somewhere in the Midwest, where they don't use pronouns.

Just to be certain, I gave her a few more clues. She got each one with minimal effort and I finally capped my pen, closed the magazine, walked over to where she was standing and handed it over the fence. She wouldn't take it.

"I hate doin' them," she said without a hint of irony. "It's like a gift from hell I got."

I wanted to strangle her. Instead I peered over her shoulder at a small gathering in her front yard. About four or five Andrea clones all sitting in lawn chairs talking to each other like they were negotiating peace with Saddam Hussein. Nearby, the only man in the group was working a Webber, trying to look cool and uninterested at the same time he was grilling veggie burgers and turkey hot dogs. I felt sorry for the guy.

"Seems a little heavy for a nice Sunday afternoon," I said.

"It's our regular get together," said Andrea, who by day worked for an exclusive hair salon on the Santa Monica Promenade, an outdoor mall that ran the length of Third Street from Colorado to Wilshire in downtown Santa Monica.

"Kind of like a club?"

"Guess ya could call it that," she snapped her gum at me. The cigarette, which she'd taken maybe four drags from, was burning to ash in her hand. "We talk about life, you know, guys and work and shit."

"I see," I watched the group for a minute, focusing on one in particular, a sun-bleached blonde, thin as paper, who sat at the edge of the circle of lawn chairs, a little further back than the rest of the group. She was staring straight ahead and it seemed to me, trying hard as hell to hold back tears.

"What's with the blonde?" I asked Andrea.

She turned to look, dropped the stub of her cigarette onto the ground and looked back at me, her expression changed from uninterested to concerned.

"Sherrie," she said with resignation. "She's got self-esteem problems. We're all worried about her."

Sherrie caught us looking in her direction. Busted, I dropped my eyes. But she barely seemed to notice. Andrea waved her over.

I was about to beg off, but I couldn't take my eyes off Sherrie. I watched her walk across the lawn, a kind of half-hearted roll to her gait.

She was wearing worn jeans, a Harley-Davidson T-shirt and a leather jacket that was older than dirt and much too big for her. It hung over her like a cape. She could hide Texas underneath it and nobody would notice.

And there was her hair. It was white blonde, cut short in no particular style as if she had shorn it off for effect or in a fit of anger. As she drew closer, I could see where the rage could come from. Her eyes gave the impression of staring aimlessly but there was a kinetic energy to them that radiated trouble and despair. They were set into her face, encircled in rings so dark it was as if they had fallen into two black holes in her skull.

"Hey," she said.

"Sherrie," said Andrea. "This is my neighbor, Zen. She's a detective. Like McGruff the Crime Dog."

I smiled at this and offered a slight wave. She gave me one back, a half-hearted motion that emphasized the lack of meat on her arms and revealed the remains of a jagged scar on her wrist.

She had the aura of the needy, a lone traveler in a barren desert searching out her oasis and knowing that no matter how hard she looked or how real it seemed to her, it would never prove to be anything more than a mirage. But she'd keep on looking. In the end that's all she'd ever have, the singular search for the thing that would rescue her from her place in the food chain.

Knowing she'd never find it was her great secret, the very thought that propped up her tough facade and gave emphasis to the sneer on her lips, both and more protecting her from the elements of real life.

They were, just like that thin, uneven wound on her wrist, proof that her problems weren't easily solved.

Andrea, seeing that we were properly introduced, retreated back to the other members of her party, leaving me to converse with Sherrie across the fence.

"Fucking cool," she said, lightly dusting her hand against her jacket to show she was impressed. A glimpse of what she must have been before life battered her to her present state. "A real private detective? You gotta gun?"

"Sure," I mumbled. "I keep it locked up in the house."

"You ever kill anybody?"

"Unfortunately," I said. "I try not to if I can help it."

"Well if you decide you need the release, I got just the asshole in mind." This made her smile, but her eyes were wet.

"I guess we all know a few of those," I said, thinking of Eddie Cooke and feeling guilty all of a sudden. I've seen people destroyed by their obsession with vengeance. That's one table I'd rather not sit at.

"You don't know Gary. They surely broke the mold," she jawed. "He's the king of the asshole kingdom."

She talked about her relationship with Gary, the dozen or so jobs she had had and lost, the ten-year-old daughter she was on the verge of losing to Child Welfare, an on and off addiction to alcohol, crack and even her failed attempt at going back to college. It wasn't surprising she had once tried to slit her wrists.

Sad story upon sad story upon sad story poured forth from this tough girl and I stood there, listening and nodding, thinking how the thin fence between us might as well have been the Grand Canyon.

Soon she was crying her eyes out, sitting on my Barcalounger. She kept looking at me through those tears with a dead-on stare, daring me to give her a reason—any reason—not to end it all right there. As if she'd give a shit if I could.

"The only thing I have," she sobbed, "is Emily. My kid. But she takes better care of me than I do of her. A ten-year-old should have friends to play with. They shouldn't worry about making sure there's something to eat for dinner. God, my mom is right, I've turned out to be a total loser, just like my dad."

I put my hand on her shoulder. I'm awkward showing emotions, especially around people I don't know. Most of the time it comes out without me even knowing it. But at times like this when I know I should do or say something, when I'm the only person in any position to bring comfort to another human being, I'm clumsy and uncomfortable. It's a part of me I hate.

"Don't say that," I said. "You've had a tough time is all. Emily sounds like a good kid. Now that's something to be proud of."

She nodded, looking around my yard. The grass was turning brown. A friend had installed an automatic sprinkler for me last spring and I've never quite figured it out. I keep having to re-set the timers and most of the time end up watering my street.

"You own or rent?" Sherrie said. I was selfishly relieved she had changed the subject.

"It's all mine," I said. "Bought it after the earthquake with FEMA money."

"Good deal," she said. "Nice place. Better than the dump we have to live in."

"Wanna see it from the inside?"

"Sure," she said, getting up and wiping her face. She fixed her hair and looked around in her coat pockets for something. She rooted around in the inside pocket, before gingerly pulling out her lipstick.

"I got too much crap in here," she said, seeming a bit nervous as she applied the pale red to her lips.

I got the impression she was hiding something in that big coat. Probably drugs. But I wasn't a cop and as long as she didn't do it in front of me, I wasn't going to hassle her.

She was an adult, albeit a sick, sad, troubled one, but as much sympathy as I had for her, it wasn't enough for me to start lecturing her on the evils of drugs.

After a brief tour of my place, she lingered over the floor-to-ceiling bookshelves that Nat and I had put in after the earthquake.

Nat owns Father's Office, the local pub where I get my regular fill of fresh microbrew beers. He's also a good friend who has been there when I needed a hand to hold or a shoulder to cry on.

Our friendship has been strained lately. My cousin Danny died in his place last winter and it's getting harder and harder for me to go back there. I know I will return some day soon, but for now the memories are too fresh. Right or wrong, I associate Nat with Danny's death and that makes everything even more awkward.

Although he will never say this, I know my absence has hurt Nat deeply. Even thinking about him now makes me sad.

I think of telling this to Sherrie, but as usual I clam up. Talking about myself is another thing I'm not good at.

"I used to read to my kid," she said, her voice drifting off and tears starting again. "Back in the day."

"Hey," I handed her a box of tissue, "Things are bound to get better. You just have to weather this. You're stronger than you think."

"I don't know what I'm going to do without Gary."

"I thought he was an asshole," I said and immediately regretted it. Sherrie began to sob louder.

"I know, I know, I know," she cried. "But I can't do this alone. He promised me this time would be different. And I believed him. What a loser."

She was sitting on my couch, her head in her hands. I was wondering how the hell someone gets mixed up in such a mess.

"You just think you can't," I sat down next to her, trying to comfort her again.

"Lots of women get on okay after breakups," I said. "You'd be surprised how many not only survive but thrive. Then when the right guy does come along, they're ready."

"I don't know," she said. She had started to leaf through my current copy of *Vanity Fair,* turning the pages quietly. Her mind was elsewhere.

Finally, she slapped one hand on the couch and used it to help herself up, the other hand holding her jacket closed. She was definitely hiding something.

"I gotta get back to Andrea's," she said. "Thanks for the tour."

"Anytime," I said, handing her my business card. "Feel free to give me a call whenever you want."

"Thanks," she mumbled, a little embarrassed.

"Sure," I said, as I followed her to my front door.

Just as she reached for the door knob, I grabbed her arm.

"What?" she said.

"I don't want to know what's inside your coat," I said.

"Hey," she said, back on the defensive. If she was a dog, she would have growled. "I don't know what the fuck you're talking about."

"Forget it," I said. "I'm not going to bust you. There's places where you can go to get help. Think of your daughter. Think of yourself. Okay?"

She just nodded, turned back to go outside and then stepped back quickly.

"What?" I said, then knew immediately what had spooked her. Through the small window next to my door: I saw Vince Lennon and his partner getting out of their police cruiser.

Lennon's weapon was holstered, but as he walked up my front walk, his hand was resting on the handle.

"Damn," I said. "I think you better . . ."

I never finished. Sherrie wasn't hiding drugs under her coat, she was hiding a hand gun. As I watched the two cops walk toward my front door, Sherrie pressed it into my ribs.

fourteen

"**Hands up,**" she hissed.

I held my hands up so she could see the palms. "C'mon, Sherrie," I said. "What's this going to get you? What about, um, Emily?"

"What do you know about my daughter?" practically spitting the words out. "Nobody knows my kid better than me and don't you forget it."

She softened suddenly, the gravity of the situation weighing on her so much you could see it in her face.

"I don't want to hurt you," she said. "But I ain't going to jail."

"Those cops aren't coming here for you," I said. "They're looking for me."

"Oh, right. That's a good one."

"It's true goddammit. Why don't you let me ask them?"

"No fucking way," she said. "I'm running out of options here."

I glanced at the weapon, looking for a way to disarm her, but the hammer was cocked back. One twitch of her forefinger and I wouldn't have a chance.

It was a Charter Arms Bulldog which is a small gun, but has a large caliber ammunition. You don't have to shoot straight to make a big mess. I recognized it from my stint bounty hunting for Bobo up in Oakland.

I wasn't sure Sherrie knew how to use it but I wasn't going

to take any stupid chances, not with a crazy woman's finger on the trigger.

She was holding the gun so tight, the veins in her hands were visible, her skin taut around her fingers. This didn't give me much confidence the gun wouldn't go off, even accidentally. Lennon was almost up the steps.

She seemed to freeze in place as we watched them approach.

"Sherrie," I said with as much toughness as I could muster with a .44 jammed into my side. "That cop out there is an asshole. Frankly, I'd like nothing better than for you to shoot him. But that's not gonna happen."

She shushed me harshly, then started crying again and for the hundredth time in the last hour, I wanted to feel sorry for her. But it was getting tougher.

Then she lowered the gun, but when I reached for it, she shoved it into my kidney hard enough to make me cry out. Suddenly, I wasn't feeling anything for Sherrie anymore. I wanted to deck her.

The sound of my doorbell made us both jump. Sherrie pulled me away from the door, shoving the gun under my chin. For the first time since this started, I wondered if she'd ever done this before.

"Say a word and I will shoot," she whispered. "Nothing personal. I just don't have any choices left."

"There's got to be an alternative," I said. The doorbell rang again.

"I'm making my own," she said. "Let's go."

"Where?"

She shoved the gun into my side again. I was really getting pissed off.

"Out the fucking back," she hissed.

"Are you nuts? Those cops are never going to let us out of here."

"Move," she said and I did.

We went out my back door and down the stairs to the alley. Behind us the cops were banging on my door. In a minute, Lennon was going to send his partner around the back.

I wasn't sure I wanted us to be there when that happened.

She led me to her car, a faded black Mustang parked in one of the spaces behind Andrea's building, directly behind Andrea's red Honda Civic.

The car had seen better days. Its paint was peeling and rusted in places, the upholstery torn and dulled. It was an 80's Mustang, part of the legendary car's forgettable years when the geniuses in Detroit came down with a case of the uglies. Devoid of anything resembling style, like its predecessor, this version was square and squat. With the top down, it looked like a Kleenex box.

I was glad when Sherrie handed me the keys. I didn't want to be the passenger in a car with questionable safety restraints, no air bags and a desperate, crazy woman at the controls.

The engine was in far better condition than the rest of the car and it whirred to life with authority.

"Drive," she said, back in her faraway place.

I drove down the alley with no sign of Lennon or his partner. When we were on Olympic, Sherrie instructed me to head for the freeway. I drove quietly, though I wondered how long I was going to have to play this out.

The situation escalated greatly when we turned onto Lincoln and down the ramp to 10 Freeway East. A police cruiser was following us, a few cars back. Brooks was right when he said Lennon knew how to be a good cop.

But he was also volatile, and if that was Lennon, it upped the ante for all of us. I knew then we were heading into trouble and I wasn't in control anymore.

So much for being in the driver's seat.

fifteen

Los Angelenos have discovered a new sport now that both the Rams and Raiders split town for riches elsewhere. It's called "freeway chasing" and it comes complete with live feeds, color commentary, and dramatic, death-defying stunts.

It's one of the many LA phenomena particular to the O. J. Era. The Juice himself led the LAPD on a multi-freeway chase on Father's Day Weekend, his buddy behind the wheel and a gun to his own head.

Now once a month or so, a flaming idiot gets behind the wheel of a car, gets flagged by the cops and once again proves how little difference there is between the intelligence of your average dog and a large cross-section of the populace.

But even most dogs know they can't outrun a car. It's bad enough that these fools endanger the lives of other drivers and pedestrians, but it's downright ghastly that people actually tune in to watch it as it happens.

Of course, maybe it's worse that news programmers feel the need to show the chases live as if it really is a regularly scheduled sporting event. Makes you wonder how far we've really come from the Christians and the lions.

There's two types of freeway bandits. One is your basic career criminal with a record longer than his pants leg with two strikes on it. If they don't run, they're staring down the barrel of a mandatory life sentence in the slammer.

Then there's those poor souls, desperate or angry, physically or mentally ill, at the end of the end of their rope, who want out of this world one way or another. Maybe they can't do it themselves, maybe they don't want to embarrass their families or lose out on the life insurance benefit. So they get on a freeway, find a cop to take the bait and run until they're cornered like a wounded animal. It's the new form of assisted suicide. Only for this kind, you don't need to call Dr. Kevorkian.

Sherrie had said she would take care of her daughter and perhaps this was the way, only I doubt she expected to have company along for the ride.

"This is no way to solve your problems," I said.

She was staring out the rearview mirror, the gun still pointed in my direction. We were now heading north on the 405 Freeway. We were driving the speed limit, holding steady in the left lane, heading up through the Sepulveda Pass.

I could see the new Getty museum complex perched on the hill far above the stretch of freeway. Behind us, our escort had grown by two CHP cars. I could just imagine what the cops were thinking.

Well actually, I knew what they were thinking, because I would draw the same conclusions. I was no longer a respected private detective. I was a possible murder suspect on the run, with a hostage.

Above us, I could hear a helicopter. Could be the cops, could be the news media, could be both. The longer we drove and the farther we went the more likely we were going to end up on tonight's 11 o'clock news, if not earlier.

"There are three cops on our ass already," I said to her silence. "Let's pull over now before this thing really gets out of hand."

"You don't understand," she said. "All that mumbo jumbo back there. Like you have a clue how I feel about my life."

"You got me there, Sherrie," I said. "But act like you're not the only one with problems."

"Fuck you," she said. "Look how easy it was to pull a gun on you. Some PI you are."

"Funny," I said, trying not to talk through my teeth. I was seething. "I outweigh you by how much? Thirty pounds? And I'm in a helluva lot better shape. I could've made my move back there, but you know what? One of us would have been dead. And I'm not gonna die for this shit."

"How very heroic," she said. "What did you think, that you could talk me out of this? Take the 101 N. *Take the 101!*"

I looked back at the road, slowing down on the transition from the San Diego Freeway to the Ventura going north, which goes all the way to the U.S.-Canadian Border, a week's drive from here.

"Faster," she said.

"I can't. Traffic," I said, then when she poked the gun into my ribs again, I swung onto the shoulder, using it to get around the bulk of the traffic and careening back onto the ramp for the 101 North. I made sure to burn some rubber—it was the only way I could show my anger.

"So mature," she said.

"Fuck you," I said. "And fuck your problems. I didn't ask to be taken on this joyride with you. You could've gone out the back without me."

"Yeah, well I wasn't thinking."

"Is that supposed to surprise me?"

"I don't give a shit about you or anyone else but my kid. And I'm not gonna sit around in prison while somebody else raises her as their own."

"And you think trying to outrun the cops is gonna change that?"

"If I didn't run, they'd have arrested me anyway."

Then it all came to me in a flash. "Please don't tell me you have an outstanding warrant."

"I won't."

"Drugs?"

"No," she said. "Surprised, I bet. If you must know, they got my picture on a Rite Aid video camera. Me and Gary, passing a stolen ATM card. We were supposed to be in court on Friday but Gary got his own lawyer and cut a deal to testify against me. So you can see I got nothing to lose."

"Where's your kid now?"

"With my Mom. Look, I don't want to talk about it anymore. What the cops want you for, anyway?"

"I've been framed for something I didn't do," I said, knowing it sounded as hollow to her as it did to me.

"Thelma and Louise."

"What?"

"The movie," she said. "We're just like Thelma and Louise."

"Not to me we're not."

We didn't talk again until we were heading through the city of Ventura. Now we were the only car on a wide-open freeway, a dozen cop cruisers on our ass and two or three copters circling above us.

Just outside of Ventura, the freeway opens up into a spectacular view of the Pacific Ocean. It's a sudden transformation of scenery and most days I find it exhilarating.

On a clear day, you can see forever in all directions, the green and brown hills rising up on the inland side and to the west, the splendid sea crashing against rocky beaches, sailboats and tankers sharing the endless horizon, surfers catching the waves along with sea lions and gulls, tourists and sometimes even a dolphin or two.

Today was such a day, and even as the afternoon was fading to evening, the sea sparkled in the sunlight, the smell of fish hanging in the air like fine perfume.

"Take the next exit," she said pointing to a half moon ramp that circled underneath the freeway. We followed the narrow ramp as it came out onto a desolate stretch of Route 1 that's more like a service road than a piece of California's most famous scenic highway.

The cops were following close behind, but keeping their distance. This was procedure, hang back and let the pied piper run out of gas, blow a tire or finally just pull over, hoping to resolve the situation once everyone had come to a complete stop.

We took a couple of more roads and I navigated them slowly, the smell of the sea getting stronger and the wind picking up the closer we got to the coast. Finally, we came to a stop on a small piece of land next to a freeway overpass. A tattered old house stood well past its last legs toward one end of the property, where over the course of the day it would get the most sun. It was mere steps from a rocky, litter-strewn beach, a prime piece of real estate to the right buyer.

Sherrie was staring at it.

"Yours?" I asked.

"I grew up here," she said. "My pop left it to me. Can't sell it. Not allowed. Some city zoning bullshit. Round here, you're supposed to keep these in the family. But who's got money to fix it up?"

She pulled a piece of paper out of her bottomless jacket, unfolded it and handed it to me.

"Read it," she said.

It was a simple will. Sherrie Sanger's last will and testament, leaving all her worldly possessions to her 10-year-old daughter Emily.

"Don't do it," I said. "It's not worth it."

"Only people who don't know say things like this aren't worth it," she said and put her hand on the latch. Behind us, the cops had parked two cars with their noses touching so they formed a 'V'. The doors were open like wings and two cops were using them for shields, pointing their 9-mm's in our direction. While I couldn't see from where I was sitting, I knew further back the SWAT team was setting up a sniper.

Sherrie reached for the door.

"Don't," I said.

"What do you care?" she cried out. "What does anybody care?"

"What about Emily?" I said. "What if she's watching this on TV right now? Do you want her to see her own mother gunned down?"

"It doesn't matter. She'll know I did it for her."

"How fucking noble," I said. "You got this whole thing figured out, huh?"

"That's right," she said. "For once in my life, I do."

"What about Gary?"

"What about him?"

"You guys lived together, right?"

"Yeah, eleven years of fun and games."

"Long enough," I said.

"You got that right."

"No," I said. "Long enough so that he can contest the will. California has shared property laws."

"You're bullshitting me."

"Nope," I said. "You can look it up."

"This will is solid," she said. "He can't take it away from my daughter. She's real family."

"That's not how the courts will see it," I said. "They might even award Emily to Gary."

"Fuck you," she yelled and we both jumped when the sound of one of the cops calling through a bullhorn made the ground shake. He was telling us to get out of the car. Like a cop movie, only there were real bullets in those guns out there.

"Better do what he says, Sherrie," I said.

"What about the life insurance?" she said. "He can't take the life insurance. I made Emily the beneficiary."

"Look, I'm no lawyer," I said. "But Emily is a minor and the courts are going to have to appoint someone as guardian. It could be Gary since he's the parent of record. And another thing, if you go out there and get yourself killed by the cops, that's gonna be considered an act of suicide. There won't be any life insurance."

"This is too damned complicated," she said and sat still for a moment thinking. I kept my hands on the steering wheel, hoping the cops would see.

We listened as the man with the bullhorn called at us to surrender. We were running out of time. I didn't want to die in this goddamned Mustang.

"What are you going to do, Sherrie?" I said.

"Gimme that," she said, snatching the will from my lap. I could see one of the cops twitch.

"Easy with the sudden movements," I said. "Or we're both toast."

She was scribbling furiously on the back of the will, talking as she wrote. "I, Sherrie Sanger, do hereby appoint Zen M-o-s-e-s to be guardian to my daughter, Emily Ann Sanger." She dated and signed it. "Now you."

I was going to argue, but she pointed the pistol at me again. I didn't think it would be legal.

"Okay," she said and reached for the door latch again. "Take good care of my daughter."

"Don't Sherrie," I said. "Wait."

She ignored me, swung the door open and I held my breath, unhitching my seatbelt, letting it uncoil at about the same moment as the door creaked open. I glanced at the side-view mirror and saw too many cops with guns and the shakes. There was no way they could hit her without hitting me in the process. And for all they knew, I was party to this whole thing.

"Sherrie," I said, but she was rising from the seat, slowly, as if she was trying to summon the resolve to throw herself out there, before the firing range.

She had the gun down at her side but she was facing away from me, looking straight at the cops. I took advantage and scrambled up so I was squatting on the seat. Mustangs have these big, low bucket seats and it was pretty simple, though not without pain, to get my feet up. Sherrie was out of the car and the cop was yelling for her to drop her weapon. She was yelling something back but with the whir of the helicopters above us and the crashing of the waves against the beach, I couldn't make it out.

I could see her indecision. It was her Moment Of Truth, and she was hesitating, taking stock perhaps in a life a minute ago she had believed was worth more dead. Behind us the cops were taking aim.

Suddenly, slowly, she started to raise her gun hand and I knew it would be over in a few seconds. I threw my body lengthwise toward the open door, slamming my sternum hard on the plastic console between the seats, scrambling in spite of the pain, crawling, scratching, grabbing onto anything my hands could find just to pull myself out of that car.

Sherrie saw me through the corner of her eye and turned, but I was faster and as I hurled myself out of the car, I rolled into Sherrie's ankles as hard as I could, hauling her to the ground.

I heard the sound of gun fire, felt a terrific, shooting pain in my right side and caught the scent of sea and sand and blood as Sherrie fought to get out from underneath me.

PART TWO

sixteen

I came to when the EMTs were wheeling me into Santa Monica hospital's emergency room, watching the white acoustic tile ceiling fly by over my head, the fluorescent lights like disco strobes.

They wheeled me into an examination room and I noticed they had patched up my side with bandages and traded my shirt for a blue-green hospital gown.

My left arm was hooked up to an I.V. drip, probably a pain killer. I was conscious, but the edges of my world seemed blurred as if I was staring through Plexiglas.

My right arm was handcuffed to the side of the stretcher.

I lay back on the bed, prone and more tired than I'd been in a long time. I knew it was the drugs affecting me and even as I tried to keep my eyes open, my lids didn't want to put up a fight. So I closed them, listening to the sounds of the hospital around me, a strange combination of silence and deafening noise.

I smelled Bobo before he touched me, but only seconds before he wrapped one of his large hands around my ankle. Like most ER's, this one was cold and Bobo's touch was surprisingly warm.

I opened my eyes. He was standing above me, paging through the chart that the EMT's had left on the foot of my bed.

"I hope you're not the doctor," I said through my drug-induced haze. My head was starting to clear and I was starting to see better. But the only thing my brain could focus on was the searing pain in my right side. "Cause then I'm in big trouble."

"The girl weighs less than a twig," he said in his deep baritone that most of the time is barely above a whisper. "Losing your touch."

"Thanks for the report card, pal," I said.

"You sure keep things interesting," he said. "Woulda been around to see it if I hadn't gotten detained elsewhere."

"I bet," I said, knowing this was true. Bobo was like my guardian angel. He had his own stuff going most of the time, but he always seemed to find a way to watch my ass, especially when I needed it most.

But he doesn't always show up. I think this is because he doesn't want me to think he's gonna rescue me whenever I'm in trouble. His theory is that the idea he might not appear on his white horse keeps me sharp.

"Please, no lectures," I said. "I'm not in the mood."

"Lennon is wandering the halls out there," he said. "Think he's afraid of me."

"He should be," I said.

"Want me to stay?"

"Nah," I said. Get outta here."

"I called Judy just in case," he said. "She's ready if you need her."

"Thanks," I said. Judy Johnson used to be Jim's law partner until she joined the public defender's office. She's one of those lawyers who still thinks the law can make a difference in people's lives.

"Not to worry," he said. "Just here to make sure you're gonna live."

"Am I?"

"Dunno," he said, backing out of the room and winking his blue eye at me. "I'll be in touch."

And he was gone.

A moment passed before Lennon came in, followed by two uniforms. He had a stern look on his face and he was still wearing his fuck you aviator sunglasses.

We took a dislike to each other from the first and it's been downhill ever since. Last New Year's Eve during a particularly trying case for me, I lost my temper and sucker punched him, breaking his jaw in two places.

It remains months later a red hot embarrassment for a cop who prides himself on being tougher than everybody else.

I rattled the handcuff. "Am I under arrest?"

"Where were you last night?"

"I asked you a question," I said. "Am I under arrest?"

He shook his head. "Not yet," he said.

"Then take these goddamned cuffs off of me."

Lennon stared down at me, but all I could see was my reflection distorted in the lenses of his sunglasses. Finally, he motioned for one of the other officers to unlock the cuffs.

I wanted to reach over and massage my wrist where the cuffs had been, but moving was excruciating. I coughed, trying to hide the tears of pain I knew were ready to fall from my eyes.

I wasn't about to give this asshole the satisfaction.

"Where were you last night?"

"On a case," I said.

"And this was where exactly?"

"Why do you want to know?"

Lennon suddenly turned to the uniforms and told them to leave. They didn't argue.

When they were gone, Lennon leaned over me, his look

menacing, and even though I couldn't see his eyes, I knew they were filled with hate. It was thick in the air around him.

Nearby I heard voices, getting louder, coming closer.

"I know you were in that house last night," he said. "And I know you killed that guy. You're going down for this and I'm gonna enjoy every single moment."

He was still leaning over me when we heard the swish of a curtain opening.

"Get away from my patient." The voice was attached to a young doctor. My uncle Sam came in behind her.

Sam was smiling though I could tell there was concern underneath it. He pushed his way past Lennon, adding a good old-fashioned glare. There's nothing like family to lift your spirits.

"I wasn't told this woman was under police custody," the doctor said.

"She's not," said Lennon, completely changing his demeanor. "Just routine questions."

"I'm sure they can wait then," she said and stared daggers at Lennon until he had no choice but to leave the room. Then she winked at Sam.

"We saw Bobo on his way out," he said to me and suddenly everything was clear. "How you doing?"

He rubbed my cheek with a dry, callused hand. Like Bobo's, Sam's hand warmed the spot on my face where he'd touched me.

Sam is my father's younger brother and except for my mom, who I haven't seen in 25 years, is all the family I have left. We lost touch ourselves for a dozen years until about a year ago. Since then, we've been trying the best we can to make up for all the lost time.

He lives not far from me, in the Marina. We play golf

Wednesday mornings and most Fridays we have dinner together. In between, we talk on the phone and try to catch the Dodgers when the Giants are in town.

It's not perfect, but we're learning.

"Thanks, Sam," I said. "And thanks, Doc. Appreciate you coming to my rescue. I owe you one."

"Your friend was very convincing," she said. "Besides, Vince Lennon's reputation isn't exactly a secret around here. Everybody knows he's an asshole with a short fuse."

"Nice to know I'm not the only person he picks on," I said. "So, what's the damage?"

"It's not too bad." She was stocky, not fat, with short-cropped hair and small features on light brown skin. The tag on her jacket said Dr. Lynn Sherman.

She peered over me, shining a pen light into my eyes. I focused on the tiny light, trying to will away the pain.

"I feel pretty good," I said, forcing a smile. My lips were dry, the buzz of painkillers making my head float.

She was done with my eyes and, after pulling the dressing off my wound, was gently poking and prodding. It hurt like hell.

"Uncle," trying to be funny through gritted teeth, but sounding more pathetic than brave.

"Sorry," she said, then grabbed a folder and leafed through it. "Ms. Moses, I'm Dr. Sherman. I suppose you know by now that you've been shot."

I nodded, winking at Sam who had taken a seat by the bed. He shook his head but his eyes, like mine always do, gave him away. They were twinkling.

"You're lucky," she said. "I know it hurts but as far as we can tell, the bullet missed your right lung or anything else vital. We're going to have to do X-rays of course just to make sure."

I laughed but it made me cough again. She gave me a drink of water, helping me to sit up a bit.

"What's so funny?" she said.

"I can guarantee you it didn't hit my right lung," I said. "Cause I don't have one."

"One what?"

"Right lung," I said and told her about the cancer.

She smiled and I decided right there that I liked her.

"Well that would explain things," she said. "Let's get you the X-ray anyway. Just to make sure, okay?"

As if I had a choice.

Dr. Sherman checked a couple more things, told Sam to wait outside and then left when the X-ray technicians arrived. She came back after they had finished their work, which included folding me into various poses for the portable machine. I felt like a contortionist with a badly pulled stomach muscle.

"I was right," she said. "The bullet missed everything important, But there's a problem."

"Of course," I said.

"It's your heart," she said. "Anybody else, it would have missed by a mile, but it barely missed yours."

People always ask me what it feels like to have only one lung and most of the time I say something flip like that's the reason we're all born with two. The truth is most of the time I don't feel any different from anybody else.

The body is truly an amazing machine, adaptable in ways I think science is only beginning to grasp. When someone loses a lung, for example, the one that's left has to take on more capacity and literally expands in order to handle the extra load.

In my case, in part because I was so young, some organs in my body were pushed into unusual positions by the bigger lung. In most people, the heart is on the left side of their chest. For me, it's now somewhere just right of center, courtesy of my expanded left lung.

I tapped my chest gingerly.

"My ribs are killing me," I said. "Feels like I broke one or two."

"You win the prize, Ms. Moses," she said.

"Call me Zen," I said. "Everybody does."

"Fine. Zen it is. As I was saying, you're correct. But I think you must've cracked a rib when you fell. It looks like the bullet entered under your right arm and somehow ended up here."

She pointed to a spot just below my shoulder, near my collar bone.

"So it's still inside me?"

"Unfortunately," she said. "Wherein lies the problem."

"Is there infection?"

"We've got you started on antibiotics, but it's a very clean entry," she said. "So far, so good."

"But?"

"But with most patients, we'd just wrap you up and send you on your way. But like I said, you're not most patients." She held up the X-ray again, using her pen as a pointer. "As you can see the bullet isn't far from the surface, but it's lodged in pretty good. See this in your neck? That's an artery. And that white crooked thing next to it, that's the pesky little piece of lead."

The picture was clear. The bullet was perilously close to nicking an artery in my neck. An inch or two to the left and I'd bleed to death.

"What's the chances that it will move?" I said.

"That's anybody's guess," she said. "It could move in the

next hour, the next day, week, maybe never. But if it does, you'll be staring up at the ceiling, coughing up blood before you ever know what hit you."

"What exactly do you suggest?"

"Surgery," she said. "It's risky but somehow I'd feel a lot better about the odds."

"I'll take my chances," I said. "No surgery. Thanks."

I knew what I was saying and not an ounce of me was undecided. Maybe it was coming out of an insane line of reasoning and maybe I was under the influence of some powerful painkillers, but I couldn't think of anything that could change my mind.

Once you or someone you love has been cooped up in the hospital for any length of time, especially after serious surgery, it becomes a place you avoid at all costs, as if merely walking in will make you sick again.

Part of it I think is the sicker you are and the longer your stay, the more you learn about the inner workings of the medical profession. And while being a doctor may be a noble undertaking, the same can't be said for the industry as a whole. It's the same reason why you wouldn't want to see the food being prepared at your favorite hole-in-the-wall restaurant.

There are other reasons why the term elective surgery has become an oxymoron, why just the scent of antibacterial soap makes me want to throw up. But I know in my case it would take years on the couch just to get to a small understanding of the emotions my illness has stirred deep within my psyche. Suffice it to say I hate hospitals. I barely tolerate doctors and unless I've no other choice, there's no way in hell I'm gonna stay one second longer than I have to. I'd rather spend a year in prison.

"I think you'd better consider the consequences," she said. I was thankful and impressed she wasn't arguing with me, just trying her best to cajole. Maybe she understood.

"I have," I said. "But I'd just as soon play this out. I'll be careful."

"It's up to you," she said. "I'll write you a prescription for some Percodan and some antibiotics. You have to remember to take them all. Also clean the wound twice a day until it heals up."

"Am I free to go?"

"I have a feeling I won't be able to stop you."

She wrote some instructions on a piece of paper and called in a nurse who started to re-dress my wound and wrap up my sore ribs. At least the painkillers they'd given me were working.

When she was finished, she had me sign a couple of forms and she and the nurse helped me to a sitting position.

"Your uncle said he'd give you a ride home. He brought this," said Dr. Sherman, handing me one of Sam's flannel shirts. It smelled of cigars and turpentine. "Please call me if you have any symptoms described on that form."

"Thanks, Doc," I said, and when I shook her hand, the movement made me wince.

"You know you don't have to prove to me you're tough," she said.

"It comes with the job," I said.

"I bet a lot of people believe that," she said. "But I noticed the bullet wound isn't the only non-surgical scar on your chest. Looks like a stab wound there as well. I'm not trying to tell you how to do your job, but just because there's no lung on that side, doesn't mean it's not vulnerable."

"I know," I said quietly. "I appreciate your concern. I'm very careful with my health. I work out regularly and I don't take stupid chances. I understand what I'm doing. Even you said that bullet might never move."

"Maybe not, but it's risky."

"I don't mind the risk," I said.

"It might kill you," she said.

I just nodded. There was no question we understood each other.

"I'll see you at my office in a week."

She left me in the room, sitting on the edge of the bed, trying to collect myself. I closed my eyes for a moment, willing my inner voices to calm, quelling the doubt I was feeling from rising up and taking over.

I thought of my mother, wherever she was tonight, and my father and first cousin and aunt, all gone from this world. I considered Sam and I, the last of our line, once strong and vibrant, now just a couple of loners hanging on to each other in some last gasp semblance of family.

I realized sitting in that sterile hospital room that taking risks was easy for me, perhaps even welcome. That settling down was as foreign a concept as working on Wall Street.

I was thinking maybe Sherrie and I weren't so different after all. She was willing to pay the ultimate price for her daughter. Maybe in the end, it wouldn't have worked out the way she planned. Her methods were wrong, dangerous, ill-conceived. But her motives were pure, direct, even noble. Here was a woman ready to give her very life so her child could have a better one than she had, than she could possibly give her.

It's exactly what I would do under the circumstances, I told myself. But would I? I knew I'd take a bullet for Sam without hesitation. I took one for Sherrie, a total stranger, and it was stuck inside me doing God knows what to the empty space where my lung used to be.

I told myself it was all part of the job I loved, taking measured chances, putting myself out there in the middle of the chaos, trying to make things right in my own corner of this upside down universe. I wondered how much of what I liked about my job was the gamble and what part was the pleasure of helping another human being out of a jam.

These were questions I didn't want to ask myself now. Not because I didn't know the answers, but because I didn't want to know.

I opened my eyes and buttoned my shirt, took a measured breath and slipped ever so delicately off the bed. Then I walked slowly out to the waiting room to look for Sam.

seventeen

Sam was reading the LA Times when I wobbled into the waiting room. He had the sports section open, but was looking up at the television.

The late news was being rebroadcast and the anchors were watching my and Sherrie's drama unfold, getting the play-by-play from the reporter in the helicopter.

Sunday had been over for more than two hours and the waiting room was empty save for one man who sat on one of the orange plastic chairs in the back, leafing through some papers.

"Hey Sam," I said. "Take a walk with me."

Visiting hours were over, but I knew my way around. I didn't think anyone would stop a gimpy woman and an old man. We went down a long, white hallway and through two double doors to get to the I.C.U.

It was dark and the indescribable scent of the sick was so fresh it was as if the walls had just been painted with it.

We got as far as the nurse's station before someone stopped us. It was a nurse dressed in rose-colored scrubs with cartoon characters on it.

"Can I help you?" she said.

"We were looking for my friend," I said.

"Unless you're looking for your bed, you aren't supposed to be here," she said. "Visiting hours end at ten."

"Listen," I said. "My friend was nearly killed Saturday night.

They say it's touch and go and that he might not make it through the night. I just want to see him, you know, just in case . . ."

I wanted to touch this woman's heart and I didn't have to try hard. Anybody could hear the cracking in my voice was real.

She gave me and Sam a real hard look-over, putting her hands on her hips. They were wide hips, but not out of proportion with the rest of her.

"I'm really not supposed to," she said. "But . . . alright. What's his name?"

"James Gray," I said, watching her face fall. It must be worse than I thought. "Is he . . . ?"

"No," she said. "He's still with us. But he's taken a turn for the worse. I can let you see him, but only for a second. If the doctors found out, it'd be my job."

Jim's room was filled with so many electronic beeps, flashes and lights that it felt like the bridge of the *Enterprise*. He looked peaceful lying there, his hands resting at each side, his feet pointed away from each other.

I stood over him, placing my hand on his. It was warm. His other hand was bandaged up. The cops found his finger at the scene and the doctors sewed it back on. The wonders of medicine.

"I'm sorry," I whispered, holding back tears. "I'm gonna make this right for you. I swear it."

I squeezed his hand. "I swear it," I said and left him to the medical rhythm of beeps and pulses, wondering if I'd ever see him alive again.

eighteen

When we went out to the parking lot to find Sam's pick-up, a couple of TV vans were lying in wait on the Street outside the ER entrance. I was glad they didn't seem to notice us.

Inside his truck, I leaned back and tried to stretch, feeling fatigue in every corner of my body. It lasted about a half a second, right until I felt the sharp, biting pain about where I knew my cracked rib to be.

I had to grab hold of myself and squeeze before it subsided. I wanted to go home and crash for a week or longer, but I knew I wouldn't be able to sleep. Not yet.

"Let's swing by SMPD," I said.

Sam looked at me, shaking his head. "Can't this wait until daylight? You're in no shape . . ."

"I'm okay Sam."

"You can barely move."

"I'll give you that," I smiled at him. "Look, I gotta do this. I'll drive over myself if I have to. Besides, I'm tough, re-member?"

"I know you think you are," he said.

He didn't argue after that, opting instead for the silent pro-test. We drove to the police station. His exasperation was like another passenger.

"Think I can see Sherrie Sanger?"

I wanted my voice to sound strong and sure, but it came

out more like a hoarse whisper instead. My side hurt like hell and I seemed to be using all my energy making only tiny movements. So, by the time I'd walked into the lobby of the police station and made my way downstairs to the holding cells, I was out of breath and coughing from the effort.

"I don't know why you'd want to." The sergeant on desk duty was a big guy, heavy through the middle with thinning light brown hair and blue eyes that seemed intent, focused and intelligent. He was one of those people who looked like what they do for a living, though there was no telling whether he had started out that way or the other way around. It made me wonder though, who had he pissed off to land the graveyard shift down here? His name was Vaughn.

"After what she did to you. . . " he stopped, looking up at me as if he just saw me for the first time. "Jeez, from the looks of it, damage was done."

"I look worse than I feel," I lied. "But to be honest I would like to go home and get some sleep. So how 'bout it?"

"Hey, you know I can't let you in there, not without the proper authority."

"Yeah, I know," I said. "You have to go by the book. But let's think this out a bit, okay? As you so astutely pointed out, this hasn't been a great day for me. I'm tired and I'm holding my insides in over here, and I'm trying damn hard not to breathe because it hurts so bad.

"And I'm here because of that woman in there. I think she owes me an explanation and that's not something I want to wait for. Not after the night I've had. Besides, you're aware that I'm on pretty good terms with some of the guys who sign your paycheck. Right now, they're all at home, dreaming about making a nice, fresh start on Monday morning. I'd hate to be the one who has to wake them up because a certain cop wasn't willing to give his okay to something they'd say was cool any-way. What's your take on it?"

The guy smiled, pursing his lips together and shaking his head as he turned a clipboard toward me.

"For the record," he said, "I know you're bluffing."

I shrugged and smiled back at him.

"Sign here," he said.

"Must be my innate charm," I said and waited while he grabbed a set of keys and led me to the back.

There are about two dozen cells in the bowels beneath the building. Upstairs are the mayor's office, city government de-partments, courts and the SMPD. The jails are holding cells, but they're state of the art. When it's called for, they can quite adequately serve as maximum security holding pens.

Sherrie was on suicide watch. She had her own private cell and a female police officer, sitting across from her, leaning back in a padded office chair. She was reading a book about seeing New York on a budget.

The guard didn't get up when we approached.

"Billie," said the officer. "Give Ms. Moses a minute here."

"On whose authority?"

"Mine," he said, a little agitated. Guess more than one person could go by the book. "Go take a smoke break or something."

"I quit," she said.

"Go," Vaughn said. "Go call Mel and tell him about all the stuff you're gonna do over New Year's in the Big Apple. You can decide what show you wanna see."

Vaughn watched her as she walked away, reluctantly.

"Don't be thinkin' you're gonna rat me out either," he called after her. "You don't want them to get the wrong idea about you losing those keys last week."

After she huffed off, Vaughn checked his watch. "You got exactly ten minutes," he said. "That's all I can spare. I don't want to have to explain this to the next guy on duty—hey, you alright?"

I felt lightheaded suddenly, my ears started ringing and spots formed in front of my eyes. I had to grab the bars of Sherrie's cell to keep from falling over.

It was another long moment before I found my equilibrium and was able to speak again.

"Yeah, just a little woozy," I said. "I just want to get this over with. Thanks Vaughn. I owe you one."

"Sure," he said. "Just be outta here in ten, okay?"

Sherrie was lying on the cot in the corner, staring up at the ceiling, smoking a cigarette. She took one look at me and scowled.

"Well if it isn't Wonder Woman," she said.

"A simple thank you might be nice."

"For what? I was trying to kill myself," she said. "Or maybe you needed a fucking road map."

"Cut the attitude Sherrie," I said. "I'm not here to give you shit."

"Gee thanks, Mom."

"I don't know what you're thinking right now and I don't really care," I said, holding up my shirt so she could see the bandages, which were blotted red in places. She looked, but then turned toward the wall. A whole day's worth of nonsense was building up inside me and I was shaking from the futile effort to keep it all inside.

"See this? It hurts like hell. So please don't get any ideas that I'm some kind of hero. I had no intention of getting myself shot. But it happened and there's nothing I can do about it."

"You'll live probably just long enough to screw somebody else's life up," she said.

I'd heard enough. It was one thing to feel sorry for this poor woman, it was another to wallow in her self-pity with her.

"If you weren't so busy with this 'woe is me crap,' you'd realize there's only one person responsible for what's happened to you," I said. "She's staring back at you in the mirror every morning."

"What do you know about my life?"

"I know things haven't always been perfect," I said. "But that doesn't give you an excuse to be kiting ATM cards. Why don't you take some responsibility for yourself and your kid before it really is too late?"

My words coming in short breaths. It was hard to breathe without feeling the sting in my chest.

"Or you can consider today as a dress rehearsal and when nobody's looking, try it again. Only this time, I won't be there so you ought to be able to get it right."

"Maybe that's what I gotta do then."

"Anybody can feel sorry for themselves. You wanna be the world's expert, that's okay by me."

"Where I stand, I don't got no choices left."

"That's where you're wrong," I said. "If you can't see it, then you're gonna have to look harder. Jesus, Sherrie. Nobody said life was gonna be easy. Maybe this is your second chance, a new lease. It happens you know. It happens to people whose lives are a helluva lot more fucked up than yours. It's your call Sherrie. Tell me what's it gonna be?"

She didn't say a word and I couldn't be sure but I thought she was crying again. I was surprised she had any tears left.

"All I want to know," I said, quietly, "is that I didn't take this bullet for nothing. Make it mean something, Sherrie. Not for me, but for you, for your kid, for whatever's out there waiting for you."

She turned back to the wall, and while I still couldn't hear, I knew she was crying again, her whole body was shaking.

"You need anything?"

"Nah," she said, finally wiping the tears. "I'd like to be by myself though."

I nodded, even though I knew she couldn't see me. I watched the cigarette she had dropped onto the floor. It was still burning, filling the small cell with the stale smell of smoke.

I called for Vaughn, but Billie showed up instead and let me out. She shut the door and clicked the lock and managed to give me a dirty look in the process.

I started back down the hallway.

"Zen," Sherrie called and I stopped and turned back to the bars. She was back to staring at the ceiling.

"Yeah?"

"You might be a lousy PI," she said, "but you'd be a good mother. I should know."

I nodded. I didn't know what else to say.

"Anyway, I just wanted you to know that, that . . . well, I've been thinking about all that shit you said."

"And?"

"I don't know," she said. "I'm just thinking about it is all. You got a problem with that?"

"Nope," I said. "It's okay. You take care, now. You need someone to talk to, you know where to find me."

I followed the long hallway back toward Vaughn's station. It seemed even colder and harsher than five minutes ago. I thought about Sherrie, about the burdens she carried, and how for some people the load was heavier and less bearable than for others.

I've heard it said that life's harshest trials are often visited upon the people who can handle it the best. Like tests to strengthen them further for what's to come. But if I ever believed it, I didn't anymore.

I'd remember thinking long after how on the surface a part of me was feeling good, like I'd done the right thing, reached out to a soul in need, made some kind of important sacrifice of a depth I'd yet to fully comprehend.

But deep down, I felt something else, a sense that some days, even the best we are isn't good enough and worse, it isn't even our best.

nineteen

Sam had to drop me off a half block from my house because reporters were already camping out on my curb. There was one big truck in front of the back entrance to the pet cemetery and about a dozen members of the news media were milling about, ready to catch me in their strobe lights.

I painfully and quietly climbed up the back stairs and sneaked in through the door off my kitchen. I kept the lights down.

If I'm not a public figure by legal standards, my job puts me in the public eye. I'm part of the story whether I like it or not. I can live with this.

I once was a journalist. I appreciate the importance of dispensing information in a democracy and understand that gaining access often gives a reporter more facts and less compulsion to fill in what's missing.

But there's something troubling about the lengths to which today's reporter will go to cover a story, get the angle no one else has and get it out faster than the speed of light. Pundits and programmers claim there's a proven audience for this kind of rubbernecking journalism, but I wonder what in the world ever happened to integrity and fairness and why reporters aren't kneeling at that altar anymore.

The truth is, it makes me mad, especially when it's me, a friend or a client who's the latest specimen jammed under their microscope.

It was slow going as I fumbled around my living room, getting used to the dark. I made my way to the front door, and turned on the timer to my new, temperamental sprinkler system.

I crawled gingerly into bed without even taking my clothes off. I had no energy and everything below my chin seemed to radiate pain.

The sprinklers came on as I nodded off, It was a soothing feeling. That and knowing right now, those reporters were getting doused, scurrying to get out of the sudden rain.

I only wish I'd been out there to see it.

twenty

I spent the next few days getting back on my feet. Mostly, I slept till noon and found my way to the couch for the rest of the day, catching up on newspapers and magazines that had piled up.

By Tuesday, I didn't need the bandages anymore and by Thursday I could actually do some housework without debilitating pain.

The week passed quietly, though my phone rang incessantly for two days straight. I let the machine answer most of them. For years, my calls were forwarded to a former client turned secretary. Vivian had been a film actress way back when and I'd helped her recover money she'd been bilked out of. But she surprised me last January when on her eighty-first birthday she announced she was getting married for the third time and moving to the desert.

She could be nosey and forgetful, but I've missed hearing her Brooklyn-bred accent and her clumsy attempts to hook me up with her young doctors. It had been more than six months since she'd left and I was just getting used to not having her around to run interference.

Andrea came by Tuesday morning, the first day I'd been able to drag myself out of bed. I had shuffled to my living room couch, where I collapsed in a pile of aches and pains and a pool of sweat for my trouble.

I had the TV clicker in one hand and a copy of the new Tom Wolfe novel on the coffee table. Everybody else was reading it, so I figured what the hell. John Hiatt was playing on the stereo. Before I could turn one of the big book's pages, I heard someone outside on my front landing.

"Are you gonna stand out there all day?" I yelled toward my door.

"Zen? Oh, I wasn't sure whether you were up." Even muffled, Andrea's shrieky voice could be heard clearly through the door.

"Oh hey Andrea," I said. "The key's in that milk box on the landing. Let yourself in."

I don't always keep the key there. I had Sam leave it there in case I didn't feel like getting up. Like now.

Andrea entered, a little sheepishly, but I didn't say anything. Maybe it was hard for her to be around the wounded or maybe she felt guilty for the whole Sherrie thing.

"Hey," she said, taking in my living room. I think it was the first time she'd been inside. "How ya feeling?" she said, playing with a loose strand of her hair. It was dyed auburn. Sunday she'd been a brunette. "This all the furniture you got?"

I looked around at my couch, the coffee table, the big chair in the corner, my lamp and the bookshelves. It felt crowded to me.

"I don't like clutter."

"You know you could really do some cool things in here. This beautiful floor and the windows, the right treatment and you'd get a ton more light. You could get something with a pastel motif. It's so you."

"Oh yeah?"

"Absolutely," she said. "Yellows, pinks, blues, greens. You could really impress the guys."

"Hold it, Andrea," I said. "See this stuff? This is me. Okay? The last thing I need is an interior decorator. Thanks but no thanks."

"Suit yourself," she said. "But maybe it would help you get a date once in a while."

I almost said something. I didn't have the energy.

"Heard from Sherrie?" I said, trying to sit up but still unable to work my sore body into that position.

"Nah," she said. "She's real sorry, you know. I came by to say how sorry I am that . . ."

"Forget it," I said. "Sherrie made her own choices."

"I knew things were bad, but like I had no idea they were *bad*, you know?" she said. "I still can't believe it. You know, we watched the whole thing on the news."

"I heard it was quite the spectacle."

"Everybody's talking about it," she said. "They let her go but she's gotta go around with some electronic thingy on her leg. And she has to see a shrink."

"That's probably a good idea," I said.

"They said they might cut her some slack if she turns her ex in," she said. "But she'd never do that."

"I thought she hated the guy," I said.

She looked at me like I was an alien from a far away planet who'd never seen a human being before.

"Boy you're pretty stupid for someone so smart," she said. "You need to get out more."

"We barely know each other, Andrea. What's with the cracks about my love life?"

"It don't take no detective to see where you're spending your nights, girl," she said. "Jeez."

She had a point there. "So have you talked to Sherrie?"

"Once. I'm tryin' to give her some space, you know? She's been worried for Emily. They took her away and put her in a foster home."

"It's probably a good thing for her until Sherrie gets back on her feet," I said.

"I don't know," she said.

"What do you mean?"

She stood her ground for a second, walked over to my chair and started toying with the fabric. It was black leather with handles and a foot rest. I like to sit in it like Captain Kirk, put my feet up and blast the stereo. Smoky cabaret when I was depressed and something more upbeat when I wasn't.

"Can I ask you something?" she said suddenly and waited until I nodded before she continued. "What if you know something but you've been sworn to secrecy, like practically a blood oath, right? But you think maybe if you tell, you might help that person who didn't want you to say anything about it in the first place? Would you do it?"

My head was spinning. "If you know something that will help Sherrie you should tell me," I said.

Andrea had her head down again, she was pouting and the hip blue lipstick she wore made it look she'd been holding her breath for hours.

"It's just that, that," she said and sighed. "Sherrie and me, we've been friends forever, you know? And I'm worried about her. But it's more than this crazy stuff. I think, well I think she's into something really bad."

"Please, Andrea." I didn't mean to sound so edgy, but I was achy and tired.

"Shegotadeaththreat." It came out so fast I had to make her repeat it twice before I heard it right.

"From who? Her ex, what's-his-name? Gary?"

"Wouldn't put it by him," she said. "But that's not the worst part. She wasn't the only one they threatened."

"Who else? You?" I looked at her as she shook her head No and suddenly it hit me. Gumshoes with new holes in their chests aren't too quick on the uptake.

"Emily?"

Andrea nodded.

"Shit," I said. "When?"

"She told me she got a letter Sunday morning when she went outside to get the paper," she said. "It was sitting underneath, on the back of a postcard of the Hollywood sign."

"She still have it?"

"Nah, she told me she burned it," said Andrea. "I told her she should've showed it to the police, but she told me she was taking care of it herself."

Maybe that's why she was carrying that gun, I thought.

"Wish she'd told me about it," I said. "Might've helped our situation a bit."

"I was hoping that maybe you could find out who sent it."

"Me?" I smiled. "I don't think Sherrie wants anyone's help right now, especially mine."

"Don't do it for Sherrie," Andrea said. Then she pulled a roll of money out of her tight jeans. They were bellbottoms, which proves that everything comes back sooner or later.

"What's that for?"

"I want to hire you," she said and I managed to shift so I could swing my legs off the couch and face Andrea.

"Listen, Andrea," I said, holding my hand up. "Sherrie's got a lot of problems right now. If she wants help, she knows where to find me."

"People like Sherrie don't ever ask for help," she said. It was the smartest thing she'd said to me. "Anyways, I can pay."

She said the last part without much conviction. I had a feeling it would be a difficult task to separate this woman from her money.

"I've got savings. You'd be amazed how much I can make cutting hair."

"Let's hold off on the money for now," I said and she was clearly relieved. "Tell you what though. I'll keep an eye on her, okay?"

"And Emily?"

"Sure," I said, remembering the paper Sherrie made me sign during our freeway adventure. "Now get going so I can get some sleep. Or I'm not gonna be in any condition to help anybody."

twenty-one

Nobody had ID'd the body in Donnell's house. His finger-prints weren't in the FBI database and nothing on him shed any light on who he was or where he came from.

No one had come forward to claim the body even though the description was handed out to the news media. He was just a faceless corpse alone in a freezer in the city morgue with a John Doe name tag tied around his big toe.

Brooks suggested they call in a forensic anthropologist to reconstruct the face, but his boss, Watkins, said the costs would outweigh the benefit. He had a point. There was so much damage it might take weeks or months to get an accurate picture and by that time routine police work might already have done the job.

Jim was still hanging on. The good news was that the surgery to reattach his finger was a success. The bad news was he might not ever wake up to use it again.

I didn't think much about any of it until Thursday morning when Bobo came by. As usual, he came in without knocking. I have no idea how he gets into my house. I think he must walk through walls.

I was sitting on the couch in my sweats, reading Cormac McCarthy's *All the Pretty Horses*.

"I love the part when they steal the kid's horse back," he said.

"Is there anything you don't know?"

"Nope," he said, plopping down in my favorite chair. He had a soft leather satchel open on his lap. "You still lazing around?"

"I was thinking about taking a walk actually," I said. "I'm starting to feel a little better."

"Don't get used to it," he said. "I hear they're looking at you for the John Doe murder."

"What have they got?"

"Beats me. Lennon's been keeping a tight lid on the case," he said, adjusting the shoulder holster he almost always wears. "I'd watch my back if I was you."

"It would help if I knew what was going on, but it's like chasing shadows," I said. "I remember going into the house and the dog and seeing Eddie and Jim. But after that, it's a blank."

"Not surprised," he said, pulling a sheet of paper out of the satchel and tossing it on my coffee table. "Your blood test came back. Rohypnol."

"The date-rape drug? That can't be right. I felt a sting in my back—someone injected me with something. Besides roofies take a few minutes to knock you out. I dropped right after I was shot."

"Lab says they musta knocked you out with something else first," he said. "Not sure with what."

I sat back, taking this new information in, trying to will my memory back. Something wasn't right.

"So it's true, Eddie was setting me up," I said.

"Looks like it. You said the guy hates you."

"Yeah," I said. "But why now, after all these years?"

"Revenge is a dish best . . ."

"Thanks, Shakespeare," I said. "But I mean it. Eddie never does anything unless he has a very good reason."

"If he's running this whole thing, why disappear? If you tell your side of the story, it's gonna look bad for him."

"That's what's so nuts," I said. "Maybe he didn't count on me waking up and wiping down the crime scene."

"Speaking of, they still don't know who that body belongs to," he said.

"What about Jim?" I said. "Where's he fit in to this?"

"Went by to see him today," he said. "Still in a coma but doctors say he's stable."

"We're gonna have to find out what he knows," I said. "Jim might be the key to this whole mess. I still don't know why Jim would get mixed up with him. If Eddie was blackmailing him, why didn't he come to us?"

"Secrets," said Bobo, who had more than most. "Everybody's got some they don't ever tell."

"Not even to your best friends?"

Bobo shook his head at me, his way of reminding me how much more about the world I had yet to learn.

"Whatever Eddie had on Jim, it's bad," he said. "Jim was thinking of closing his practice and moving back to Minnesota."

"Maybe he was sick of the grind," I said, feeling suddenly sorry I'd let our relationship lag. In the modern world friendships are often the first casualties.

"Maybe," he said. "I found a plane ticket to Minneapolis in his desk. He was supposed to leave Monday morning. It had something to do with a twenty-five-year-old murder case that took place on some Indian reservation back there."

"You think that has anything to do with all this?"

Bobo shrugged.

"What you gonna do about the cops?"

"I don't know," I said. "I gotta find Eddie Cooke first."

And I knew just where to start. When Eddie was a big-time sports agent, he had a big-time mouthpiece who handled the press for him.

Marty Bergstein was a hardass like his client, but he was always fair. I can't remember a time when he wasn't honest with us, even if that meant not saying anything at all.

Bergstein still represented Eddie and there wasn't a chance in hell of me getting in to see him. But it was nearing 12:30 and Bergstein was a creature of habit. I knew exactly where to find him.

twenty-two

While I was in the shower, Bobo took off. His note said he had something he wanted to follow-up on. I put on jeans, a crisp white cotton blouse, my Nikes and my black leather jacket—nothing special, but for the first time in nearly a week I wasn't wearing sweats.

I steadied myself, found I could move around without passing out and headed out the back. It was time to get reacquainted with the rest of the world.

I was sore and the rib was still bothering me, but overall I was beginning to feel like my old self. I silently thanked Bobo. Then I cursed him.

When I was just starting out in the detecting biz, Bobo took it upon himself to train me. It was a grueling process that took the better part of six months. We worked on everything from your basic hand-to-hand combat, American marine style, to a host of disciplines Bobo had picked up in his many travels around the globe.

Bobo worked me harder than anyone ever has, before or since, his theory being if I could stand his rigorous demands, I could stand anything. And he wouldn't have to worry about me more than he had to.

I spent the entire six months living with him at a cabin he keeps up in Mammoth, at the end of a long dirt road that winds up into the Sierra mountains fifteen miles and nearly 10,000 feet. It's a desolate place, snowed in eight months of the year and surrounded by stubby evergreen forests filled with mountain lions and red-tailed hawks and assorted other creatures that do what they can to get by in the unforgiving cold.

I'm not a gung-ho kind of person. The anger and violence that I summon up when necessary comes from personal fires inside me that get stoked when someone does wrong to a client or someone I love. I hated every moment of the training with Bobo, and for months afterward I wouldn't speak to him. To this day, we don't talk about it.

The worst part was this ritual we had at the end of each day. Bobo and I fought outside in his yard. No gloves, no man-made weapons, no rules.

For the first couple of months, Bobo beat up on me. I still have marks from those fights. But gradually, as time wore on, I learned to fight back. While I never really got the best of him, he couldn't get me either. There were moments when I was able to get the upper hand and take a few whacks of my own. For six long, cold as shit months, those were the moments I lived for.

I know now Bobo was doing me a favor. He was preparing me to battle bigger, stronger opponents, to be able to take punches and get up. He was teaching me how to survive.

And while I wouldn't admit it even under extreme torture, days like today I'm grateful.

I drove my Alfa north through Santa Monica toward Sunset and the elegant confines of the vaunted Riviera Country Club.

I parked the Alfa on a quiet street near the club and cut through the back nine to get past the security gate.

The clubhouse attendant was unavoidable. He looked me over with an air of superiority which he only dialed down slightly when I told him who I was there to see.

"Mr. Bergstein didn't say he was expecting someone," he said.

"Gives me more time to get lunch," I said. "But we do have an appointment. It's not like I just walked in here."

He looked me over as if he knew I was lying, but he let me go anyway. One reason was the crisp Benjamin I deftly placed in his palm and the other was something else I hadn't counted on but should've.

It's one thing to be a member of a rich man's club, it's quite another to be one of the people who has to serve them. Maybe the idea of me interrupting one of his better client's lunch time tennis matches was too good to pass up.

"We never talked," he said to me without lowering his chin even a millimeter. "I've never seen you before."

I nodded.

Riviera is one of those stately old golf courses where membership costs somewhat more than most mortgages. It's not the kind of place where you can just walk in off the street — somebody has to invite you. Once a year the pros come through to play for a six-figure purse in what used to be called the LA Open.

Not so long ago, Riviera was also a place where only white people could play as long as they were praying in the right church. But now the club is owned by the Japanese, and while they still play pro tournaments there, it's now named after the Japanese carmaker who sponsors the event. Oh, and the membership still finds the tournaments a nuisance. The more things change, the more they remain the same.

I found Bergstein in the midst of an intense rally. I walked quietly up to the court, and stood back from the fence, waiting for them to finish huffing and puffing.

Marty Bergstein is about fifty-five, tall, lean as a pole, all arms and legs. When he walks, he stoops a little, which makes him seem awkward, but out on the court he is fluid motion.

I waited patiently, a few steps away from the fence, maintaining proper tennis etiquette. The two men were in a heated match. When Bergstein nailed a forehand into a far corner, his opponent groaned in agony.

"That's $150 you owe me," said Bergstein.

"Double or nothing," his opponent said.

"You're on."

I wasn't going to wait for the grudge match to begin.

"Marty," I said as he was collecting balls at the edge of the court. He looked up, did not smile.

"What the hell do you want?" he said.

"How are the kids?" I said.

He walked over, limping. He had a scar on the inside of his knee. War wounds, they were everywhere.

"Cut the bull," he said. "How'd you get in here?"

"What makes you think I'm not a member?" I said.

"Cause they don't let people like you in," he said. "Besides, I'm on the membership committee."

"I need to see Eddie," I said.

"Call his office," he started to walk back to the service line.

"He tried to kill my friend," I said.

This stopped Bergstein in his tracks.

"That's some accusation," he said. "I doubt you can back it up."

"What if I could?"

He didn't say anything. He was leaning on his racquet, an oversized graphite model that was so big you could use it to volley a basketball.

"You have two minutes," he said. Friendly, matter-of-fact.

There was no threat in his tone, just the quick, short breathing of someone who had been exerting himself.

"I can wait until your match is over," I said.

"I don't have time," he said. "We can do it here."

He returned to his place on the court, gathered himself and then whipped a herky-jerky serve over the net. He was a strategic player, going for angles, spin and placement rather than power. The kind of player power hitters hate to face because you can never get a good enough beat on the ball to crush it.

"You now have 1 minute, 45 seconds," he said even as he returned his opponent's volley. I moved closer to the fence and spoke quietly, wary of offending the other players on the courts. Like libraries and churches, tennis courts were places for reverent tones.

"I want to have a meet with Eddie," I said. "It's time we aired this thing out."

"Do I look like Don King to you?" he huffed between strokes. I was caught between watching him and watching the action. Like most people observing a tennis match, my head bounced back and forth, along with the little yellow ball. I felt like an idiot.

"I'm his lawyer not his babysitter," he said, grimacing as he scooped a low, short ball up over the net and headed in behind it. "Why don't you call his wife? She always knows where he is."

"She reported him missing a week ago."

"Oh?" He was up at the net, had his opponent pinned deep and hit a ball that the other player had to half-volley just to get back. With emphasis, Bergstein slammed it into the surface of the court. His point. "That's news to me."

"Listen Marty," I said. "You know your client isn't exactly

a choir boy. I got a story to tell and it's gonna make that Greeley thing look like a misdemeanor."

"I don't take kindly to threats," he said. "Especially from small-time private eyes."

Asshole. "Just answer one question."

"You have thirty seconds," he said, grunting this time on his return. I noticed beads of sweat forming on his brow. I couldn't help but wonder if he was getting nervous or just tired. He looked like he could go five sets easily.

"Have you seen Eddie since Friday night?"

Bergstein went low on a ball again but couldn't dig it out. It sailed into the net. "Damn," he said, returning to the service line. "If I answer, will I be rid of you and your lunatic ravings?"

"For the time being."

He put up his hand and asked his opponent for a quick break. The other guy was sweating profusely and it didn't look like he minded. He went for his water like he'd been stuck in Palm Springs on the hottest day of August.

"You have a good game," I said. "I'm impressed."

"The answer is no," he said, ignoring my effort at congeniality. "But there's no reason why I would."

"And the last time you saw him was . . ."

"A week ago Friday night, at a charity function he talked me into going to," he said, obviously unhappy he'd gone. He leaned his massive racquet against the fence and was wiping his face with his towel. "It was at that hotel on the beach, what's it called. I forget. It started early, around six, and ended before eight. Eddie and I left at the same time, he said he was going over to the Promenade for a drink, Jiggy's, I think. I went home."

Jiggy's was a new sports bar on the Third Street Promenade

in Santa Monica. It was a members-only hangout for current and former sports celebrities.

"You wouldn't happen to know where the family dog is, would you?"

Bergstein looked at me, exasperated, like a law professor admonishing a student who should know better. "No. It's not my day to walk him. Is that all, Ms. Moses?"

"Aren't you at all concerned that no one has seen Eddie since that night?"

"I don't know that that's true," he said, picking up his racquet.

I was running out of time.

"When do you start wondering if it is?"

"When his bills are late," he said and jogged back to the court. "This interview is over."

He punctuated this by his serve. Unlike his last few, he belted this one with such force that it hit inside the server's box on the other side of the net, skidding low, underneath his poor opponent's backhand lunge.

Bergstein turned to me and smiled the grin of a middle-aged man high on testosterone.

I left him and his moment to find my way out.

twenty-three

I rolled out of Riviera onto Sunset Boulevard feeling like I'd been had, but not really knowing how or why. Bergstein is a lawyer and by nature lawyers are crafty, devious and not to be trusted, especially if they have a high success rate. There was no doubting Marty Bergstein was one of the best.

But his reputation, like Jim, was as a solid lawyer who managed to keep his ethical balance in a profession where things like ethics are easy casualties. There are a lot of reasons why Eddie Cooke would want to be hard to find, not the least of which is that people with money and fame will sometimes do almost anything for a few moments of privacy.

Maybe he really was trying to stick it to his wife, hiding out somewhere, living it up and holding on to Noodles just to make Marcy miserable. As if their contentious divorce isn't enough.

If he was just lying low, then Bergstein's refusal to cooperate with me made sense. It wasn't as if a major crime was being committed and I doubted a judge was going to put someone in jail for stealing his own dog. But I admit it was tough to say whether Bergstein was hiding anything.

Under the constraints of the interview I couldn't know for sure if he was sweating from exertion or worry. I was pissed that I let him have the upper hand.

And if Bergstein's reactions were genuine, he certainly wasn't worried that one of his big clients was missing.

Eddie Cooke's whereabouts weren't the only thing on my mind. I'd been thinking a lot about Sherrie lately, particularly after my visit from Andrea. I was feeling guilty about not being able to reach out. Andrea's concerns were serious, especially if the threats were real. There wasn't much I could do at this point.

Sherrie knew where to find me and she hadn't called. It was best to let her have her space, work it all out from her end. I could check in on Emily, keep an eye out for her, but other than that, there was little else to be done.

But Andrea did plant an idea in my head that had been growing ever since my adventure with Sherrie. A lot of her problems seemed to go back to her ex-boyfriend. I decided it couldn't hurt to pay him a visit. Under the circumstances, it was the least I could do.

Gary Barnhill worked at a gas station down on Pacific Coast Highway across from Santa Monica's beachfront. I had a civilian I know at SMPD run a check on his record. Mostly small-time stuff, though he served six months for hacking into the Bank of America's main computer. He also had an arrest for hitting Sherrie, though the charges didn't stick.

The worst thing he got caught doing happened when he was still a minor and the records were sealed. But a probation officer I knew remembered Gary's case well. It was hard to forget. He tortured an old man out of his ATM card, using cigarette butts to burn holes in his victim's forehead. Nice.

They say the sea has powers of redemption and I felt in need of some. It was with some promise that I headed west toward the coast. Along the way, I stopped for lunch at a Caribbean fast food joint for a Cuban sandwich of ham, pork, Swiss cheese, and pickles on pressed bread with a side of rice and beans. I washed it all down with ginger beer, sitting outside at a high-top table, gazing down at the Santa Monica pier below. It was a decadent lunch, but it was the best meal I'd had in a week.

Then I drove down scenic PCH looking for Gary Barnhill's gas station. A mile or so north, between a biker bar and an organic pet store, is the gas station where Gary Barnhill works. The afterglow of my pleasant lunch stop was wearing off when I pulled into the Chevron, I was feeling downright ornery, determined that this interview be more fruitful than the first.

I needed gas anyway, so I pulled up to the full-service pump and got out of the car. I rubbed my sore ribs but except for the occasional twinge, I was feeling pretty good. I still wanted to get this over with in time to get some Z's.

The Chevron had recently been remodeled, but because it doubled as an auto body shop, had the depressingly gloomy look of places where somehow most things that come in to be fixed don't ever come out.

They had two repair bays, both occupied by cars up on lifts and another half-dozen vehicles parked along one side of the cramped lot, all in various states of disrepair, all waiting for a turn that might never come.

"Fill 'er up?" a voice said behind me and I turned to see a scruffy, skinny kid in a black Metallica T-shirt, dirty blue jeans, a frenetic display of tattoos down both arms, slicked back hair and a pathetic attempt at a beard. His name tag said "Gary B." It said something else, too. It said "Manager."

Oh, brother.

"Yeah," I said. "Fill it, 87 is fine."

He nodded, checked out my car which seemed to pass his muster, then loosened my gas cap and started the pump.

Just before he finished another car, a bright, clean Mercedes, drove up and slid in front of the self-service pumps. A well-dressed woman, partly attached to a cell phone, got out and pushed her credit card on Gary. She never even looked him in the eye and it made me feel sorry for him. "That'll be thirteen bucks even," he said to me when he finished pumping my gas, and I handed him a twenty. "Hang on, I'll get you your change."

I watched him walk back toward the cashier's station for a second and then followed him. I didn't say a word until we were inside the tiny room.

"So, Gary," I said. "Nice place you got here."

"It ain't mine," he said. "The Gook who owns it is never here though. Hey, how'd you know my name?"

I wasn't feeling sorry for him anymore.

He was behind the counter, making change in the cash drawer. He still had the Mercedes' woman's credit card, had placed it on the top of the counter and he looked up and squinted at me.

"Do I know you?"

"We have, um, mutual friends," I said, and his reaction was immediate and swift. He jerked his hand forward under the counter and I had a sinking feeling whatever he was reaching for was deadly.

But he was slow and much smaller than me and I was faster, bigger and stronger. I reached over the counter, grabbed his arm and twisted it at the elbow in the way it's not supposed to bend.

He yelped and something metal crashed to the floor behind the counter.

I held on until he stopped fighting me, then loosened my grip a little. The maneuver had caused me to slam my ribs against the counter and I bit down on my lip to hide the pain.

Finally he was still.

"Are you gonna reach for that gun?" I asked him and he shook his head No, defeated. What did Sherrie see in this loser?

"Good." I let go of his arm and he rubbed it, trying his best to give me the hard look of a tough guy who could back up his threats. Even though we both knew it was a lie. "Gary, your reaction was way out of proportion, don't you think? What kind of friends could you have to make you shoot first and ask questions later?"

"Either you know or you don't," he said. "If you don't, you ain't gonna hear it from me."

"Like I care," I said, though the fact was I did. I wondered who he might be involved with and whether those same people were the ones who had threatened Sherrie and her kid. "Our mutual friend you weasel is your ex-girlfriend."

"What's that crazy bitch want from me now?"

"Her name is Sherrie," I said. "Not crazy bitch. And you will address her as such in my presence or I swear I will break both your arms."

"What the fuck do you want?" He said this as a dare, but it was half-hearted. He was a dumb kid, but not so dumb he wasn't taking my threat seriously.

"I want to know who's threatening Sherrie and her daughter."

"How the hell would I know? I haven't seen the bit . . . I haven't seen her in weeks."

"Word I hear is that you got her involved in some big jam up," I said. "If that's true, you're gonna find a whole lot of trouble."

"You have no idea what trouble is." He said this quietly, like a man twice his age. Wisdom in a little punk. Would wonders never cease?

I decided to play that card. "Listen, Gary. From our little demonstration, I think you understand that I'm good at what I do, so if there's anything you want to tell me, I might be able to help you out, too. I just don't want to see anyone get hurt, especially a mother and her daughter."

"Sherrie can take care of herself and so can that kid of hers. So can I," he said. "I don't got nothing else to say to you."

Just then the Mercedes woman walked in, having finished pumping her own gas. Gary hit a couple of buttons and out came the receipt. I watched him; his whole demeanor changed in a nanosecond. Suddenly, he was the sweet gas station attendant. He turned the charm on so high, by the time he was done processing the transaction, he had her complete attention. I watched, amazed.

While they were talking, I saw Gary discreetly, expertly, palm the credit card and slip it under a display box of Slim Jims and the motivations behind his sudden attitude adjustment became clear in an instant. She signed her receipt and walked back to her car.

We both watched her from the window.

"Very smooth, kid," I said, still staring at the woman. "Are you gonna tell her or should I?"

"Tell her what?"

"That you just stole her credit card," I said. "You got five seconds."

He stood his ground for a second, looking from me to the woman like he was watching a Ping-Pong match.

"Fuck it," he said, grabbing the card and running out the door. "Must've slid under the box. Didn't even see it."

It was the first time I'd seen him smile.

I left my card on the counter. Maybe Gary would get tired of lifting credit cards and give me a call.

twenty-four

I had a fitful nap that lasted until after sunset and I awoke in the darkness of my room with the sound of the wind blowing outside. The Santa Anas had returned.

I took a bath, filling the tub up with fragrant bubbles and soaking my sore ribs until my fingers and toes were wrinkled like prunes.

Bobo called when I was drying off. He'd been doing some research on Jiggy's for me. It was owned and managed by a former pro football player named Lunde who'd made a killing running a string of strip joints near the Los Angeles airport.

Now he was considered respectable and Jiggy's had become a hip hangout for Hollywood's in party crowd.

"They have a pretty exclusive membership," said Bobo. "Don't know how you're gonna get in."

"I need to find out if anybody saw Eddie that night," I said.

"Maybe you should ask the mayor," he said.

"She's a member? You're kidding me."

"The mayor, the police chief, even Captain Watkins."

"Watkins? Well, bless his political ass."

"If you say so."

"Forget it, Bobo," I said. "I gotta go. I think I have a date tonight."

An hour later, I was sitting across from Jonathan Brooks in a booth at the back of a noisy Mexican restaurant on Pico.

"Thanks for doing this on such short notice," I said, leafing through the multi-page menu. I was already halfway through a shot of Hornitos and ready to order another.

Brooks was nursing a bottle of *Negro Modelo*.

"I'm surprised you called at all," he said. "I was beginning to think you didn't like me."

"I like you," I said. "We're friends aren't we?"

"Yeah," he said.

"Besides, I felt bad for having to cancel on Tuesday, gunshot wound or no."

He smiled at this, and even in the dimness it lit up his features. He had a regal face. Everything on it seemed to match perfectly in size and shape.

We ordered a second round of drinks, then a third and finally put in our food orders. I was getting tortilla soup and a couple of soft tacos. Brooks was going with the enchiladas.

We made small talk, but mostly we just kept to ourselves. It was awkward and silly, it felt like we were two prizefighters scoping each other out.

"So," he said, "I heard your father ran a cigar shop."

"We lived above it, me, my folks, Danny, his folks. It was a zoo, but we were very close."

"I know Danny was special to you," he said. "Wasn't right the way that whole thing went down."

"Yeah," I said, tapping my heart. "I miss him and my Dad every day."

"I know how you feel. My Mom passed nearly six years ago and I still pick up the phone to call her sometimes."

"Your Dad?"

"He's still kicking and screaming," he said. "He taught freshman English at George Washington for thirty-five years, retired a year ago and moved to Hilton Head. He gets up every day and plays a couple rounds of golf. Then he goes home, sits on the porch and re-reads the classics. He's got a nice place, a view of the water."

First dates are always difficult for me. I don't like people to know too much about me, mostly because I'm uncomfortable talking about myself. This quality has gotten stronger as I get older.

My strategy is to ask as many questions of my date as possible, so I quizzed Brooks.

He grew up around affluent white people in Washington, D.C., the son of a college professor and a lawyer. Brooks went to George Washington University on a basketball scholarship and earned a degree in Criminology.

A summer modeling job after his senior year brought him out to Santa Monica where he tried to break into the movies, working days walking the beat for SMPD.

He was engaged briefly to an actress he met his first week in California, but she broke it off when he decided to stay with the police department.

He's got a sister, Susie, who married an ex-rodeo star and lives on a ranch in Montana, and he talks to his Dad nearly every day by phone.

"It's funny, but we used to fight all the time. I mean serious. A few times we even came to blows," he said, rubbing his chin. "He was golden glove. Man he could throw a punch. Now we talk like brothers."

"That's cause you're not in competition anymore," I said. "Me and my Dad never got there. I didn't grow up fast enough."

"I keep trying to remember when we stopped trying to take each other's heads off," he said. "But I couldn't pinpoint it with a flashlight and a map. It just changed, that's all."

I smiled at him. I liked hearing him talk, partly because it helped me forget about my problems. I had to admit he had some wonderful qualities. He was direct, honest and he seemed to be trying, which is a lot more than I can say about ninety-nine percent of the men I date.

"I envy you and your Dad. It took finding Danny a second time for me and Sam to find that kind of relationship. I keep wondering if it's too late."

"Not as long as you're both still breathing," he said.

"It's hard, though," I said. "I'm having difficulty getting used to having him around."

"Only cause you make it that way," he said, smiling. The food came and I had to wait for the bus boy to leave before I could say anything.

"What's that supposed to mean?"

"C'mon, Zenaria," he said. "You're a loner. You'll always be a loner. Sometimes I think it kills you that you have to spend time with the rest of us."

"Now you're a shrink," I said. "Am I gonna get charged per hour?"

"It depends," he said.

"On . . ."

"On you telling me the truth," he said.

I looked up from my soup, trying to read his expression, wondering how much he knew about Saturday night. All of a sudden I wasn't hungry anymore, not with visions of faceless bodies in my head.

"What's the matter?" he said. "You look like you've got in-digestion."

"Nothing," I said. "What truth are we talking about?"

"I just wanna know why you invited me out tonight," he said.

"I told you . . ."

"Cut the crap. You've been dodging me for months and don't tell me you weren't relieved when you had to cancel Tuesday. Now all of a sudden you're calling me up for a date. You must think I'm an idiot."

He was playing with me, but underneath he was being serious. If I didn't say the right thing, right now, I was going to ruin the evening. And I hated to admit it, but I was having a great time. The tequila was working wonders, the food wasn't half bad and I even found myself absently sizing Brooks up, wondering what he'd be like in bed.

For the first time since we met, I thought we might just have a chance. Now I was gonna fuck up everything.

I thought about my bike ride, the moment when it was just me and a 360 degree view of pure beauty.

But like the dirty air hidden on the horizon, I knew it was an illusion, an oasis in an ugly world. Reminders that nothing is ever quite what it seems, and evil is everywhere.

"You're right," I said, waving down the waitress for the check. "Let's get out of here first. I don't want to talk about it in here."

I looked across the booth at Brooks. The muscles in his jaw tightened and he turned away from me. He didn't want me to see the disappointment in his eyes.

twenty-five

We silently walked the two blocks to where Brooks' car was parked. After we got in, we both sat there, staring out the window, letting the tension build up between us.

"Well," I said.

"Well," he said.

Then we looked at each other and I started to say something, but he reached out his hand, placed it on my cheek and bent toward me. It seemed the most natural thing in the world. It never happened. Brooks' cell phone went off like a siren.

He didn't move but the moment was gone. He let the phone ring itself out.

"Not going to answer it?"

"No," he said. "If it's important, they'll page me."

Outside the car the winds were picking up again. Inside, the windows were fogging. It made me think of a Springsteen song from my childhood, something about young lovers and the backseats of '57 Chevies.

"I'm sorry, Jonathan," I said to his brooding silence. "If it makes you feel any better, I had a great time. I mean it."

"Forget it," he said. "I just wish when you wanted something, you'd come out and ask for it."

"I figured I could kill two birds with one stone," I said. "Besides, I forgot how you always seem to know when I'm hiding something."

"What's on your mind?"

I hadn't planned on telling Brooks about Saturday night, but I felt I had no choice now that he knew I was only taking advantage of him. It was suddenly important to me that he knew that I felt I could trust him.

"Saturday night," I said. "The night Jim was shot."

He waited. I could hear his breathing. It sounded loud inside the car.

"I was there," I said. "I didn't see everything, but I was there."

Brooks turned to look at me so fast I thought he might pull a muscle in his neck.

"Christ, Zen," he said. "You can't be telling me this. I'm a police officer. I have to report it."

"Wait, Jonathan," I said. "Please wait. Hear me out first, okay? Then you decide. I won't stand in your way. I promise."

I told him about Jim and how he hired me and Bobo to find Noodles. I told him of the stakeout, the break-in, and seeing Eddie Cooke torturing Jim.

I told him of waking up next to the corpse, leaving out the part about wiping down the baseball bat.

"They drugged me, Jonathan," I said. "It was a set-up and I walked into it like a fucking lemming."

"Why didn't you tell this to the police?" he said. "That story could be easily checked out. You said you even have a blood test."

"Eddie Cooke was reported missing several days before I saw him," I said. "I was worried it would look like I was making the story up. Plus, Lennon's on the case. You can see how that would make me a little reticent. He's just looking for a reason to lock me up. And . . ."

"And, what?"

I touched Brooks on the arm, squeezing his biceps until I got him to look at me.

"I don't remember what happened," I said. "I can get pretty worked up. This is ridiculous, but a part of me isn't sure that I didn't, that I . . ."

"I saw that body," he said. "The Zen Moses I know wouldn't be capable of that. I would've given you the benefit of the doubt."

"Are you sure?" I asked him.

He stopped at this. I'd touched a nerve. Without meaning to, I'd hit on the one obstacle that stood between us. It was an insight not lost on either of us.

His voice was low and soft when he spoke again.

"What do you want me to do about all this?" he said. "I'm going to have to give it to Lennon. If I don't, I could lose my job."

"I know," I said. "I was hoping you'd see through to doing me a favor first."

"I don't like the sound of that."

"Hear me out," I said. "Eddie Cooke was last seen at Jiggy's. I'm sure you know the place. Anyway, you'll never guess but Watkins is a member."

"Captain Watkins? You're kidding. How does he afford that?"

"His wife, remember? She's some hotshot real estate agent," I said. "I found out she gave him the membership for his forty-fifth birthday."

"Where do you get this stuff?"

"Friends in low places," I said. "So are you in?"

"On what?"

"Did you know members can invite guests there, even if they're not on the premises?"

"Oh, no. No way. You must be on crack. You want me to ask Watkins? He'd never go for that."

"I didn't say ask him first. I just want to get in there, talk to some people, see if we can find out anything about Eddie. I hear it was his regular hangout."

Brooks sat back in his seat, considering my request. I could tell he wasn't happy about it. But I knew, too, that I almost had him. Almost.

"Jonathan," I said. "I don't know what happened to me Saturday night. But whatever it is, I know I saw Eddie Cooke in that house. If he's the one who framed me and nearly killed my friend, I can't rest until I find him. You'd feel the same way if it happened to you, badge or no badge."

"Oh brother," he said, but he was almost smiling. Maybe he agreed with me or maybe the thought of putting one over on his boss was too much to resist.

"The night's still young," I said. "A round of pool, a beer or two? We might be able to salvage the evening after all."

He started the engine. "Perfect," he said. "I can kick your ass at nine ball and brag about it to our cellmates later."

twenty-six

Brooks parked his car near Jiggy's and as we walked down
the alley toward the club, Brooks took my hand.

"I want to get my money's worth out of this date," he said
and winked at me. I had to smile.

It was a busy night. We had to wait behind two other cou-
ples before we were inside, facing the hostess, a tall, well-
endowed woman wearing an impossibly short sequined tank
dress and not much else.

Behind her, a beefy guy with a beer gut, pony tail and patch
of hair for a beard, stood silently, eyeing everyone who walked
in. He had a headset on which was attached to a radio at his
belt.

There were No Smoking signs prominently displayed
throughout the room. The state of California had recently expanded its ban of smoking in public buildings to bars and
restaurants, but no one at Jiggy's seemed to have gotten the
memo. The place was thick with a fog of cigarette and cigar
fumes and a few minutes after I'd walked in, I could feel a
burn at the back of my throat.

"Good evening," the hostess said. "My name is Tiffany, may
I help you?" She had a toothpaste commercial grin pasted on
a face that was thick with makeup, which up close barely covered the lines from too many nights in dark, smoky rooms like
this one.

She gave me a brief once-over, but seemed more interested

in Brooks and she gazed at him like a dog baying at the full
moon.

"Evening," he said, showing his badge as covertly as possible. "I'm a friend of Bob Watkins'."

Tiffany's smiled seemed to grow impossibly wider.

"Well, he didn't leave word tonight," she said, giggling. "But we always try to extend our warmest hospitality to the boys in blue. We feel so safe when you're around."

I rolled my eyes at Brooks so only he could see and he squeezed my hand to warn me to quiet.

"Unfortunately, only members are allowed upstairs, but we have pool tables and dining in our main room," she said. "Please feel free to partake."

"Tell me," I said to her. "Is Mr. Lunde around this evening?"

"Are you thinking of joining the club tonight?" she said, still looking at Brooks. Any minute, her tongue was going to drop out of her head. "You'll find our rates for Santa Monica's finest to be quite reasonable, thanks to Bobby of course."

"Bobby?" I mouthed to Brooks, then turned back to Tiffany.

"Yes," I said, snuggling closer to Brooks. A woman protecting her turf. "Honey, don't you think we should sign up?"

Brooks wanted to say something, but I knew he couldn't and it made me want to laugh again.

"Captain Watkins talks about how much he loves this place," said Brooks, recovering. "I've been meaning to check it out."

"That would be so excellent," she said. "You'll find Mr. Lunde is always here on Thursday nights. He's in our pool room. Through that door over there, below the exit sign. Sir, if you'll give me your card, I'll be happy to have it brought over to Mr. Lunde."

"That's all right," he said. Tiffany looked dejected. "Thanks just the same."

Brooks dragged me away before I could say anything else to her. I could tell he'd been enjoying himself, but no doubt he was also worried about the fallout if "Bobby" ever got wind of this. He'd be relegated to bicycle duty in no time.

The crowd on the main floor was eating late dinners, and working on pseudo martinis and overpriced cigars. It was still too early for the bar to fill up. LA's movers and shakers were still partying elsewhere.

We went into the back room, which was about three-quarters full, and grabbed the pool table closest to the bar. There weren't many empty stools, but I recognized Lunde from his strip club TV commercials.

Squat and once powerfully built, he was just another chubby guy pushing past middle age with the grace of a two-toed sloth.

Lunde had his back to the bar, smoking a stogie and surveying the room as if he was a casino pit boss looking for cheaters.

I pointed him out to Brooks and as we watched him, two men walked up to him and shook hands. I noticed one was a young actor gaining some recognition on and off the screen. Brooks saw him too and chortled. I imagined he'd had run-ins with him.

A waitress came for our drink order. Like the hostess, she was showing more skin than clothes. I ordered beers for both of us and asked her about Eddie.

"Eddie Cooke's a friend of yours?"

"Sort of," I said. "We heard he hangs out here."

"I haven't seen him," she said. "Come to think of it, I don't think I've seen him for a while. Funny, he usually comes in a few times a week."

"When was the last time you saw him?"

She thought about this a minute, absently playing with the strands of her hair. "Friday night. A week ago. I think that's right," she said. "I remember now. Some guy was in his face. Georgie had to throw him out of the club."

"Did you know the guy?"

"Nah," she said. "Never seen him before. Ask Mr. Lunde. He and Eddie are buddies."

She went off to get our drinks, and me and Brooks watched Lunde, casually starting a game of pool. At least it began that way. Brooks was pretty good, but so was I and we got into an intense match, our competitive juices and the evening's alcohol intake adding fuel to the fire.

The drinks came and then the bouncer came in and crossed to where his boss was sitting. Then the two of them strolled over to our table.

"Hi folks," said Lunde, his voice higher than I expected. He was dressed like a mobster who was color blind: blue pin-striped suit, blue shirt, blue tie. A sparkling pinky ring on his finger reflected the light like a disco strobe when he moved his hand.

He had the stub of the cigar between his teeth and he reached a fleshy hand out at Brooks. "My name's Harry Lunde. I'm one of the owners. I wanted to welcome you to the club."

"Jonathan Brooks, nice to meet you. This is, uh, my date, Zenaria."

Lunde's hand was cold and wet and when he touched me it felt like one of those soft toys you squeeze to relieve stress. "Zenaria. What an unusual name."

"My parents were unusual people," I said.

The bouncer was standing still behind his boss, but he was glaring pretty hard at us.

"So, you're friends of Bob Watkins," he said. "Funny he never mentioned you."

"We work together," Brooks said. "He's been telling me to try this place out for months. So here we are."

"That why you were quizzing Margo?" It was the bouncer.

"Let's not make a scene, Georgie," said Lunde.

"Yes, let's not, Georgie," I said, giving him my best conciliatory smile. I don't know why, but it didn't seem to be working.

"At least we agree on one thing," said Lunde. "But that doesn't mean I appreciate people waltzing into my place under false pretenses. Why don't you tell me why you've gone to all this trouble?"

Brooks started to say something, but I jumped in. I wanted to insulate him. It was the least I could do for getting him into this mess in the first place.

"We really are on a date," I said. "I'm looking for Eddie Cooke. I was hoping to find him here tonight."

"Maybe you should call his secretary," he said. "This is a private club. The operative word here being private."

"Eddie's been reported missing," I said. "He was last seen here."

"Are you implying I had something to do with his disappearance?" he said. "I think you'd better leave. As I said, I'd hate for there to be a scene."

"I wasn't implying anything," I said.

"Mr. Cooke is a member of this club," said Lunde. "Members expect to have their privacy respected. If we can't provide that, we're finished. Now get the hell out of my club before I . . ."

"Call the cops?" It was Brooks. "I am the cops."

"In here, you're nothing but a pain in my ass," Lunde backed away, but he was only making room for Georgie.

Georgie seemed to perk up suddenly, like he was itching for a fight. He lunged forward, grabbing my arm roughly.

"Get your hands off me," I said in as normal a tone as possible, stamping hard on Georgie's foot. I did it so discreetly only the four of us knew what had happened. Georgie let go and stepped back, his eyes tiny dots of rage.

He advanced on me and Lunde stepped aside. I guess a scene wasn't out of the question after all.

Brooks stepped in front of him, holding a pool cue. "Back off," he said. "We'd be happy to let ourselves out."

Lunde walked to the bar and took his seat, leaning over to say something to the bartender. Two more sides of beef came into the room. The crowd of pool players behind us were whispering and watching. The smell of a fight was thicker than the smoke.

Brooks' jaw was twitching and I could tell he was having a battle in his own head, stay or go. He looked down at me, but I shook my head. "It's not worth it," I said.

Before he could answer, I got sucker slapped on the side of my head and went crashing into the pool table. Then Brooks threw a punch of his own. The fight was on.

Brooks reacted quickly, breaking the pool cue on Georgie's shoulders, but when he went down, the other two guys took his place. Brooks was quick, strong and agile and even with a few beers in his system, was holding his own.

Me, I was just holding my head. I shook off the sting on my cheek and, feeding off of adrenaline only, grabbed a pool ball in each hand and jumped into the fray.

I nailed one of Brooks' opponents in the teeth and felt a few break off, the warmth of his blood on my hand. Then someone grabbed me from behind and squeezed and the pain on my ribs almost made me pass out. In desperation, I slammed both hands, still holding the heavy balls, and boxed my attacker's ears as hard as I could. He let go and I fought to get my breath back, turning to see Georgie holding both sides of his head. I put one of my boots in his gut and when he doubled over, slammed him on the back of his neck with both hands. He went down in a heap.

Someone else grabbed me by the arm and I turned to throw a punch, but it was Brooks. "Let's get out of here," he yelled, and I followed him as we caromed through the main bar and out past Tiffany, who was still wearing that toothy grin.

We didn't stop running until we were down the alley and around the corner and leaning against Brooks' car, giggling and breathing so hard, our laughter was coming out in fits and spurts and coughs.

It was late and the wind howled between the buildings, but it was so clear you could count every star and the sky formed a velvet blanket above us that was majestic. Brooks pulled me into his arms and when we kissed, I didn't notice any of it anymore.

It was the first time all day that I wasn't thinking about Eddie Cooke.

twenty-seven

In the distance, the sound of sirens brought us back to the present. I pulled away from Brooks' embrace. It took some effort.

"What?" he said.

"Not here, not now," I said.

He started to argue, but he knew I was right.

I wasn't disappointed in the evening. But I was confused and tired. It had been a long day for me, my first out of bed in a week and I was sore from the fight. All I wanted to do was crawl under the covers. By myself.

"Now that I've seen you in action," he said, "I can see why you're always in need of medical attention. Shoulda seen that coming."

"Hey, I saved your ass," I said. "Besides, I thought I was pretty darn creative."

"That one guy you nailed in the mouth? He's gonna need a flashlight to find all his teeth."

"You're not so bad yourself," I said. "At fighting I mean."

He pulled up to my house and opened the door for me. I slid out, achy and dead tired. Brooks walked me to the door.

"I hope you don't get in too much trouble tomorrow," I said.

"Ah, forget it. Those guys care more about their reputation than anything else," he said. "And I'm not so sure Watkins wants to broadcast his membership at Jiggy's."

"I hope so, for your sake," I said. "Thanks for a wonderful evening."

"Yeah," he said. "Maybe we can do this again some time when you're not working a case. At least it will be safer."

Then he reached over to my cheek, where Georgie had whacked me. A welt had formed just under my left eye.

He bent down and started to kiss me again, but suddenly he stopped, stood up straight. I turned around to where he was looking.

Lennon and two uniforms were coming up my front walk.

"What now?" I said.

"Zen Moses?" Lennon said as he drew closer, then he saw Brooks and an evil grin spread across his face. "What have we here? The lieutenant and the private eye. How sweet."

"What do you want, Vince?" said Brooks.

"You guys smell anything?" it was one of the uniforms.

"Smell wh . . . ," I didn't have to finish. I'd been too tired, too preoccupied to notice anything. But when I did, I realized it had been in the air since we got there. One of those smells you only have to experience once to remember it forever. And as I tried not to breathe it in, I had to suppress the urge to vomit. It was the scent of something on fire, something awful on fire. It was the smell of burning flesh.

I fumbled with the alarm on my door and I saw that the indicator light was out. So were all the lights in my house, which was completely dark. The sky was so bright, I hadn't even noticed that the porch light wasn't on. I tried the door; it was locked.

"How long were you waiting for her," Brooks asked Lennon.

"Not long," he said.

"Actually, we've been here for almost three hours, sir."

"Thanks, Macy," said Lennon. "We didn't see anything if that's what you're getting at."

"The fuse box is on the back porch," I said. "I'm gonna go 'round the back and check it."

"Macy, Richmond. Follow us," Brooks said to the two cops. But I was already around my fence heading for the alley and my back steps. The closer I got to my back door, the stronger the smell became. My knees were starting to feel weak. Dread rose up in my stomach.

Brooks and the two uniforms joined me around back and somebody handed me a flashlight. They followed me as I climbed my backstairs, toward whatever was giving off that awful smell. It was so bad at the top, that I held my hand over my mouth.

One of the cops stopped halfway and threw up.

The first thing I noticed was the landing, which was wet as if someone had soaked it with a hose. Water was dripping off the stairs and onto the pavement below. In the dark quiet of the alley, it was like water torture.

There was a puddle at the top of the stairs and my fuse box was broken open, the circuits melted and mangled, still hot. Tiny clouds of smoke were floating off its surface, like a smoldering fire.

Below it in a heap on the ground was a body, it too giving off smoke.

I shined the light over the slight, motionless figure and the familiar big leather coat, now scorched black in places, jeans, cowboy boots and the short, white blonde hair. One arm lay awkwardly, as if the person was raising her hand, stopping just short of the back fuse box. The fingers and wrist were blackened and I moved the light down the body to the boots. Both had black marks on the soles.

Beneath the body, my new porch was charred black in a rectangular pattern and I noticed that my straw mat had been moved. Someone had draped it over one of the railings.

"What is it," Brooks said quietly behind me.

I turned off the light and told him to call it in.

I didn't need the flashlight to tell me who the face belonged to or even what caused this person to die. I knew immediately who was lying dead on my back porch, somehow electrocuted by my own fuse box.

Less than a week after trying to force her own public execution, Sherrie Sanger had finally found death. I don't know why, but as I stood over her, I cried. It was partly for Sherrie and all those like her for whom death seems an easy way out.

But it was also for me and the overwhelming sense of failure and guilt that gripped my heart, the irrational feeling deep down that it was all my fault.

PART THREE

twenty-eight

In less than a half hour my house was crawling with cops. It was close to midnight, but the neighbors were out, milling about, sticking close to their property lines, peering at my place like rubberneckers.

I was standing outside in my front yard, watching the scene and trying to stay out of everybody's way. Watkins was around and so was Lennon, who was waiting off to the side, a reminder he had unfinished business with me.

Andrea came home late from a night out just as the cops arrived. She pushed past us into the house. It took me and two other cops to restrain her, but by that time she'd already seen too much. Her wailing seemed as loud as the police sirens and harder to forget.

Seeing her flail and cry out was gut-wrenching and a part of me wanted to join her. It was a long while before she calmed down again.

The news media had returned to their vigil in front of my house. Though I noticed they stayed clear of my front yard.

I couldn't stand all those cops trampling over my private space and so I sneaked over to check on Andrea, ignoring the reporters who were yelling questions at me. I had changed into a sweatshirt and jeans and slipped on my Nikes and as soon as I stepped out into my yard they were hounding me.

Most were calling me by my last name, but one guy was yelling "Zen," over and over again. I wheeled to get a look at him. He was the lead reporter for one of the local news stations.

"Zen," he said again, as if I was his best friend. "Help us out here."

I walked over to the edge of my lawn, stopping just on my side of the yellow police tape. The reporters moved forward like a herd of cattle and in a matter of seconds I had strobe lights burning holes in the back of my eyes.

I put my hand in front of them to shield the light.

"Turn the cameras off," I said, but nobody moved. "Turn them off or I'm not talking."

After a minute, the lights went out. But I waited until they lowered them. Then I pointed to the man who was calling me.

"You," I said. "Do I know you?"

He flashed a smile, the one he uses every night on television. All teeth, no soul.

"I'm Brent Majors. Channel 2," he said.

"Have we ever met in person?"

"I don't think so," he said. "You probably recognize my face from TV—"

"Don't call me Zen," I cut him off.

"What?"

"You were calling me Zen," I said. "That's my first name. My friends call me Zen. My colleagues call me Zen. You're not in either category."

He looked at me as if I'd taken away his kid's puppy. A cameraman, sensing some action, started to raise his camera.

"Don't even think about it," I said.

"We have every right to be here," said Majors, getting back his nerve. "You used to be a journalist, you should . . ."

I grabbed him by the collar.

"Are you going to quote the Constitution, now?" I said "A

woman died here tonight. You people are turning it into a Goddamned circus. And you, you yell at me across my yard like we're old buddies. Well, we're not and we never will be. And if I ever have to see your face out here again . . ."

I pushed him away from me.

"That's a threat," he said, more to his colleagues than to me. "She threatened me. Everybody heard it."

"It warms my heart," I said, "to find out you're more of a wimp than I thought you were."

There were a couple of chuckles, somebody snorted. I could see some of the reporters bowing their heads to hide their reactions.

I walked away. Behind me Majors was still making noise. The farther I got, the louder he became.

Andrea was sitting on her front step, drinking beer from a bottle and trying to stop crying. Her makeup was smeared under her eyes, marking the path where her tears had run down her face.

"Hey," I said, plopping down on the stoop next to her. She had a small cooler filled with ice and beer and I helped myself to one. "You okay?"

She shrugged, holding off the tears with a long swig from her bottle.

"I know that guy," she said.

"Who, Brent Majors?"

"Yeah," she said. "I do his hair. He's so full of himself."

"Big surprise," I said.

"Wish I was as tough as you," she said, then grimaced toward the cameras that were now trained on us. She first glared at them, then flipped them the bird and found a hesitant laugh under her tears.

"Guess we're gonna be on the news tonight," she said. "I'm

so used to watching what's on TV. Guess I never realized they're talking about real people."

"Yeah," I said, turning away from the cameras so they couldn't see my face or read my lips, if that's what they were trying to do. "It's never real for most people until it happens to them."

"Yeah," she said.

She fell quiet again and I left her to her thoughts. She drank down the beer and put it on the stoop next to her, aligning it in a neat row next to two other empties. She reached into the cooler for another, twisted off the top and downed about half of it in one swallow. A lot of it missed and dripped down her chin, but she wiped it off with the back of her hand.

I put my hand around her bottle and gently tugged it out of her grasp. She didn't fight me.

She put her head in her hands and cried and I put my arm around her shoulders, pulling her close to me. We both sat on her porch, holding each other until we were too tired to cry anymore.

The she stood up, wiping her face and bending down to pick up the empties. She was turning back into the old Andrea, but when she suddenly hurled one of the bottles at the cameras, I knew the old Andrea would never return. Nights like this one change people in ways they don't fully realize. Some only get it years later, when the passage of time heals their wounds enough to let them look back with an objective eye. But others never do.

I wondered which category Andrea fit in and hoped with all my heart it was the first. I wanted, no *needed* her to not only survive, but thrive. To help me deal with the loss and guilt that was renting a space in my head the size of Rhode Island.

"I know I'm acting crazy," she said to me. "But Sherrie was

my best friend, you know? She was always there for me, even when she was having her own problems, even during this whole mess. Did you know that my birthday was today?"

I looked up at her.

"Yeah, funny huh? Sherrie came by, dropped off a gift. It was just what I wanted. I don't even know how she was able to afford it, but I could never give it back. That would have broken her heart. That's the way she was."

"Did she say anything? I mean did she give you any indication that . . . ?" I left the thought unfinished.

"No. At first, she seemed okay, very quiet but okay. I was thinking maybe this thing would help her get her life back together. But when she hugged me good-bye, I knew."

"Knew what?"

"That I'd never see her again," she said.

I finished off the last of my beer, the sour flavor leaving a bitter taste in my mouth. It seemed like another bad omen.

I saw Brooks on the landing in front of my house, talking to Watkins. They both looked in my direction and Brooks waved me over.

I got up, squeezed Andrea on the shoulder and tried to think of something to say. The only thing in my heart was guilt and I didn't want to talk about it. I felt like a jerk but no matter how hard I tried, I couldn't find the words that might give this girl comfort. So I didn't say anything at all.

"She wasn't just my best friend," she called to me as I walked back toward my side of the fence.

She was looking down at the ground so I couldn't see what was in her eyes. I didn't have to.

"She was the only real friend I ever had."

twenty-nine

I walked back through the gauntlet of neighbors, cops and journalists and met Brooks and Watkins on the front stairs of my house.

Brooks looked grim. Watkins just looked pissed. But he always looked like that. I nodded at Brooks and reached out a hand to Watkins. He ignored me.

"Why are you always somewhere around dead bodies?" he said.

"Must be a phase I'm going through," I said. "It didn't used to be this way. Come to think of it, you're always there with me. Think there's a connection?"

"This isn't funny, Moses," he said, but his tone wasn't confrontational, which was unusual for him. "I need to know where you were tonight."

"Out on a . . . ," I caught Brooks' warning wave just in time. "Out with a friend. We had dinner, drinks, pool, that sort of thing. Nothing very exciting."

"And your friend will back this up," he said.

"Absolutely," I said.

"We're going to need to know what time you left your house this morning and what time you returned," he said.

I pointed to Lennon, who was standing a few feet from us. He was talking with one of the lab technicians, but he had his head bent in such I way I knew he was eavesdropping.

"Why don't you ask him?" I said. "He and two uniforms were waiting for me when I got home this evening."

Watkins looked at his protegé, then waved him over.

"You were here tonight?"

"I was following up on some evidence we found at the Donnell crime scene," he said. "We were waiting for Moses to take her in for questioning."

"With two uniforms?" said Brooks.

"She has a reputation," said Lennon. "But I guess you already know that."

"Fuck you," said Brooks. He shoved Lennon and the detective shoved back. They were on the verge of an actual scuffle when Watkins and another uniform stepped between them.

Out on the street, the reporters had suddenly perked up. It was sweet that Brooks thought he had to defend my honor, but I didn't need it, or want it.

"What the fuck is wrong with you?" said Watkins.

"Brooks was with the suspect," Lennon said. "Maybe we should look into *his* whereabouts."

"Get a grip, Vince," said Watkins, turning his protegé red. "Tell me again why you didn't clear this with me."

"It was late, sir. The evidence is quite compelling," he said, trying to fend off his embarrassment at being grilled in public by a superior. "Time was of the essence."

"A moment, please?"

Watkins took Lennon aside. Brooks and I watched silently. We couldn't hear what they were saying, but Watkins was doing most of the talking.

"You fucking idiot," Watkins said, suddenly aloud. "How's it gonna look when I have to tell the press that we had three cops parked outside while some poor kid was being murdered?"

"What's the deal with him?" I asked when Watkins returned. From his look, I knew it was a mistake to ask.

"Don't push me, Moses," he said. "I'm not saying he had no reason to be out here. You're just lucky he fucked up. Maybe you'd like to explain why your fingerprints were found in the Donnell house?"

I looked at Brooks, but he left me hanging. As well he should, considering he'd probably hear it from Watkins in the morning, if not sooner.

"I can explain that," I said. "But I'd rather do it in the light of day with my lawyer. All you need to know is that I didn't kill anybody."

"All I need to know? You got fucking balls, I'll tell you that," he said. "I'm sick and tired of this game you play, Moses. This is an open police investigation. If you think holding back information gives you grounds to do your own digging, you're mistaken. I'll lock you up just to keep you off my ass. Do you understand?"

I didn't say anything. I'd already done enough damage. A minute ago, I'd thought he was on my side.

"You don't want to get into a pissing contest with me," said Watkins. "Stay the fuck away from the Donnell investigation. That's all you need to know."

He was talking to me, but all three of us knew this was directed at Brooks. He paused for effect, letting it sink in long enough so there wouldn't be any question as to his meaning.

Then he headed toward the media to give a statement. He crossed my yard and as he got closer reporters perked up, cameras were raised and strobes got turned on.

Another night in LA. And another camera junkie in the middle of it.

"He's in his element," I said.

"That's for sure," said Brooks. He was leaning against the railing, looking down my street toward the freeway, though I doubt he saw any of it very clearly. He was somewhere else.

"Jonathan?"

He turned toward me, looked down at Watkins who was staring back at us and then back at me again.

"Jonathan?" I said. "You gonna tell me what happened?"

He looked toward Watkins again.

"Didn't you hear him?" he said. "Christ, you don't quit do you?"

He went inside and I heard the echo of my screen door slamming in the night, leaving me standing alone outside my own house. The word "No" formed on my lips.

thirty

I went inside myself a few minutes later and grabbed a cigar to smoke outside on my front porch. I sat on the steps, staring up at the sky and making the cops and lab technicians climb over me.

It was my house after all.

A few hours later, everyone was gone, except Brooks who was drinking a cup of coffee out of one of my mugs. The reporters had stayed long enough to get film of Sherrie's body being brought out on a stretcher.

She was already in a body bag, there was nothing to see but a slight form underneath the black cover. But when the coroner's technicians carried her out, the media went into high gear, lights, camera, action. Another LA tragedy to lead the morning news.

Brooks and I were both sitting on my porch, listening to the wind. It had picked up steam in the last couple of hours and was blowing a warm breeze over us. Neither one of us had spoken since he'd come out. My cigar had long faded to ashes, but the smell still lingered and it made me think, as it always does, of my childhood.

"I see you found the coffee," I said.

"Didn't think you'd mind."

"Are the lines of communication shut?"

He shrugged. "Watkins is my boss, last time I checked."

"This is fucking personal," I said. "And you know it."

"Everything's personal with you," he said, his words were cutting. But I wasn't sure I could argue against him.

"Sherrie was screwed up," I said. "But I thought maybe there was some potential, that I could save her. At least, help her save herself anyway. It was arrogant and naive of me, but that's how I felt.

"Now she's dead and I want to find out who murdered her," I said. "I owe it to her."

"You just want to get rid of your guilt," he said.

"That's my problem," I said. "Look, if you don't want to help me, then say it. But don't turn this into a therapy session."

I got up to go back inside, but Brooks grabbed my arm. I yanked it away from him. One step forward, two steps back.

"Sorry," he said. "I just want you to know how it feels. Every time I give you information, it comes back to bite me in the ass."

"A woman was murdered tonight, Jonathan. On my own porch. She wasn't perfect, but I liked her. And now she's dead."

"I'm sorry," he said again. "Tell me: what makes you think it was murder?"

"Where do you want me to start? My back porch was wet and it hasn't rained in two weeks. It was charred black underneath Sherrie's body. I bet if I looked at the ground wire to my fuse box, it would be cut.

"Here's what I think happened," I continued. "Somebody loosens my fuses, rigs it to the doorknob, cuts the ground wire and attaches it to something else conductive, something you would have to stand on, a mat of some kind. Then they laid it out in front of my back door. Just to make sure, they hose down the back porch. Anybody touching the back doorknob or reaching into that fuse box would get, well, you saw what they would get."

Brooks didn't say anything. It was late, probably nearly four a.m. and my second wind had long since petered out. I felt like I could sleep for days.

"Well," I said impatiently.

"That's pretty close to it," he said, getting up and stretching. "But you're missing something."

"Like why Sherrie was trying to get in my back door in the first place?" I said. "That's a good question. She might have been trying to circumvent the alarm, but even third-rate burglars know that won't work. They run on different currents."

Brooks was standing at the foot of my front steps, shaking his head.

"There's something else."

I thought for a minute but couldn't see what he was getting at. I was too tired to think anymore.

"When we got here this evening and you saw the lights were out," he said. "What's the first thing you did?"

"I went to check the fus . . . ," I said, finally getting it. "That's why Watkins went so easy on me."

"Somebody wanted you to come home, see the lights were out and try to get in the back door. And if you decided to stick your hand in the fuse box, even better," he said. "What I'm saying is somebody wanted you dead."

He handed me the coffee mug, now empty, then pulled his jacket tighter.

"Sleep well, Zen."

thirty-one

I went straight to bed, but didn't fall asleep right away. I stared up at the ceiling replaying the last three days like a movie without an end. The only clear thought in my head was that somebody was trying to kill me.

Finally, as the winds died down and the morning fog rolled in, covering the sun's first attempt to show itself for the day, I closed my eyes from sheer exhaustion.

I woke up around 9:30 to the sound of a ringing phone in my ears and a pounding headache within.

I rolled over and grabbed the phone without thinking. For a moment, I'd forgotten the previous night's events but when the sharp, all-business voice spoke my name into my ear it all came flooding back.

"This is Zen Moses," I said. "Who are you?"

"My name is Leslie, from Marcy Cooke's office," she said, barely stopping for a breath. "Ms. Cooke expects you in one hour. Do you need the address?"

"Expects me? Marcy Cooke never made an appointment with me," I said. I was tired but not so tired I wouldn't remember a meeting with Marcy Cooke.

"Marcy Cooke doesn't make appointments with anybody," she said, completely serious. "She is accustomed to people seeing her when she requests it. We'll expect you at the Bel Air address in one hour."

Now I was wide awake.

"Don't hold your breath," I said. "Nobody summons me. Not the President of the United States, not the fucking Queen of England. She wants to see me, she can make an appointment like everybody else."

I slammed the phone down and stretched, noting that my ribs were feeling much better. I stopped. I swore I heard a sound in my living room, the creak of floorboards and the strange sensation someone was close by. It was probably my cat, but just in case I grabbed my backup piece from my bedside table where I'd put it the night before.

I listened, but everything was quiet again.

I yawned, pulled my sleep shades back on and dragged the sheets up to my neck, turning on my side and cradling the Walther under the covers. I planned on sleeping for a week.

Maybe when I woke up again, everything would be different and my back porch wouldn't look like used firewood. And nobody would be trying to kill me.

It only lasted an hour. I was dreaming I died but couldn't get into heaven so they sent me to this place that looked like my house, only everything was on fire. The walls, the floors, the ceilings, they were all burning in slow motion and I was trapped in the middle, feeling the heat on my face and holding my breath to keep the smoke out.

The funny thing is that while the whole world was burning around me, I wasn't on fire myself. I was passing through a gauntlet of fire, untouched. But then I saw my fuse box and I reached out to touch it even though I knew it was the worst thing I could ever do. In my mind, I tried to stop my hand but I had no control and when my fingers touched the hot metal, it exploded like fireworks.

I pulled my hand away but it was too late. I was on fire and in my nostrils, I could smell my flesh burning. I screamed, waking myself up from my nightmare.

I yanked off my mask and sat up. And almost had a heart attack. There, sitting in the big chair in my bedroom, reading the morning paper and drinking a Coke was Bobo.

"Point that thing somewhere else," he said.

"Jesus, Bobo," I said. Without thinking I'd trained the Walther on him. I lowered the gun. "Do you always have to go sneaking up on me? It's creepy, like you're a ghost or something."

"It's my nature," he said. "Never let the bastards sce you coming."

"How long have you been here?" I said. "Wait, I remember. When I was on the phone with Marcy Cooke's secretary, I heard something in the living room."

"Must have been the cat," he said.

"Yeah, and look what she dragged in. You're here for what exactly?"

"Heard about the electrical accident."

"Where were you when someone was rigging my fuse box?"

"Here and there," he said, holding up a manila folder.

"What's that? My horoscope?"

"Ballistics report. That freeway accident."

"It wasn't an accident, it was a justified shooting. Sherrie was waving a loaded, cocked hand gun at the police," I said. "And why would I care about it anyway. I'm lucky to be breathing."

"You don't know the half of it," he said. "Cops on the scene, they were told to fire above the subject. They had three snipers with beanbag rifles. Figured it was all they needed to take down a skinny kid like that."

"That's bullshit," I said. "I got hit with a real bullet. Wanna see the X-rays?"

"That bullet you were shot with? It came from Vince Lennon's gun. Maybe you know the guy."

"What? Gimme that," I sat up, threw the covers off. I was wearing a T-shirt and XX-L basketball shorts that went down past my knees.

Bobo leaned a long arm over and gave me the folder. He was in his usual attire: black jeans, black jacket and a T-shirt with a saying on it. This one was "Hate is not a family value."

It was there in black and white and I didn't believe it. Lennon had shot me. While the cops might say different, I knew in my heart he had hit me on purpose.

"Imagine that," he said. "Couple dozen uniforms, a SWAT unit, all those guns, all those trigger fingers and the only bullet that finds a target comes from the one guy in the whole force who can't stand your guts? What are the chances?"

"I can't believe it," I said. "I know he's a hothead, but try to kill me? It's crazy."

"Probably didn't plan on it. Saw an opening and couldn't resist."

"How did you get hold of these anyway?"

"I have my sources," he said. "What are you going to do about it?"

"For now? Nothing," I said. "Lennon can wait. I got other problems."

"That's for sure," he said and then the phone rang.

It was Brooks.

"This is a courtesy call," he said. "You're wanted for questioning on the Donnell case in an hour."

Not even a hello. I looked at my watch. "I'm doing fine, Jonathan. Thanks for asking."

"This is serious, Zen. You can bring your lawyer if you like."

"Do I need one?"

"It wouldn't hurt."

"I told you I didn't do it," I said. "Don't you believe me?"

"It's not for me to say," he said and hung up.

I had the phone about six inches from my ear and I was staring at it.

"Something wrong with the phone?" said Bobo.

"That was Brooks. I'm supposed to go down to the station for questioning.

"I guess I'm gonna need these reports now, after all," I said. "I got a feeling Brooks didn't buy my story. If he doesn't, Lennon and Watkins aren't going to either."

"Can't blame them," said Bobo.

"You, too?"

He shrugged. "Just saying it looks bad. That's all."

"Fuck you," I said.

I glared at Bobo then went into my bathroom and slammed the door so hard, the walls of my house shook. It was a childish thing to do, but it felt good. Damn good.

thirty-two

I stayed in the shower longer than necessary, but the heavy spray felt almost religious as it massaged my sore body. Maybe if I could stay under it long enough, all my troubles would wash away, too.

I was glad to see Bobo. Despite the fact that he can be a real pain in my ass, I always feel better when he's around and not just because he's great at watching my back. He's a trained killer, deadly and quick when he wants to be, and I've never seen him hesitate in life and death situations.

I also value his counsel even when he's the only person I know who will tell me things I don't want to hear. He disappears often, off to places I can't pronounce much less locate on a map. I don't ask what he does or when he's coming back.

I don't want to know. I'd worry too much. I'd be lost without him.

Bobo had brought breakfast, warm, sweet donuts he gets from his older sister who, outwardly, lives the life of a soccer mom in the Valley ferrying around her two kids in a minivan and staying home to cook dinner for a husband who manages a recycling plant.

But looks can be deceiving. Bobo doesn't like to talk about it because it scares the shit out of him, but his sister practices some kind of ancient black magic.

He agreed to do some checking to see where the cops were

with ID-ing the John Doe. Unlike me, Bobo didn't have many enemies on the police force, none that I knew of anyway. But that was because they were all afraid of him. Who says cops aren't smart?

After Bobo left, I called Judy Johnson's office and arranged for her to meet me at the police station. I had a feeling I was gonna need her.

Judy was waiting for me on a bench outside the station and she motioned me to sit beside her. She had a scuffed briefcase open on her lap, and she was digging through it, trying to keep papers from flying away in the wind.

"Morning, Zen," she said. "Any word on Jim?"

"Same," I said. "They say it's a good sign that he's made it this far."

"He's a good man, a good lawyer . . ." She trailed off and I half expected her to finish the sentence with something like, 'despite what they say.' I don't know why. Maybe it was her tone or just me being overly suspicious. I felt like Fox Mulder, looking for conspiracies everywhere.

Regardless, I couldn't let it go.

"What do you mean, Judy?"

"Just what I said. Jim's a standup guy." She was staring straight ahead, but she was wearing sunglasses so I couldn't see her eyes anyway. I like Judy. She is tough but very warm, and she smiles often. Her soft, dark skin only makes it seem that much more intense.

But she's a lawyer and lawyers are to be suspicious of, always. Nothing personal. That's the nature of the beast.

"There's a 'but' missing, Judy. You say he's a great guy, but. But what?"

"Nothing," she said. "Let's go over your stuff. I want to make sure I'm prepared in there. I have the papers Bobo faxed to me. They're here somewhere."

She was rustling through her briefcase, but the wind whipped up suddenly and a couple of papers flew out of it. She tried to grab them before they got away, but she only toppled the briefcase, sending papers flying everywhere.

I jumped up and grabbed as many as I could, but we were fighting the Santa Anas. It was like trying to rake leaves with your hands.

We finally picked up all the papers and got them back in Judy's briefcase. She started searching through it again, but I made her close it up.

"You're jumpy as my cat," I said. "What's going on?"

"It's just a rumor," she said. "There's no basis in fact. I mean, you know how lawyers are."

"Are you gonna tell me what it is or do I have to hang around all day at the courthouse water cooler?"

"It's just rumors," she said again. "Jim's under investigation by the state bar. Something about perjury."

"What, like lying in court?"

She shrugged. "Could be that, could be a lot of things. All I heard was perjury."

"When did you hear this?"

"I don't know. I guess maybe I first heard it a couple of days ago."

"Is it true?"

"I have no idea. Like I told you—"

"I know, I know. It's only rumor," I said. "Can you find out?"

"Me? Doubt it. That stuff is usually kept on the QT. I'm surprised people are even talking about it," she said, a layer of sweat forming on her forehead. "Lawyers are paranoid. You know, there but for the grace of God and all that."

"Well, you gotta help me out here," I said and she started to shake her head. "C'mon Judy. You wouldn't be here if it wasn't for Jim. And you know that."

She was pulling her blue silk shirt so the cuffs were longer than the sleeves of her gray pin-striped jacket. Then she took off her sunglasses, folded them and put them in the side pocket of the jacket.

"I'll see what I can do," she said. "Now can we forget about it and talk about you?"

thirty-three

I went into the squad room nodding to the desk sergeant who grimaced at me like he hadn't brought enough antacid for the shift. Some days you can never bring enough.

When I walked in, the place was buzzing. Brooks was talking to a couple of plainclothes detectives and Watkins was in his office, with two people, one a tall, rangy guy with glasses and a bald spot the other a round, older woman.

Watkins' color wasn't good. I could see red blotches on his face all the way across the room.

A few feet away, sitting at a desk, was Lennon. When he saw me, he glared at me so hard I was expecting smoke to come out of his ears. I flashed him a thumbs up sign and smiled.

"Hey, Detective," I said. "I'm here for the powwow."

"What? No mouthpiece?" he said.

"My lawyer's outside making a phonecall," I said, winking. "Don't worry, she's a real ass kicker."

"It won't matter to me," he said. "No lawyer's gonna be able to help you where you're going."

"Lead the way," I said, keeping the smile on my face. I was determined not to let this guy get the best of me. That's what got me in trouble the last time.

"Interview number three," he said, brushing past me toward the back of the squad room. Lennon's only an inch or two taller than me, but he's got a barrel chest that's been going soft, sliding toward his belly. He's got the remnants of some monster biceps, but he's not as solid as he probably once was.

He smelled strong of aftershave, a musk scent that would never be confused with cologne, and of sweat and something else I couldn't quite get. Something dark and mean, like a junkyard dog. When he walked by, I shivered.

I waited until he was a few steps ahead before following.

I went toward Brooks, who frowned when he saw me and I returned it with a shrug and a smile. The two detectives took off as soon as they saw me coming.

"Bad day?" I said.

"It is now," he said.

"I thought we were friends," I said. "What happened?"

"This happened," he said, waving a sheet of paper at me. I grabbed at it, but he yanked it back. "I've been suspended."

"What? Why?"

"Believe it or not, they are investigating our relationship and whether I had anything to do with whatever happened at the Donnell house."

"You weren't even there," I said, lowering my voice so only he could hear. "Who's behind this? Lennon? That's just not fair. I'm gonna . . ."

"What? Look, Zen, don't do me any more favors right now," he said. "This is my mess. I'll take care of it."

"I can't believe it," I said. "It's bullshit. I'm just gonna have to tell that fuck what happened Saturday night. You know, he's not going to believe me."

Over his shoulder, I could see Watkins trapped in his office, doing most of the listening. The tall guy was waving his hands and pointing. I nodded toward Watkins' office.

"Who's reaming your boss in there?"

Brooks looked over his shoulder, turned back. He was still frowning, but he had a twinkle in his eye and I had to drop my head so he wouldn't see me grinning.

"The Mayor and the head of the city council," he said. "They don't like to see murders North of Montana on their watch."

"Everybody's a critic," I said as Watkins rose, abruptly ending the discussion. He opened the door and pushed Councilman Ted Golenberg and Mayor Martha Matthews out of his office.

Golenberg is a commercial real estate developer and Matthews is an ex-hippie who runs a landscape company. The two represent the innate contradiction that is Santa Monica: those that welcome Banana Republic retail stores and the taxes they bring, and those who think the debate over development should be where to put the parks.

Watkins hurried the two out the door, a fixed smile on his face and one eye focused in my direction. As soon as they were gone, his smile faded and he headed straight for us. On the way over, he caught Lennon's eye and called him over.

"Just the person I was looking for," he said to me.

"I'm here as ordered," I said.

"Yeah," said Lennon. "We were about to start the . . ."

Watkins waved him off.

"That won't be necessary," he said.

"What the hell?" said Lennon.

Lennon's face fell, his moment of triumph suddenly robbed from him. He was trying to mask his emotions, but he wasn't very good at it. His lower jaw was quivering and his eyes were burning, but you could feel his anger. A blind person could tell he was pissed off.

"And on behalf of the Santa Monica police department, I'd like to apologize," said Watkins.

If this were a cartoon, my tongue would have been dragging on the floor.

"What? Why?"

"We were mistaken. You're not the murderer," he said.

"Works for me since I didn't do it," I said, not sure where he was going with this. "Taking smart pills today? What tipped you off?"

"More like who. Turns out it was your rat bastard lawyer," he said, the smile returning, and I realized Watkins was enjoying himself.

"What the hell are you talking about?" It was my turn to be pissed. "He's in a coma. Somebody tried to kill him."

"Was in a coma," he said. "'Bout an hour ago he regained consciousness. He wrote down his confession."

"I don't believe you," I said. "It had to be coerced. The guy's practically on life support."

"He volunteered the information," said Watkins. "Before this, he wasn't even being considered a suspect."

He said this last part to Lennon, who was starting to smolder.

"How can this be true?" I said to no one in particular.

"We have the murder weapon," said Watkins. "A baseball bat. It's been wiped clean, but preliminary results show Gray's fingerprints and blood type on the handle. Once we get the final report, we'll be able to proceed."

"Wait," I said, pausing for effect. "I was there that night."

This was a new one to Watkins. The color was starting to creep up his cheeks, but he managed to keep it under control. Lennon, too, seemed to perk up, but his expression was less surprised than Watkins. As if he knew something none of us did. It made me feel deeply uncomfortable.

"I was worried about Jim," I said. "I saw him and, of all people, Eddie Cooke, go inside. When I followed them in, Eddie was torturing Jim. Then somebody knocked me out. That's the last thing I remember until I woke up. So before you jump the gun, why don't you get the story from Eddie Cooke?"

"Eddie isn't going to do much talking," said Lennon. "Not where he is."

I looked at him but spoke to Watkins.

"The dead body? That's . . ."

"Eddie Cooke," said Watkins. "Seems so. Teeth don't lie. We got a match this morning."

My heart caught in my throat. Images circled and played in my head. Could Jim have killed Eddie? It didn't make any sense. Even if it was in self defense, how could Jim have gotten from the basement to where I'd found him, especially in his condition at the time? Unless there was a third person, an accomplice. But who's? Jim's or Eddie's?

"I don't believe it," I said. "Jim's covering for someone."

"Yeah," Lennon sneered. "It's probably you."

"Would you shut your monkey up?" I said. "Before I make him eat a banana backwards."

Lennon started at me, but Watkins held up his hand.

"It gets better," said Watkins. "We have an eyewitness who says your thumb-sucking lawyer threatened Eddie Cooke a few hours before he died. She's already given a statement, on the record."

"Is this true?" I asked Brooks.

He shrugged. Even Brooks was out of the loop. I looked at Lennon, who was stewing. He had backed off, was sitting on the corner of somebody's desk, his arms folded, and he had a wild dog's look in his eyes.

"Who's your witness?"

"None of your business," said Watkins. "Wait, there's more. He threatened Cooke in a crowded barroom."

I remembered what the waitress at Jiggy's had said and I suddenly knew where Watkins was getting his information.

"I don't believe it," I said again. I didn't know what else to say.

"I don't give a damn. The only thing I want to hear from you is why you shouldn't be arrested for leaving a crime scene."

"There won't be any arresting of anybody," said a voice behind us. It was Judy. She moved toward us with the confidence of a woman who has been in the trenches long enough not to notice it anymore.

"Who the hell let her in here?" said Watkins.

"Judy Johnson," she said. "I represent Ms. Moses. Heard about your worst nightmare? Triple it and you got me."

"I don't know how long you were standing there," Watkins said. "But your client just admitted to a crime."

Judy dropped her briefcase on the nearest desk and clicked it open with her thumbs. She pulled out a folder and handed it over to Watkins.

"I think you'll find some interesting information in here," she said. "One is a toxicology report showing high levels of the drug Rohypnol in my client's system on the night in question. She was in no condition to make any kind of cognitive decisions, much less murder anybody."

"That doesn't excuse the fact that a crime was committed," said Watkins.

"Perhaps you should read on, Captain. There's another document that might make you think twice before charging my client."

Watkins paged through the folder. His eyes seemed to grow wider suddenly and then the red cloud marched up his cheeks again. He seemed to hold his breath as his fury quietly built to a crescendo. Any minute I expected his head might explode.

"Where the hell did you get this? I could have you up on charges . . ."

"What matters," she said, calmly cutting him off, "is that's not the only copy."

Watkins looked it over and then stared down Lennon, but when he spoke again it was to Judy.

"Get her out of here," he said.

"Let's go, Zen," said Judy, but I didn't move. I was still in shock.

"There's been a mistake," I said to Watkins. "Jim didn't do it. I know him."

"Not that well apparently," he said.

"What's that supposed to mean?" Watkins was getting under my skin. I knew I was veering into trouble, but while my head said go, my gut wouldn't let my legs move.

"Maybe you should take a look at his background," he said. "Bludgeoning seems to run in his family."

"What are you talking about?"

"Let's go, Zen," Judy said again.

"Why don't you ask him?" he said. "Your loyalty is so touching. When you're not out with my cops, you banging your own lawyer? That how you arrange payment?"

"Tell me again how you got to be Captain," I said to him, knowing I was making a mistake but unable to contain my anger any longer. "Lose track of how many asses you've had to kiss to get here? I know it wasn't old-fashioned police work 'cause you don't know the first thing about being a good cop."

He lunged, grabbing my jacket by the collar, leaning his face in so far I could see his nose hairs.

"Who the fuck do you think you are?" he said. "Lawyer or no lawyer, I'll lock you up."

Brooks started to separate us, but I blocked his way with my knee. Then I grabbed Watkins' fleshy biceps and dug my nails in.

"Arrest me for what? I could sue your ass so fast," I said. "And I got witnesses. You wanna talk about loyalty? Let's see how many guys stand up for you right now. My money's on half this room sitting on their hands."

"Fuck you," he said and we stood there, holding onto each other like a couple of Sumo wrestlers looking for an advantage. I have strong fingers from years of piano lessons as a kid and I was pinching him hard on the soft part of his upper arm. He was trying not to show the pain, but his face was turning redder with each passing second, sweat was beading up on his upper lip and his arms were beginning to shake.

The room got quiet all of the sudden, around us cops were poised. We were on the edge of a blowup and every one in the room knew it.

Somehow, in the middle of our stand off, Watkins' face changed, softened and I think, he started seeing me in a whole new light. Maybe I was tougher than he thought I was. Maybe he didn't want to get his head blown off.

"Tell you what," I whispered. "I'll let go first. You save face and then we can start over again."

He nodded, but before I could move, I saw something in his eyes that scared the shit out of me. A moment later, Lennon's voice broke the silence around us.

"Freeze, mother-fucker."

"GUN!" someone shouted and almost in comic unison, everybody in the room hit the ground, diving behind desks, cabinets and chairs, many going for their weapons, too.

I could only see Lennon from the corner of my eye. He was standing in classic firing position, aiming right at me.

"Put the gun down, Vince. I can handle this," Watkins said, fully expecting Lennon to lower his weapon, but he didn't.

"Back away Captain," said Lennon. "Back away so I can take care of this."

I could see fear and disbelief in the faces around me. Brooks, snatched a gun from one of the uniforms standing near him and had it aimed in Lennon's direction.

"Drop it, Vince," he said.

"The boyfriend speaks," he sneered and I felt the heat running up my face. I realized how far this thing between us had gone and I cursed my part in it. You can't escalate with guys like Lennon. For them, it's only about winning at all costs and the point of no return is always closer than you think.

Watkins had a confused and angry look on his face, directed at Lennon, who perhaps he didn't know as well as he thought. Or maybe he did.

In the middle of this, Watkins and I were still in a clench. Another time, another place it would be funny.

"What now?" I whispered to Watkins.

"We're gonna let go," he said, then repeated it so everyone could hear. "You hear me Vince, Moses and I are going to let go of each other and you're going to lower that pistol. That's an order. Do you understand?"

Lennon didn't answer. But Watkins took this to mean he'd understood, then he nodded at me and I slowly started to take my hands off him.

"Fuck," he cried and through the corner of my eye I saw his hand tense and instead of letting go of Watkins I dragged him with me to the floor. Above us, a single shot whizzed by, ripping through the back of a chair and lodging harmlessly in the wall, right through a picture of the governor.

Brooks returned fire and Lennon went down. When Watkins and I got to our feet, two cops were struggling to keep him still. He was bleeding from a wound in his thigh.

"What's the deal with you two?" Watkins asked me.

"I wish I knew," I said. "We never really got off on the right foot, I guess."

"Get him some medical attention," said Brooks to no one in particular. "Everybody else okay?"

"Wait," said Watkins, who turned to me and nodded before walking over to Lennon.

"I know what happened on the freeway last week, Vince. I was willing to say it was just a coincidence but now I understand. Maybe you need some time to think about your future. As of now, you're off the Donnell case."

He reached over and unpinned Lennon's badge.

"Get him out of my sight," he said and I watched with no joy at all as they dragged Lennon out.

"Do me a favor," he said to me. "Get out of here before I really get mad."

"What about Jim?"

"Brooks," said Watkins. "Get your badge back. I want you on the case. Report directly to me. And I don't want to see you two together. Understood?"

Brooks just nodded. Then Watkins looked back at me.

"I'm cutting you some slack here because one of my cops nearly blew both our heads off," he said. "But don't take it like this makes us buddies. I don't know what you were doing the night Cooke was killed but I'm gonna find out. And if I find you anywhere near this investigation, you're gonna wish Lennon was still on your ass. Now get out."

I squeezed Brooks' shoulder on my way past and mouthed a 'thank you.' He didn't smile when our eyes met. He didn't say anything at all.

thirty-four

When I got out of the police station, I sat in my car for a long time. I was in shock.

Getting shot at was one reason but this whole thing about Jim confessing was crazy. It just didn't feel right.

It was a relief that Watkins wasn't looking at me for the murder, but now I was having to face the possibility that my good friend was responsible for a horrible crime.

Jim might be able to kill someone if he thought his own life was in mortal danger, but beat a guy to a pulp? With a baseball bat? When I saw him that awful night he could barely talk. He was practically in a coma when I found him.

Watkins said something about Jim's family history being violent. If this were true, it was news to me. Maybe Jim was protecting someone or something in his past. It was time I found out.

I half expected to find Jim sitting up in bed catching up on his caseload, but he remained in I.C.U. still, the doctors said, fighting for his life. The nurse would only let me see him for a minute or two.

The smell of disinfectant hit me in the face when I walked into his room, the beeps and clicks going full blast. Everything was the same as before except he was breathing on his own. Only his breaths were weak and half-hearted, as if he was on the twenty-fifth mile of a marathon.

He opened his eyes when I came to the side of the bed and smiled. Motioning with his good hand to the side table. There was a cup of ice and I used a plastic spoon to place a cube on his tongue.

I touched his hand. It's coldness scared me.

"You're not supposed to talk," I whispered. "So I'll make this quick and try to stick to yes and no questions, okay?"

He nodded, tried to say something, but I stopped him.

"Me first," I said. "The cops said you confessed to murdering Eddie Cooke."

He nodded again.

"Are you saying you beat him to death with a baseball bat?"

He didn't move.

"I knew it," I said. "What the hell were you thinking?"

He slowly lifted his hand a few inches off the bed, pointing toward me.

"Me?" Then it hit me. "You were trying to protect me?"

He nodded, then he started to speak. He shook his head when I tried to stop him.

"Set. Up." he said, but he could barely get a word out. I had to bend down to hear him. It was heartbreaking to see Jim like this. I felt my own tears welling, one drifted down my check.

"Eddie . . . brother . . . he . . . knew . . . I . . . my . . . fault. . . ."

A machine suddenly went berserk, flaring up in a barrage of beeps and clicks, and in seconds the room was filled with doctors and nurses. One of them pushed me out the door. I stood on the other side of the glass, hearing Jim's last words over and over like a nonsense mantra, feeling the tears burn my cheeks, helplessly, watching my friend die.

thirty-five

My grief was almost too much for me to bear, but it was infinitesimal compared with the anger and guilt I was feeling.

I hurried down the hallway, afraid at any moment I would break into tears or throw a chair through a window. I wanted to get as far away from this place as possible.

"Excuse me!" someone called. "Excuse me! Miss!"

I didn't want to turn around. It was the nurse from my first visit, the night I got shot.

"Please, wait," she said, half jogging toward me. She was top heavy and the cartoon characters on her shirt were bouncing up and down as she ran.

I looked at her but didn't say anything.

"I know he was your friend. I'm very sorry," she said, then as if she realized how hollow her words sounded to me, abruptly pushed a plastic shopping bag into my hands. "These were his."

"I think they should go to his next of kin," I said.

"He was injured during a crime," she said. "That means all his stuff goes to the cops first. And that one cop who came to see him, I didn't much like him. I don't think Mr. Gray did either."

"What cop?"

"Some detective. He said his name. I forget. I don't know why but it reminded me of the Beatles."

"Lennon?"

"That could be it," she said. "Yes, that's it."

"When did he come by?"

"This morning," she said. "He was there when Mr. Gray woke up. He stayed about five minutes. After he left, more cops came and they say that's when he wrote up his confession. You don't believe he did it, do you?"

"No," I said. "I don't."

"He seemed like such a nice man. I really am sorry."

There were so many questions I didn't know where to begin. I knew some of the answers had just died along with Jim but I couldn't believe he was a killer. I wouldn't.

When I got to my car, I left word for Bobo and phoned Myron at Jim's office to break the news. It was among the hardest things I've ever done.

"Oh my God," he said, his voice cracking. "He was like a father to me."

"I'm sorry Myron," I said.

He started crying softly and I waited him out, trying not to join him.

"You okay?" I asked.

He sniffled. "Is that why all the cops are here?"

"What are you talking about?"

"They had a warrant . . .," his voice faded off. "I can't believe this is happening. They say he confessed to murdering someone. It can't be true."

"Of course not," I said, though if I could feel the uncertainty in my voice, surely he could hear it. "Call Judy Johnson. She'll tell you what to do."

"Someone has to notify his family," he said. "Oh, God, I don't think I could."

"I'll take care of it," I said. "Give me the number."

"His mother's dead. But he's been in touch with his father lately. He lives in Minneapolis. Here's the number."

"Thanks. Hang in there, Myron."

"Zen," he said, crying again. "He's innocent. You know he could never hurt anyone. You can't let him . . . go like this. It wouldn't be right."

"I know," I said. "I won't."

But when I hung up the phone a part of me wasn't so sure. I felt like I was going to cry. I covered my face, forcing the tears away, putting them away for another time, another place when I could afford them.

The plastic bag the nurse had given me was lying next to me on the passenger seat. I stared at it a long time before looking inside.

In it was a Mont Blanc fountain pen, Jim's wallet, assorted change and a piece of paper with a phone number in Minneapolis.

I looked through his wallet, feeling a little dirty, like I was invading my friend's privacy. The usual credit cards, a few large bills and two pictures, one of two teenagers leaning against an old car. It was worn and faded, but one of the kids looked a lot like a younger version of Jim.

Inside with the bills was a schedule of his meetings for the last two weeks. None mentioned Eddie's name, but he did have an appointment with Eddie' wife, Marcy Cooke. It was scheduled for today at one o'clock at a place called The Ivory Cafe.

I looked at my watch. It was just after noon. Plenty of time to make Jim's appointment for him.

I was surprised to see Marcy's name. There was no arguing that Eddie was an awful human being, but his wife wasn't much better. If Jim had an appointment with her, he probably had a good reason.

Besides, it was an opportunity to see what she had wanted from me. I'd never met Marcy Cooke, but her lineage was legendary.

The former Marcy Louise Jansen, the only daughter of one of California's last oil magnates, broke family tradition—and her father's heart—by becoming first a very good model and then a very bad actress before settling into the most unlikely position, as a television personality.

Marcy is a gossip monger of the worst order. Five nights a week, she appears on a nationally syndicated tabloid news show and dishes dirt with the glee of an arsonist watching his work go up in flames. She has a natural advantage reporting on a world with which she is not only intimate but, by birth, a lifetime member. Access she has in spades, and she uses it. Like paparazzi gleefully clicking their shutters in the brutal aftermath of a grisly celebrity disaster, she shoots first and makes excuses later.

I was dying to know what part she had to play in this whole thing.

The Ivory is how the hipsters refer to the Ivory Café, the chi chi restaurant that was the new favorite of the current 'in' crowd. It was the sort of place where crab cakes the size of silver dollars cost fifteen bucks and your status determines where you sit and vice versa. Producers of the latest hit TV show get escorted to the choice tables in the main room, away from the bar but not too far so you can't be properly noticed. After all, what's a great seat in the trendiest restaurant in town worth if you can't be seen sitting there?

Of course, when your show gets canceled, you can't expect

anything better than a table in the back room or the high tops facing the bar where, in between, the waiters wear out the carpet running back and forth from the kitchen to serve those more fortunate than you.

Still, you go and hide your face in the latest copy of *Variety* just in case the competition walks in. Of course, the suffering is all part of the game and this is a town chockfull of experts in the fine art of anguish and heartache, both real and imagined. It's just another role to be played in the big live-action movie that is the City of Angels.

thirty-six

The urban sprawl that constitutes the 400 square miles that is Los Angeles can be tough to navigate and this is only partly due to the fact that there are just too many damned cars on the road.

Another is the uncanny sameness of streets and neighborhoods that can make them blend together in a homogenized mess. Santa Monica Boulevard resembles Wilshire, which looks kind of like Pico which in turn looks very much like Lincoln. Even savvy natives can get tripped up.

West Third Street is one of those thoroughfares that stretches across the city for miles, and changes so subtly only a keen observer can really tell when one neighborhood turns into another.

In West Hollywood it runs by the Farmer's Market near Fairfax Avenue and passes by the massive Beverly Center, a multi-story mall that dwarfs everything around it, even the overly ornate Sofitel Hotel next door.

In between it's like a lot of streets around LA's Westside, which have trended upward and are lined with an array of small restaurants and precious specialty shops that sell everything from antiques to beauty supplies and cookbooks.

The Ivory is on such a street, in between a hair salon and a sundries shop that sells retro greeting cards and handmade gifts.

The place was in full lunch-hour swing when I walked in. The Ivory is owned by Janna Margolis, a woman of no particular age who is known to wear tight jeans and fluffy see-through blouses and hug any and all males who walk in the door—which makes most women who come in hold on to their dates like vice grips.

She adores, abuses and mocks her guests and they all love her for it. Go figure. It's another form of therapy, LA style. And hell, you at least get to eat during your session.

"Oh my, now this *is* a treat," she said, crossing the tiny room to me as if we were best friends. We'd never before met and yet she recognized me immediately.

I quickly put my finger to my lips. Thankfully, she dropped her voice and led me to the bar, loving the role of complicity. "Well, if it isn't LA's most famous private detective. Don't tell me you're here on a case? Oh, how cool is that? I think I could just die."

Fame is a bitch, I thought. I wondered how long before the whole freeway chase would melt into the city's collective memory. Thank God LA's attention span isn't much longer than your average music video.

"You must be Janna," I said. "I've heard so much about you."

"Not half as much as I've heard about you," she said, actually winking one of her long-lashed eyes at me. "It's totally disrespectful of you not to have shown your face sooner. It's hurtful."

"I'm more of a beach bum," I said. "I rarely venture out this far from the ocean."

"At least you're here. How delicious."

I couldn't tell her age, but I knew her to be ten or fifteen years older than me. She could have been younger. Her skin was smooth, hardly any lines and she wore very little makeup, except for her eyes and mouth. She was wearing an off-white blouse that didn't do enough to hide the black bra she had on underneath.

"Are we dining alone this afternoon?" she asked me.

"Actually, I'm meeting someone. Would it be too much trouble to wait at the bar?"

"Are you sure?" she said. "For you we have a lovely table in the main room."

I nearly rolled my eyes. Zen Moses, the celebrity. I even rated a hipster table. What was the world coming to?

"I'll just sit at the bar," I said and after some doing, managed to get rid of her. I wanted to sit at the bar and feel sorry for myself.

I watched the lunch crowd, wondering what it must be like to have a career that revolves around power lunches, ass-kissing and disappointment. Then again, it seemed a lot like being a private detective.

I was on my second glass of sparkling water when Marcy Cooke made her entrance. Actually, it was much more than just that. She swept into the room like Julie Andrews cavorting on the hills of Austria.

She was wearing a tight dress of white stretch rayon that sparkled when she moved and had long, sheer attachments that billowed behind her like wings.

Janna pecked Marcy solemnly on both cheeks, European style, and then led her to the best table in the restaurant. It took a while to get there. Like a foreign dignitary at a state dinner, all eyes were on Marcy as she stopped to greet someone at almost every table. I wanted to throw up.

People didn't just consider her, they fawned over her. Partly this was because she wielded so much power and could be dangerous in a way a carjacker with a loaded .44 could never be. To people in this room, that was something that happened on the news every night to somebody else less fortunate than you.

But she had something else. She had the gift of presence. Her auburn hair glistened, framing silky tanned skin that set off the subtlest make-up job I've ever seen. She was taller than I'd imagined, had an inch or two on me but much more slender. Her figure was so perfect it was as if it had been sculpted from a medical textbook.

Her table could accommodate four people, but Marcy had it all to herself. She checked her watch. On the drive over, I'd called her secretary to say Jim was feeling better and would be making his appointment. Very little about Jim's condition was released to the press, mostly because that's how Watkins had wanted it. Even Marcy would have had to do some digging to find anything about him. I hoped she hadn't bothered.

I had to gulp down the rest of my drink to keep from crying again. I was going to have to bury this pain in my heart until I had time to pay it mind.

I waited until they brought her a martini and she took out a stack of papers she had brought in under her arm.

I left a couple of bills on the bar and walked through the main room toward Marcy's table. I passed Janna on the way and she started to say something. It was obvious where I was headed, but I discreetly tucked a twenty into her hand and squeezed, hard.

Everyone, I suppose has their price, but with Janna, I knew better. She was more interested in the developing scene than in getting her palms greased. The money was just an added bonus.

I sat down at Marcy's table and it seemed to me that the din quieted suddenly. But it might have been my imagination. To her credit, Marcy didn't even look up from her reading. A very cool customer.

"You have the wrong table," she said.

"I think not," I said and tossed my card so it landed on top of her papers. She started to move it away, but she stopped as if she were reading it, and re-reading it. She looked up. Gotcha.

"Is this some kind of a joke?"

"No," I said. "You asked to see me. Here I am. End of story. Actually, I'm surprised to see you here. Shouldn't you be in mourning?"

"Everyone grieves in their own way," she said. "I am a journalist. I can't stop my work for personal matters. Besides, if it's any of your business and be assured it is not, I have a lunch date."

"He's not coming," I said.

"And he sent you in his place? How charming."

"He's dead."

This barely seemed to register.

"Who do you think you are?" she leaned forward and hissed her next words and the way she said it made my skin crawl. "Don't you know who I am? I could make your life very difficult, Ms. Moses."

I laughed quietly, leaning back in my chair. She stared back at me, disbelief on her face.

"You would be wise to take me seriously," she said, downing the rest of her martini in one delicate sip. Anyone else would have spilled it or gulped or made a face. But Marcy was a tough one and I made a mental note to remember that. "I can make good on my promises I have a feeling you quite cherish your private investigator's license."

"They aren't promises," I said evenly. "They are threats and I don't like threats. Just like I don't like being summoned like a servant. You will find, Mrs. Cooke, that I am immune to your browbeating, that I work outside of the world where you wield your so-called power. So save your breath for someone who actually gives a damn."

If I'd cut into this battleax's veneer, it was impossible to tell. I found her belief in herself and her own private cause to be downright frightening, yet somehow wondrous as well. Her single-mindedness was admirable, even if it was focused on hurting people.

"I know people like you," Marcy was saying. "You live on the edge, never quite making it, always fighting for the underdog. It's quite charming somehow, but also quite pathetic, don't you think?"

"You don't want to know what I think," I said as the waiter appeared out of thin air to bring Marcy her martini. "Let's dial down the chest-pounding because despite what you think, you can't win. Know why? Cause we're in a public place and I'm in no mood. My friend is dead and I believe with all my heart that your husband killed him. So I've got nothing to lose here. Do you understand?"

She was gripping the stem of the martini glass, wanting badly to throw it in my face. I could see everything about her pull tight like an instant face-lift. I tried to be cool, to relax, but my heart was pounding in my chest so hard I thought everyone within five miles could hear it.

"What do you want?" she said.

"I want to know what Eddie had on Jim."

"How am I supposed to know?" she said. "We were getting a divorce. Whoever killed Eddie did me a favor."

"Where were you Saturday night?" I said.

"None of your damned business," she said. "If you're implying that I had anything to do with what happened that night, you're greatly mistaken. My lawyers eat people like you for lunch."

"People like you often underestimate people like me," I said.

"You're so smug," she said. "The way I hear it, your friends are dropping dead like flies."

I didn't move, didn't flinch, didn't even blink. Just because she nailed me between the eyes, didn't mean I had to give her the satisfaction of knowing she had. Beneath it all, my very soul was burning.

"I know why my husband didn't like you. There's something we agree on."

"How nice for you both," I said. "Why did you summon me?"

A cell phone rang before she could answer. Everyone in the restaurant except me reached for their phones, even Marcy. It was funny, really, to see a roomful of diners going for their phones simultaneously, each in their own way trying to be discreet and cool about it. It was a real riot, that is until I realized that the phone that was ringing was mine.

"Zen Moses," I said, quickly, quietly, feeling embarrassed, but as I looked around, everyone was back to doing their own thing. A cell phone ringing in the middle of a power-lunch crowd was about as foreign to this group as a traffic jam at rush hour.

"It's me," said Bobo. "Where are you?"

"With the widow," I said. "What's up?"

"Been talking to some people," he said. "You were right. They couldn't ID Eddie by his prints cause they couldn't find a match."

I looked up at Marcy, who was pretending to ignore me, but an idiot could see she was trying hard to eavesdrop.

I wondered again how this woman could be so cavalier when the man she'd spent the last fifteen years with was lying in the Santa Monica morgue without a face. Even in the midst of a contentious divorce, it would be a hard thing for most people to take.

But then Marcy Cooke isn't like most people. Most people have actual feelings. Hell, it's not like Eddie deserved any sympathy.

"You telling me the ID is wrong?" I whispered into the phone.

"No, the dental records matched," he said. "But the prints are no longer on file. Nobody knows why."

"That's weird. They always take your prints when they arrest you."

"Uh-huh," he said, then I heard voices in the background. "Gotta blow. Out."

Damn. I hate when he does that. I looked up at Marcy. She wasn't even masquerading anymore. She was staring at me, sipping her martini and holding my gaze like she was trying to put a hex on me.

"Where was I?" I said quickly. "Oh, right. Leaving."

I stood up.

"Where are you going?" she demanded.

"I'm going to clear my friend's name," I said.

"Tilting at windmills. How quaint."

"You won't be so arrogant if I find out you had anything to do with this," I said. "And that's not a promise. It's a threat."

I hurried through the tightly packed crowd of diners and out of the Ivory. All I could think about was getting some air. When I made it outside to the sidewalk, I stopped to suck in the grimy Hollywood ozone as if it was as clean as the first day on Earth. I felt as if I'd been holding my breath for hours.

In the restaurant, sitting across from Marcy I got this uncomfortable sensation, as if something sinister was nearby. It was a feeling I'd had once or twice before and it wasn't without irony that one of those times was in the presence of Eddie Cooke.

It didn't give me any solace that he was now dead. But it did make me consider that matches weren't only made in heaven.

thirty-seven

By the time I got back to my place, the news about Eddie was all over. When I walked inside, Bobo was sunk into my couch with his feet up on my coffee table watching CNN. They were doing a piece on Eddie's life.

The cops hadn't released Jim's name yet. Watkins was giving me some time to notify his family first, which was quite decent of him. But then again, if he really was smart and I sometimes got the feeling he was, then he'd be as suspicious of the confession as I was.

Lennon had gone to see Jim just before Jim told the cops he was the murderer. I didn't know what went on in that room this morning, but obviously Jim felt he had to act.

I couldn't ask Jim and now I couldn't even get to Lennon. Not only was he on administrative leave, but he was forbidden to go near me.

I thought about Lennon and our first of what has been many confrontations. I wasn't an innocent bystander. I knew how to push his buttons and I rarely let an opportunity to do so pass me by.

Lennon was a dangerous man. But I suppose I really had no idea just how dangerous and unbalanced he really was. He was a small-town cop running loose in the big city, looking for some way to ease the chip on his shoulder. Looking for somebody to dare to knock it off. He was a barroom brawl waiting to happen, a redneck tough guy masquerading as a cop. And he hated my guts.

I went into the kitchen and tried Jim's father's house again. No answer. I got an Anchor Steam from the fridge and sat on the couch next to Bobo.

The sound was down, but the images that flashed on the screen—Eddie, his late partner Bud Greeley, John Dennis Moore—didn't require words. A real who's who. And now almost everybody involved was dead.

To most people, it was another celebrity of excess coming to a horrible end. To the news media, it was the final tragic chapter of another story in the annals of LA history.

To me, it was reminders of a friend who was now dead, and all I could think about was that the man who was responsible was getting called the victim. Eddie Cooke had once again had the last laugh.

It was like being forced to watch the instant replay of a grisly train wreck.

I turned off the set and threw the clicker on the table, slumping down next to Bobo on the couch. It wasn't hot, but I was sweating. I hadn't gotten much sleep and that and the stress of the last couple of days was starting to get to me. I felt like I'd gone a few rounds with George Foreman.

"You're looking peaked," said Bobo, who had my Walther in pieces on the table in front of him. He had all my cleaning supplies there, too: a brush, silicon cloth, gun oil and a strong-smelling solvent.

"I'm okay," I said, gesturing to the TV. "When did they announce it?"

"Not long after our talk," he said.

"And now the cops think Jim did it," I said. "They got a

witness who puts Jim with Eddie a few hours before he was killed. And a bunch of people at Jiggy's saw them together."

"Funny, the odds were you did it."

"Yeah, I know," I said. "It's not like I didn't want to. But I didn't have the chance. He was already dead."

"Whatever you say," he said.

"Thanks for the vote of confidence," I said.

He had the barrel up to the light and was peering inside.

"I cleaned that thing a couple weeks ago," I said.

"Uh-huh," he said, which was his way of saying I was full of shit. He soaked a piece of cloth in the solvent and used the brush to push it through the barrel. It came out as clean as it went in.

"See?" I said. "You could operate in there."

"Uh-huh," he said again and then he stopped.

So did I. We both heard it. Quiet creaks from outside my door. Footsteps. Someone was creeping up my landing.

Bobo quietly placed the barrel on the table and reached quickly for his own, which was in a holster he wore on his shoulder. He trained it on the door. And we waited.

The footsteps were so quiet it was amazing we heard them at all. Whoever was out there was either a midget or barefoot—or someone like Bobo who was trained to be light on his feet.

We heard the steps go silent and after a minute, the click, click of someone trying to pick my lock. I was lucky Bobo had schooled me about guns. I could put a Walther together blindfolded, which is pretty much what I had to do. I worked quietly, never taking my eyes off the door.

I finished the job just as the knob turned. I raised the Walther. Then as the door swung open, Bobo and I both hit the floor in opposite directions, rolling up to a firing position so we were not directly in front of the door, but still had an angle on whoever was about to walk in.

I looked at Bobo, who nodded.

"Open that door one more inch and you're dead," I said. "I'm pointing a loaded firearm at the door. And I won't miss."

The door stopped in mid-swing and we heard a small, muffled voice behind it. Maybe it was a midget.

"Whoa, don't fucking shoot!" it said. "I'm not packing."

"That's a good thing," I said. "For you. Here's what we're gonna do. When I say so, put your hands over your head and push the door open with your foot, gently. Understand?"

"Hey I ain't no idiot. I speak English," the voice said, it was high-pitched, not scratchy but it warbled a little, like a child's. It was also vaguely familiar but I couldn't place it.

"Okay, so we don't need to hire a translator," I said, looking at Bobo and rolling my eyes. He just shrugged. "Okay. Ready?"

We both had our guns raised again.

"We doin' this today? Or next year?"

"On three," I said. "One. Two. Three."

The door swung open slowly, revealing the person who had just successfully gotten through my dead bolt. Bobo's jaw was slack and he had the tiniest grin on his face. On another human being, his mouth would be open.

Standing in my doorway, holding up both hands, one holding a professional lock pick, was a skinny, young girl with short red hair and freckles, green eyes, a Snoop Doggy Dog sweatshirt, enormous baggy jeans and high-top Jordan basketball shoes with the laces undone.

She had a purple and yellow Lakers duffel over one shoulder.

"Damn, you two maniacs or something? This looked like an okay neighborhood to me." The kid was putting on a brave face, but she was shaking a little.

I looked at Bobo and he looked back at me and then we lowered our guns.

As soon as we did, she came inside, closed the door and headed straight for my kitchen.

"Man, that's more like it," she said. "I hope you got some decent food in here. 'Cause I'm starving."

"Who the hell was that," said Bobo as soon as she'd left the room. He went back to the couch and sat down, though he didn't put his gun away. Instead, he laid it on the coffee table. Within easy reach.

I went over and checked my lock. It's not difficult to pick a dead bolt when you know what you're doing, but I didn't expect it to be an easy job for a little girl.

"Never seen her before," I said.

"Ugh, all you got in here is health food crap," she yelled from my kitchen. We heard some rustling, the sound of dishes clinking and my refrigerator door being slammed shut. "Tree hugger food. Great, we got ourselves a friggin' nature girl."

I couldn't help but smile at this kid. She came out, with a can of Diet Coke and a sandwich made of the rest of the ham and swiss Sam had brought over.

Bobo and I were both sitting on the couch. The kid shed her duffel, grabbed my clicker, plopped down on my big chair and started running through my channels. Almost all of them were doing live reports on the death of Eddie Cooke.

"Don't you got Nintendo or something?" she said.

"Sorry," I said, getting up. I walked over and grabbed the clicker. "Entertaining smartass juvenile delinquents isn't on my schedule today."

"Hey," she said. "What's your deal?"

"Hey yourself," I said, turning the set off.

"You don't have to be rude," she said, taking a big bite out of the sandwich. "Jeez."

"I was just taking lessons from you, kid," I said.

"Yeah, well you're supposed to know better."

"I can do whatever I want," I said. "You just broke into my house and stole a ham sandwich. That's a felony."

"Like the cops don't have anything better to do but bust a kid for stealing ham," she said, then pointed the uneaten portion at Bobo. "Does he talk?"

"Very little," I said. "But I think you and me, we're gonna have to."

"You got that straight," she said. "You the big time private eye?"

This surprised me. "I'm an investigator, yeah. Why?"

"You're um," she pulled a worn business card out of her pocket and read from it, "Z-Z-Zen Mos-es?"

"Yes that's me," I said.

"What kind of name is that?" She put the sandwich down on the floor, wiped her mouth with her sleeve and stood up, unzipping her duffel. Then she turned it upside down and emptied its contents onto my hardwood.

"My name is Emily," she said with the slightest tinge of melancholy. "Sherrie Sanger is my Mom. I know the scumbag who killed her and I want to hire you to burn his ass."

Bobo and I both stared down at the floor at Emily's feet where she had dumped a sizable pile of money, all in nice, neat, crisp one hundred dollar bills.

"If you know who did it," I said quietly, unable to take my eyes off the cash. There had to be a least a hundred grand, maybe more. "It's better to go to the cops."

"Not for what I want." she had her arms folded across her chest, tough-guy style, but her bottom lip was sticking out, a child's pout. I doubted she even knew she was making the face. It was probably the last dying remnant of a childhood she seemed to have abandoned ten years too soon.

"And what is that?" It was Bobo and his tone surprised me more than hers had. He spoke so softly, it was almost a whisper. As big and scary as he was, this little kid with a adult-sized attitude problem had gotten to him. I knew Bobo had a big heart, bigger than most, but I didn't get to see it laid bare like this too often.

"The guy who killed my Mom," she said defiantly. "He's my Dad. I'm not hiring you to bring him in. I want you to kill him. I want the bastard dead."

She picked up the duffel, unzipped another pocket and pulled out a .9-mm hand gun, held up the magazine to show it wasn't loaded, then dropped both to the floor with a thud.

A single tear rolled down her freckled cheek, but she swatted it away before it even got halfway down her face. She stood before us, trembling, on the outside tough as nails but on the inside a mangled mess of emotions and feelings she wouldn't come to understand if she spent the rest of her life in therapy.

We were watching a kid wrestling with the lousy hand she'd been dealt, coping the best way she knew how and daring us to say she didn't deserve to be so angry, so full of hate.

But I knew in my heart we were watching something else, something you never want to see in someone so young, who should be home with her friends, giggling about Leonardo DiCaprio and watching *The Lion King* on cable. She was somewhere else far away from all that, breaking into peoples' homes with stacks of money and handguns in her duffel bag.

We were looking into the eyes of a childhood lost, of a kid on the edge literally, of the end of innocence.

thirty-eight

It was a long while before any of us spoke again. There was Emily, holding her own on one side of the room and me and Bobo trying to swallow the scene whole without choking on it.

"Well," Emily said finally, glaring at us homey style. "You gonna do it or do I have to?"

"Nobody's doing anymore killing here. There are ways . . ."

"Ways of dealing with it? Oh, yeah. Right. Like what happened to my Mom. The cops really helped her out, huh? Please stop me from running to the phone right now and calling 911."

"You got some mouth on you sister," said Bobo, again his tone soothing, safe, not at all threatening. "Maybe you should show us a little props here. We're on your side."

She bounced down on the chair again, pouting. "If you're on my side, why won't you kill him?"

"Cause it's not our job," I said.

"Don't tell me you never kill'd nobody. I sure bet he did."

"That's not the point," I said, exasperated. "That's self-defense. It's different."

"Yeah, whatever." She got out of the chair and knelt on the floor, starting to collect the cash, shoving it back into the duffel. It started as a pretty simple exercise, but it didn't take long before she was crying. She tried to ignore the tears, but she was having trouble seeing through them and it made her task harder. Some of the cash was going in the duffel, some falling back onto the floor.

"I'm gonna do it," she said, crying. "I'm gonna shoot the shithead. You just watch."

I crossed the room to Emily and gently tried to pull the duffel out of her hand, kicking the gun toward Bobo.

"Stop it," she said. "That's mine."

We had a brief tug of war until she finally gave up and let go, falling to a sitting position on the floor and dropping her head to cry. The ten-year-old had finally showed herself.

I cautiously approached her, put my hand on her shoulder and she swiped it off, but it was half-hearted. I gathered her into my arms and as I rocked her gently, the only thing I could hear was Emily's sobbing and the silent sound of my heart, breaking in half.

I don't know how long we sat on my floor like that, but it was long enough for the afternoon shadows to fade into evening. And as night took the last of the light, Emily fell asleep in my arms.

Bobo got a pillow and blanket from my hall linen closet and we let her lie there on my floor, hoping if the sleep wasn't peaceful, it would be dreamless.

We went into my kitchen to talk. Bobo poured himself a cup of stale coffee and I went to the fridge for an Anchor Steam.

"What are we going to do with the kid?" he said.

"Wash her mouth out with soap?"

"There's that." Bobo was holding up one of the bills from Emily's stash to the light, checking it out.

"Counterfeit?" I asked.

"Nah," he said. "Looks real enough to me."

"So what's a ten-year-old kid doing with this much cash?"

"You're the detective," he said. "You tell me."

"Why don't we ask her?" I said, peering into the living room. She was still in dreamland. "When she wakes up."

Bobo nodded. Then he asked me how my meeting with Marcy went.

"Sounds like a real nice lady," he said. "I don't know why a couple so made for each other would split up. They don't know how good they had it. Still no sign of the dog?"

"Fuck the dog. We gotta find out who's framing Jim."

"That and who tried to kill you the other night. Your porch was rigged. Nice, clean job. Somebody who knew what they were doing."

"So good the wrong person got killed," I said. In all the hubbub I'd forgotten about the attempt on my life. It seemed months ago. I took a long sip of the beer. It felt cool and clean going down the back of my throat.

"Does it fit anybody's MO?"

"Nobody I know of," he said. "Creative though."

"Yeah, but it didn't take the cops long to figure out it was rigged," I said. "If they were really creative, they would have done a better job to hide it."

thirty-nine

Emily woke a few hours later. Bobo was in my kitchen read-ing the paper. I was standing on my broken back porch, look-ing out across Santa Monica toward the mountains.

The wind was howling fierce, blowing a cold wind across the city. It matched my heart.

It had been nearly a week since my bike ride to one of its peaks but it felt like I hadn't been up there in years, like the last trip had been in another lifetime, when I was a different person.

I was thinking of Vince Lennon's eyes.

I told Bobo about Lennon's implosion. I was glad to have Lennon off my back, but I couldn't get the wild look in his eyes out of my head. It made me wonder how deep his hatred of me went and how long it would take before he let it go, if ever.

I had a feeling I had not seen the last of him.

I went back inside and tried Jim's father's house again. No answer. Part of me was glad. I didn't want to be the one to break the news.

But the other part knew this was one thing I was going to have to do in person. I said this to Bobo.

"Maybe we'll find out what he was running from," I said, looking in on Emily who was watching TV.

"What are we gonna do about Emily? We can't take her with us."

"I'll call my sister," he said. "She can stay there until things quiet down."

"Fine," I said. "I'd better check the flights."

"I need to get some things," he said, looking at his watch. "Be back to get you in an hour."

I grabbed a bottle of Anchor Steam and took a couple of long sips, trying to calm my anxiety. It didn't work. It never does. Emily shuffled in, rubbing sleep from her eyes with her fists. She came in quietly, pulling herself up onto one of my kitchen stools.

"You okay?"

"I guess," she said. "You mad at me?"

"Nah," I said. "But I do have some questions. First, you want something to eat? Drink?"

"I'll have what your having," she said.

"No you won't," I said. "It's Coke, water or nothing."

"Coke, I guess," she shifted in her seat, dropping her head.

I got a can of soda out of the refrigerator, opened it and put it in front of her. Then I sat down on the other side of counter, waiting her out.

"Sorry I busted in," she said.

"You coulda knocked," I said. "Forget about it. I'm more concerned about where you got the money and the gun."

"That stuff's mine," she said. "Sort of."

"What's that mean? Don't tell me you stole that money."

"Well, it's kinda a long story," she said, taking a long sip of the Coke. Some of it spilled down her chin, but she didn't clear it off.

I watched the tiny coffee-colored droplet sit on her chin, fighting the urge to wipe it off myself. "Why did you come here? To see me? Last I heard, you were a ward of the state."

"Fuck those foster homes," she said and I cast a sharp glance at her. "What?"

"You're too young to be talking like that," I said. "Why don't you give it a rest at least while you're around me, okay?"

"Whatever you say, Mother Theresa," she smirked.

"So you ran away from foster home?"

"Yeah," she said. "But they won't miss me 'til tomorrow. They put us to sleep and went out to the movies."

"They left you alone?"

"For a private detective, you're pretty dumb," she said, echoing the words her mother had said to me what seemed like weeks ago. Maybe they were both right. "You think them dorks are there to take care of us? Gimme a break."

"Okay," I said. "Let's move on. The money, the gun?"

"I got 'em from my Mom."

"She gave them to you?"

"No. Dog, you are a dumb shit," she said.

"Enough," I said, both my impatience and my irritation rising. "I don't know what kind of relationship you had with your mother or the folks at the foster home, but it's time you showed me a little respect.

"If you think that smart-ass street punk jive of yours is gonna win me over, you got another thing coming. I'm not beyond spanking your ass."

"You can't scare me," she said. "I seen a lot worse."

"You know I'm trying my best to feel for you," I said. "And I want to help you. But you're making it real difficult. You've just had the shock of your life and from what I gather, that's saying something. I'm not expecting you to cry all day, but giving me this attitude isn't fooling anyone. You're just a kid, Emily. A ten-year-old kid. Do yourself a favor and act like one. Believe me when you get to my age, you'll be glad you did."

"Whatever," she said, but I could tell she was giving in. Her edge was wearing off. "It's too late for me."

We both fell silent. What if she's right? I didn't want to believe it. I couldn't.

"Listen, Emily," I said. "I sort of made a promise to your Mom that I'd watch out for you. I'm gonna follow through on that promise but I can't do it without you. Maybe you don't like or trust me much but I need you to at least try, just for a little while, okay?"

Her nod was noncommittal, but it was a start.

"Can we try this again?"

She nodded again. "I guess."

"Good," I said. "Tell me again where you got the money."

"It belongs to my Dad," she said. "My Mom found it a few weeks after he left us. It was underneath a floorboard in the closet. She took it and hid it. She said she wanted me to know where it was in case, in case . . . something happened to her."

"Are you sure it was Gary's money?"

"Yeah," she said. "It was hidden in this duffel bag. It was his favorite."

"Where'd he get the money?"

"He's ripping off credit cards," she said.

"How do you know?"

She looked at me like I was an idiot. "He's been doin' it for a while," she said. "He used to get 'em from those dummies at the gas station. But now he's working for somebody else."

"What makes you think that?"

"My Mom had a fight with him about it," she said. "'Bout a week ago. It was loud and he was yelling at her. I heard him say they'd kill us if he didn't give them their money."

"That doesn't mean your Dad did it," I said.

"He hates us," she said.

"Listen, Emily," I said. "I need you to hear me out, okay? Your Mom was killed by accident. Whoever killed her was trying to kill me. Now that doesn't mean that your father didn't have anything to do with it. But I got a feeling he wouldn't do that to you."

I thought of Gary and his credit card scheme, his ratty clothes and attitude to burn. I couldn't see him having the brains to pull it off.

"Why are you sticking up for him?"

"I'm not," I said. "Why don't you let me look into this for you, okay? Meanwhile, you gotta do me a favor and stay out of trouble. Don't be trying anything on your own."

I checked my watch again, then got up and tried Jim's Dad's number again. Still, no answer. Just as I put the phone down, it rang and I snatched it back off the cradle.

It was Bobo. "My sister's on her way. She's coming in from the back so nobody sees. I'll be parked out front. Is the kid ready?"

"She will be," I said.

"Ten minutes," he said and rang off.

"What's going on?" she said.

"I gotta take a trip," I said.

"I get to go?"

"No," I said. "It's too dangerous. So is staying here."

"I ain't going back to those foster fucks," she said. "I mean those . . . sorry."

"Forget it," I said. "Gimme the number. I'll call them and tell them you're staying with family tonight. I want you somewhere where we can keep an eye on you. You're going to go stay with Bobo's sister Lorraine and her family for a couple of days. Don't worry. She's got two kids your age and they have Nintendo. Sit tight. I gotta get some things together."

I went into my bedroom and got out my black overnighter, filling it with a couple of days worth of clothes, my toiletries, the last of my antibiotics, my Walther and extra ammo.

"What's in the bag?" she said.

"Some stuff for our trip," I said.

"I don't wanna go," she said. "No friggin' way. Can't I stay here? I can take care of myself."

I didn't doubt she believed that. Not for a minute.

"It's that or the foster home," I said. "Your choice."

"It's not fair," she said. "You're just trying to get rid of me. You ain't coming back."

I started to say something but something about the look on her face stopped me. It told me what she couldn't; here was a kid who'd had more dashed dreams and broken hearts than people five times her age. I wanted to comfort her, but I didn't know how I could break through the hard shell of cynicism. Why would she even want to believe? She'd been fooled a hundred times before by people just like me.

"One second," I said and went into my office, opened the safe where I keep my Walther when I'm not using it and rooted around for my mother's cameo.

It was at the bottom, wrapped in an old-fashioned embroidered handkerchief, the only thing I had left of my mother. It was the cameo that her mother had given her on the day she got married. It was very unusual. The background was a light shade of peach. Around the edge was an intricate pattern of fine, gold inlay.

It hung on a delicate gold chain which sparkled in the right kind of light. I wrapped it back up and closed the safe.

When I went back into the kitchen, I grabbed a stool and sat next to Emily, handing the cloth bag to her. She opened it up and looked inside and for the first time since I'd met her, I saw the wonder of a child in her face.

"That is the only thing I have that belonged to my mother," I said. "I want you to hold it for me."

She pushed it back at me. "I can't," she said. "It's too nice. I'll lose it."

"No," I said, closing her small fingers around it. "You're right. Why should you trust me? Well, I wanted you to see that I can trust you. That cameo is very important to me. I know you'll watch it for me. Plus, at least you know I'll be sure to come back."

She smiled and held the cameo to her heart.

"I won't let you down," she said.

"Neither will I."

And I prayed in my heart for it to be true.

forty

I hate to fly. I hate it with a passion. Mostly, it's the waiting.
Waiting to check in, waiting to board, waiting to take off, waiting to land, waiting to get to the gate, waiting, waiting and more waiting. And of course, once the waiting is over, you actually have to fly.

And being 35,000 miles above the ground knowing that your safety is riding on a handful of fallible human beings is not my idea of travel.

So while Bobo meditated, I read the in-flight magazine, watched a movie about ants and tried not to wonder how the hell this fifty-ton machine was staying up in the air. The rest of the time, I tried not to think of the task that lay before me.

We landed in Minneapolis in the dark of night, an hour or so before dawn. Winter hadn't yet come to the Twin Cities, but it was hovering close by. The temperature was dipping south of forty degrees and the piercing wind that slapped at us as we trudged over to get a rental made the Santa Anas feel like a tropical breeze.

We didn't even bother checking into a hotel. We weren't planning on this taking any longer than half a day. Before we left Los Angeles, I cross-checked the phone number Myron had given me in Minneapolis and got an address in suburban St. Paul.

The Twin Cities occupy about 100 square miles of mostly flat lands dotted by more than two dozen lakes and split by the Mississippi and Minnesota rivers, which gouge a winding path between the two.

We rented a cookie-cutter sedan with a V-6 and it rumbled quietly along the empty freeway as we headed north past the center of St. Paul toward Como.

Twenty minutes later, as daybreak approached, we were driving on a narrow road that snaked through a tranquil suburban landscape rendered desolate by the seasonal ravages of autumn.

The road ran between a golf course which was dotted with a few early-morning duffers, and the park and greenlands that fronted Lake Como. They were connected by a series of paved paths used all four seasons by joggers, cyclists and pedestrians who don't curtail their outdoor rituals even in the middle of the coldest winters in the country.

Out Bobo's window stood a line of homes that ranged in size from two to four bedrooms, but even the most modest seemed to give off the stately air of affluence. It was merely an illusion. The neighborhood had always been home to the blue collar class, a place where construction workers and school teachers, bank tellers and young starter families lived out their lives with only a fence and a driveway between them.

The address we were looking for was off a wide, tree-lined street of similar single-family houses with big yards and stand-alone garages. I don't know if it was the leaf-blown trees, the gray morning sky, the wet, brown lawns or my reason for coming here, but the place was depressing me.

People like to say LA burns brightly twenty-four hours a day in a way even Las Vegas doesn't. I never fully understand what they mean until I'm away, standing in places like this where whole seasons of darkened, drab skies blanket the heavens until it's nearly impossible to separate day from night and hope from despair.

Bobo pulled up in front of a cream-colored stucco house with a brown shingled roof and brown awnings over the windows and doorway. A long, narrow driveway ran along one side of a large front yard, coming to a stop at a detached two-car garage.

There was one car parked in the drive, a beat-up Ford station wagon circa 1970, with faux wood panel sides and a garbage bag for a rear window. It was early, but in the distance, we heard a dog bark, doors slamming, engines idling, the squeal of children playing and the whine of a garbage truck: the sounds of a city waking.

There was no name on the mailbox, which was empty. It was bolted to a tree that rose up next to the front walk and in summer probably served nicely to shade the front yard from the hot sun.

The screen door squeaked when I opened it and I pushed the doorbell. I could hear the chime echo back at us, making me imagine that inside the house was as empty and desolate as I felt.

We heard sounds inside and waited. Then the door opened and the smell of sickness and death slammed into the clean, morning air like a train wreck. It reminded me of hospitals and I had to fight off the queasy feeling in my stomach.

Standing in the doorway was a large brown woman in a green cotton nurse's uniform and a well-worn sweater that was heavy enough to easily handle the LA winter.

She had mid-length hair that was pinned up and a pair of round glasses rested on her forehead. Her frown was neither friendly nor antagonistic. Though she took a good, long second to look us over.

Bobo was in his usual attire, black jeans, T-shirt and jacket though he was wearing a sweater underneath it. I was in boots, jeans and a heavy fleece pullover that wasn't doing as much as I thought it would to ward off the biting wind.

"May I help you?" she said. "You're obviously not from around here."

"We're looking for Mr. Gray," I said. "It's urgent we speak to him."

"I'm afraid he's not well," she said, then: "Wait a darn minute. You're that detective from LA, aren't you?"

I looked at Bobo. "Yes ma'am." I dug out my card and showed it to her.

She nodded but didn't take it. "I thought you were a man."

"A lot of people who don't know me think that," I said.

"Jim said you'd be coming," she said, cryptically. "Hold on one minute."

She disappeared inside the house, leaving us standing outside in the cold.

"You think they already know?" I asked Bobo.

He didn't answer. The woman returned and let us into the house.

"Mr. Gray will see you now," she said. Inside the house was toasty warm, but the smell of illness and mildew grew stronger. I had to use the wall to steady myself.

She led us through the neat, modestly furnished house. It was filled with Native American items, paintings, photos and other mementos. Pictures of Jim and his family were all over the place. I knew a little about his upbringing, that his mother was Italian and his father part Dakota. They divorced when Jim was a kid. It only made the loss I was feeling seem deeper.

A narrow, carpeted hallway ran toward the back of the house and ended at a candlelit bedroom.

An enormous oak four-poster bed stood in the middle of the

room, around it a half-dozen fragrant candles that were close to burning out.

Bowls of incense were burning, barely masking the awful hospital smells and lofting a billow of smoke toward the ceiling. I had to swat away the smoke so I could see into the room.

It was only then that I could see, almost lost in the eerie effects of the room, a man lying in the bed. He was old and frail and his hands were resting on his chest, crossed, as if he was posing for the death that was surely close at hand.

But when he spoke, his voice carried through the room with surprising strength. I don't know why, but it scared me.

"Come. Sit," he said and the nurse nudged me toward the old man. There was a step stool next to the bed and I sat down on it.

"You're a friend of my son's," he said.

"I am," I said.

"Let me have your hand."

I gave it to him and he grasped it and like his voice, his grip was strong and sure and solid. Mr. Death must have quite a fight on his hands.

"You are a strong person, patient but perhaps not always so wise," he said, running his fingers along my hands, as if he were trying to commit every ridge and vein and bump and crooked finger to memory. "You're very stubborn."

I smiled but didn't say anything.

Behind us, the nurse spoke.

"His father and grandfather were both what you might call seers," she said, as if to explain a crazy, dying old man's idiosyncrasies. "Sometimes he just amazes me but I don't know."

For some reason, I didn't share her doubt. I had a feeling this man knew of things on heaven and Earth that I could never fully understand, would go nuts trying to.

I thought of Jim, born to an Indian father and Italian mother and how much of their particular blood ran through his veins. I didn't have to wonder which was dominant.

"I knew you would come," he said.

"You know who I am?"

"The private detective named for a philosopher and a philosophy," he said. "Zen Moses."

"It was unintended," I said.

"You may think that," he said. "That is why we call our God *Wakan Tanka*, the Great Mystery."

He took a fitful breath, seemed to fall into himself for a moment and I was afraid he was fading on me. The shades were drawn and the light from the candles flickered wildly, seeming to broadcast images onto the walls and furniture.

"I feel you have a great burden," he said. "You have suffered great loss."

I felt the tears start, but I knew in the dark he wouldn't be able to see them.

"It is you who have suffered a great loss," I said. It came out so softly, I was afraid he might not have heard. But he merely nodded.

"I felt him go," he said. "I felt my son die. You were with him?"

The nurse gasped and held her hand to her mouth.

"It's true," she said, starting to sob quietly.

"I was nearby," I said, thinking of the glass wall that had stood between us. Single tears were running down my cheeks. "I'm so sorry."

"Then I am pleased," he said. "One should not die alone. Did he say anything to you before he died?"

"Yes, he did. His last words were 'Eddie, brother, he knew, I, my, fault.'"

The old man managed a smile.

"I know why you have come and I am grateful." He let go of my hand and stretched a bony arm for a framed picture on his bedside table, but he couldn't quite reach it. I handed it to him, but he waved me away.

"Take it," he said. "It will help you understand."

I turned it toward me. It was a framed certificate, a copy of Jim's California law license. Tucked in the corner was an old black and white snapshot of two teen-agers, leaning against an old Chevy pickup truck, the kind with big rounded fenders and a wide grille that looks like a grin. The boys were grinning too, holding up bottles of beer. It was the same photo Jim had carried in his wallet.

It's the saddest kind of picture: both are young and strong with the sturdy build and the bright faces that come from living under the wide, open sky. Built into those faces is the indomitable spirit of youth.

But you realize somehow that this is only a momentary illusion caught on film. It's all but certain this is the last time they will ever have that look, and it breaks your heart.

Scrawled on the back it said "Jim and Billy, Morton Falls IR, August 29, 1971."

"What's IR?"

"It's an Indian Reservation, couple hundred miles south as the crow flies," said the nurse behind us. "Jim and his brother spent summers there."

I looked back to the old man. His eyes were closed, but I could hear his breathing, faint, irregular, but steady.

"What's this mean?" I held up the certificate.

"Mary," he said and the nurse came forward to his bedside. "Please leave me alone with the philosopher."

It was a moment before I realized he meant me. Mary led Bobo outside and I waited until the old man spoke again.

"I will tell you a story," he said. "It is a sad story but it is also filled with great sacrifice. There are no heroes or villains, only hard choices and broken dreams.

"I will tell you this story, but you must promise me one thing."

I nodded, not sure what he was asking or if I could ever make good on it. It made me think about how this whole thing had started, with a favor. A promise to Jim. It seemed like a long time ago and in a way it was. I was thinking how Jim had changed in my eyes since then and wondering if I had changed in his. I would never know.

What was left in the void was merely our friendship, our belief in each other even when we couldn't show our best side, when circumstances meant we had to operate in the dark. But wasn't that the ultimate kind of friendship? The kind where you just show up because you are called and for no other reason? The rest is supposed to work itself out.

"Jim lost his way," he said, bringing me back to the smoky room. "You can help him. But you must remember we are all, in our own way, long travelers. You must accept this no matter what, even though it may go against all your instincts. Do you understand?"

I nodded again, but the truth was I had no idea what he was talking about. I could only hope that when the time came, I would understand. The old man squeezed my hand and then without pretense, he began to tell a story. A story that would help me learn more about Jim and why he had set off on his journey.

Much later, I would realize how it would guide my own as well.

forty-one

It was a two and a half hour drive to the Morgan Falls reservation, and for most of the trip Bobo and I shared a serene silence. The old man's words were ricocheting around my head and I was trying to rein it all in.

It was almost too much and I was thankful Bobo was the kind of person who wouldn't ask about it. He would wait until I was ready. It's one of the reasons I love him.

Instead I spent most of the drive staring out the window at miles of flatlands and corn fields that flew by with amazing consistency. Every so often, a farm town that was little more than three stop lights, a gas station and a strip mall, would break up the monotony. Moments later, it would disappear behind us, replaced again by open fields.

It was late afternoon by the time we passed through the tiny town of Morgan and Bobo pulled over into a gas station. I got out and used the payphone to try the number Mary had given me. It rang almost a dozen times before someone picked up. My heart skipped a beat when I heard a voice that sounded eerily like Jim's on the other end.

"Billy? Billy Gray?"

"Who is this?" he said.

"My name is Zen Moses. I'm a friend of Jim's. Your father sent me."

"Oh God," he said and was quiet for a moment. "Jim's dead, isn't he?"

The whole family had ESP. "I'm sorry to bring this awful news," I said. "But I need to talk to you."

"I don't understand," he said.

"Jim stands accused of a horrible crime," I said. "I owe it to him to clear his name."

"What's it have to do with me?"

"I'm not sure," I said. "Can we talk? I'm not far from the reservation."

I heard a sound on the other end and for a moment, I thought he'd hung up. It sounded like a sigh.

The phone booth was old fashioned. It had a door, but all the glass was missing. The late day's winds were kicking up the dust around the gas station and I had to cover my mouth to keep from swallowing dirt.

Bobo was gassing up the rental, finding something to talk about with the kid at the pumps. He was no more than sixteen and it was tough to tell if he was from the reservation or one of the surrounding farm towns. He looked like a normal suburban kid. He had short blue-black hair, and was wearing baggy jeans, stylish boots and a Vikings jersey with number 84 on it and MOSS on the back.

"Where are you?" he asked and I told him. "I'll come to you. Wait there."

I called Bobo's sister and she said Emily wanted to speak with me. She gave me some of her attitude but it was softening some. I had no doubt Lorraine wasn't going to tolerate any back talk.

"What's with Lorraine, uh. Mrs. Frazer?"

"You mean her little uh, hobby?" I had to smile. Lorraine was gentle, loving and, unlike her brother, one of the most gregarious people I know. But she has the La Douceur genes and she can intimidate when she wants to. Nothing intimidates more than her mysterious voodoo, which could frighten a rampaging black bear.

"Uh-huh," she said. "It scares me."

"Good to know something does," I said. "Heck, it scares me, too. That's why her kids do their homework and eat their vegetables."

"She's nice, though. I like her," she said. "So any progress on my case?"

"Hey, I just left," I said. "Give me a day or two."

"Oh," she sounded dejected.

"Chin up, girl. Maybe I'll have something to tell you tomorrow."

"You mean it?" She sounded so hopeful, it was heartbreaking. I didn't spend a lot of time around kids, especially damaged ones like Emily. I wasn't used to every word, every sentence carrying so much meaning. But it was a small world they lived in, even Emily's which was larger than most. I'd have to remember that.

She was used to being disappointed but it didn't make it any easier to take. I didn't want to be just another person who let her down.

"Yeah," I said. "I promise."

"Am I gonna have to go back to that crappy foster home?"

"Don't know," I said. I had called the home before we'd left for Minneapolis, fed them a story about having to put Emily in protective custody. After all, her mother was murdered. I knew I was walking a fine line and while I didn't say I was a cop, I didn't not say it either.

But they weren't too anxious to take Emily back and it made me angry. They seemed more upset that the window on the back door had been broken. And when they found out Emily was missing and her room had been overturned, they assumed she'd lost her temper. It wasn't like she didn't have one.

If she was going to have to go back to a foster home, I was going to make sure it wouldn't be this one.

"You're probably going to have to pay for that busted window," I said.

"What window?"

"Didn't you break the backdoor window?" I said.

"No way," she said. "I walked out the front door."

"You didn't mess up your room either?"

"I can't believe you listen to those dork heads," she said. "I thought you trusted me."

"I do," I said, though that old feeling of dread was creeping up my spine again. "You're right about those people. They are dorks."

"I'd like to stay here," she said, very quietly and it almost made me cry.

"Just don't go running off anywhere," I said. "Okay?"

"I can take care of myself," she said. "This neighborhood is a piece of cake."

"Whatever you say, tough girl," I said. "Put Lorraine back on."

She didn't say good-bye. All I heard was a thud, the sound of Emily putting the phone down. A moment later, Lorraine picked up.

"Keep a close leash on her," I said. "I got a bad feeling in my gut."

"You and your bad feelings," she said. "Come over sometime and I can cure you of that. I have the perfect mixture . . ."

I didn't let her finish. "Forget about your mixtures," I said. "Just keep an eye out. That kid's a handful."

"She's okay. A little fire in the belly, but that's a good thing," she said. "We're not letting her get too far. Not to worry."

"Wish it were that easy," I said, hanging up and breathing in a fistful of sand and cold wind. I shivered, knowing the brutal wind wasn't the only thing that was making me feel uneasy.

forty-two

Bobo moved the car off to the side of the station and we waited. Ten minutes later, a shiny midnight blue Ford pickup pulled up, sliding next to the rental. Billy got out of the truck, took a good look at Bobo and walked up to me.

"Billy?"

"Yeah," he said, tipping his cowboy hat. He was a bigger, younger version of Jim, with long, black hair and the skin of a man who spent the bulk of his life under a big, open sky.

"Let's walk," he said.

Bobo looked at his watch. The last flight out was at 11:30 and we both wanted to be on it.

"Don't be long," he said.

"This won't take much time," he said and I followed him behind the station where the broken pavement gave way to dirt and gravel. We had to pick our way through the overgrown weeds to avoid stepping on broken glass and twisted car parts. We came to a clearing where the weeds had been tamped down by foot traffic, and strewn around a rusted oil drum lay crushed beer cans, cigarette butts and used condoms.

The lot next door was in even worse shape, covered in vegetation and old tires and mangled shopping carts. I guess the big economic recovery had yet to find its way down here.

Billy was wearing jeans, cowboy boots and a parka with a furry collar. Underneath it, he had on a blue work shirt.

"Tell me about my brother," he said.

I told him everything I could in such a short span of time and he listened patiently, his head bent forward as if he was trying to position his ears so he'd get the right frequency.

"He didn't kill Eddie Cooke," I said. Billy was looking straight at me as if he was trying to see what I was thinking.

"Why are you telling me this?" He took off the hat and wiped sweat off his brow. I was amazed he could sweat in this weather. It felt like it was getting colder by the minute, as if the temperature was tied to the very passage of time.

"Your father told me how Jim lied to keep you out of jail," I said. "Eddie must have found out about it and Jim was watching your back."

He turned away. I'd hit a nerve—I could see the veins tense up on the back of his neck. And then it came so fast and furious, I was amazed I hadn't thought about it sooner. I grabbed him by the shoulder, spun him toward me.

"You knew," I said.

The look in Billy's eyes was filled with remorse, sadness, guilt and it tugged at my heart. I knew how he felt.

"Eddie came to see you. Did he threaten you?" I tried to soften my words, but the blow had already been struck. And for Billy and his brother, it was a wound almost as old as they were. One they'd carried around forever, never to be healed.

He snatched his arm from my grasp and walked away toward the abandoned lot and kicked an old oil can into the overgrowth of weeds where it disappeared. Then he sat down on the oil drum.

"I don't know who Eddie Cooke is," he said. "Some woman called me. You don't know what it's like to hear someone else tell you your family secrets. I thought my life was over. There's no statute of limitations on murder.

"I changed. I got help. I've been doing good here. All that

would be ruined. I didn't know what to do. Then Jim called, out of the blue. He said not to worry, he'd take care of it."

He looked down at his boots.

"Part of me wanted it to come out," he said. "I'm tired of carrying it around like an extra limb."

He was rubbing his temples with his palms. "I didn't think it was going to get Jim killed."

"It's not your fault," I said. "Jim made his own choices. He felt as guilty as you did."

The wind kicked up another notch, I zipped up my pullover and tucked my chin inside the warmth of the collar. I thought about what Jim's father had told me and I felt both of his sons' pain. "What will you do?"

"I don't know," he said.

The invisible sun was beginning its final descent, turning the gray-white sky darker by the minute. Far off somewhere I heard the squeal of a car, but in my cold ears the wind was wailing and my heart was pounding.

I dug my hands into my jeans for warmth.

"I talked to Jim that day he got shot up," he said abruptly, and stood up. The laces from the hood of his parka flapped in the breeze, but unlike me didn't bother pulling his collar tighter.

"He said he'd caught a break, that it was almost over."

I thought about finding Noodles and wondered if that's the break Jim was talking about. It made me feel even more guilty.

"I better be gettin' back." He reached out his hand and I took it. Despite the elements, it was warm. We held onto each other listening to the wind and our own thoughts. "Thanks for coming. Maybe when all this dies down, you can come back and tell me more about my brother. We'd lost touch."

"What will you do?" I asked him again. "All this might still come out."

"I know," he said. "I'm gonna have to think about it. You know, I run a school for disadvantaged kids. It's a good program. We even have kids coming from outside the reservation. Going on twelve years now. The kids go to school, learn about horses and farming, their Indian and American heritages."

"Sounds wonderful," I said and it did.

"I guess my wife could run it . . ." He trailed off, shrugged.

"Why don't you hold off doing anything for now," I said. "Maybe we can keep this where it belongs. Dead and buried."

He looked up at me, his eyes wet, his face contorted in anguish and I thought again of the photo his father had given me, a glorious moment in time, frozen forever. It was a tease really; an awful and agonizing feeling to remember a thing so vivid, but in the end so fleeting.

When I looked at Jim's brother, I saw his need, his desire to recapture that memory, make it real, start all over again. How many of us carry this in our hearts, the regrets of life? The hunger to take back the bad things we did, heal the people we've hurt?

This was what Jim had been protecting. His brother had gotten that second chance and Jim wanted him to have it forever. It was his last gasp at some kind of true redemption. Few of us ever get that kind of chance. When Billy let go of my hand and turned away from me, I knew suddenly what the old man had meant.

He had lost his eldest son who, a long time ago, had saved his only remaining son. And now, he didn't want to lose him too.

Nothing could've moved me from my spot. I stood my ground, watching him walk away, wishing him Godspeed.

forty-three

We made our flight and as the bright lights of Minneapolis disappeared behind the cloud cover, I wasn't even thinking of my fear of flying.

It wasn't every day you get to stand in place and still move someone's world. I felt like I was Jim's private earthquake.

Eddie Cooke had gotten to Jim through his brother. That's what they had argued about that night in Jiggy's. Eddie had to have gone pretty deep to turn up this family's personal tragedy and I had a sneaky feeling who he had gone to for help.

Marcy Cooke ruled the world of gossip. It would be child's play for her to have dug up Jim's past, especially if she were given some place to start. Billy had said a woman had called him.

Marcy might even have been the driving force behind this whole thing. After all, right now she was the only one standing.

Jim and his brother spent half of their childhood on the Indian Reservation where their father lived and worked. But in the 60's and 70's times were tough. Reservation living was desolate and depressing. Houses were decrepit, running water was scarce and the scourge of many of their denizens was alcohol.

But for Jim and Billy, the summers at Morgan Falls were happy times. Jim was older and when he went off to college, Billy was left to fend for himself.

He began to drink heavily. Billy got arrested one night for

disorderly conduct and when he called Jim to bail him out, his brother told him to sleep it off.

The next night, Billy went back to the same bar and got into a fight with the local loudmouth, a bigot named Joe Conrad. No one is quite sure what happened that night, except Conrad ended up dead.

Billy woke up after a drunken blackout, lying face up in an empty parking lot. Joe Conrad lay next to him, his head caved in by a tire iron.

Billy called his brother and Jim knew immediately Billy was looking at hard time. It didn't matter that Conrad had threatened Billy in front of witnesses. What mattered then was that Joe was a white man and Billy was not. Jim suspected an underage, drunk Indian wasn't going to get the benefit of the doubt.

Besides, Jim felt responsible. He'd let his brother down, embarrassed him in front of his family and friends. And he knew Billy was volatile.

There was only one thing he could do. Back then, they had agreements with the local sheriffs that anything that happened on the reservation was handled by the Indian counsel. The confines of the res was out of bounds for the state and local cops. Jim knew he had to stage the "accident" on the reservation and force the locals out of it.

But Jim would be paying a price of his own. He was covering up a crime and destroying evidence. His hopes of a career in law would be lost if any of it got out. Even if it didn't, it would always haunt him.

I couldn't help but see the symmetry between Billy's story and what had happened to me the night I followed Jim into Susan Donnell's house.

Perhaps it was sharing that feeling of waking up not knowing if you were responsible for taking another man's life. Or perhaps it was simply knowing Jim, now his father, and seeing what Billy had accomplished since that terrible night. Whatever it was, I knew in my heart that I would do whatever it took to keep this family's secrets.

I would do it for Jim, for his brother, for myself. I would do it because whatever code I held dear at that very moment was telling me that this was the right thing to do. Sometimes, that's all there is to it.

They'd kept their secrets so far. Billy got help and quit drinking and he and his wife started the reservation school. Jim got his law degree, moved to California and never looked back.

Then someone came around and stirred the pot. Billy was right—there's no statute of limitations on murder, even if there was no telling what really happened that night. Jim would lose his license, perhaps worse. Both of them could go to jail and for what?

Eddie's intentions may have been evil, but for Jim, it was a watershed in his life. He told Billy he planned on moving back to Minnesota for a while, spending more time with his family.

It made him want to take a deeper look into his own soul. To examine what he had done as a lawyer, as a person and to stand up and take responsibility for his actions.

I couldn't help him do any of that now. But I could make Eddie and Marcy Cooke answer for theirs.

forty-four

I slept fitfully for most of the flight back to LA. I had so much on my mind, I was sure I wasn't going to be able to sleep, but I'd been up for nearly thirty-six hours straight, and the fatigue won over.

We landed in LA much the same way as we'd left it—in the middle of the night. Translucent clouds dotted the sky, casting a film over the stars that seemed to make them sparkle even more. But the screen was temporary and they were moving out quickly. When we walked across the roof of the parking garage where Bobo had parked his car, the wind was blowing in our faces.

I called Brooks from the car, surprised I caught him still at his desk.

"Up late?" I said.

"Working overtime," he said. "Building a case against Jim Gray, I'm afraid."

"You mad at me?"

"What do you want?"

We were out on Sepulveda Boulevard, heading for Lincoln Boulevard. Bobo was driving quietly. He was listening to some chanting music on his stereo.

The road was mostly empty, though I noticed a black Jeep Cherokee a few feet behind us. I wouldn't have thought twice about it, except for two things. It had roof mounted spotlights which were legal but used mostly on search and rescue vehicles and the front window was tinted, which is illegal for obvious reasons. It's also favored in some places by drug dealers and gang members, for reasons equally as obvious.

"He didn't do it," I said.

"You sound like a broken record."

"It's true," I said. "Tell me one thing: that witness of yours. It wouldn't by any chance be Marcy Cooke, would it?"

"I wouldn't tell you if it was," he said.

"You don't have to," I said, catching sight of that Cherokee again. I pointed it out to Bobo and he nodded. He probably had seen it yesterday.

"I know it's her," I said into the phone. "Maybe you should be checking her story a little closer."

"Maybe you should leave the police work to the police," he said.

"I think she was blackmailing Jim. It was her and Eddie, maybe both."

"More reason for Jim to kill Eddie," he said. "Listen, I might even be able to eke out self-defense, but this thing is off my desk tomorrow. We got plenty of cases where the suspect is still alive."

"I'm not gonna let you ruin Jim's reputation," I said.

"You ever think for a moment that he might be guilty?" he said. "He wrote a confession. Nobody twisted his arm."

"I'm not so sure about that," I said.

"You making an accusation?"

"No," I said. "Forget it."

"Anything else?" he asked.

"Actually, yeah," I said. "Got any leads on Sherrie's murder?"

"A few," he said. "Nothing substantial. It was a professional job. Even an electrician coulda missed it. She did have an interesting piece of paper in her pocket though."

"And what was that?"

"Suppose I can tell you," he said. "You'll find out anyway. It was a will of some sort and some kind of declaration naming you as the guardian for her kid."

"That kid was her life," I said.

"So maybe you'd be interested to know that the kid has disappeared," he said.

"What are you talking about?"

"She ran away from her foster home," he said. "Now, I went out and talked with these people and frankly, I'd a run away too. Which makes me wonder."

"About?"

"Maybe she had help. Like maybe from a pain in the ass PI I know."

I didn't say a word. There was nothing to say.

"Silent treatment? That's just great," he said. "I suppose if I go over to your place she won't be sitting there watching Nickelodeon."

"Go ahead and look for yourself," I said. "I don't have her."

"I want to believe you," he said. "But I don't."

"What happened to trust?"

"You gotta earn it," he said and hung up.

"You're not going to get laid that way," Bobo said after I rang off. He winked at me. It was almost as much as he'd said on the entire trip.

On the drive back to Minneapolis, I'd told him about Jim and his father and about my suspicions. He took it all in without saying much. That was Bobo. The strong, silent type.

I thumbed at the Cherokee, still on our tail. "Somebody you know?"

"Nope," he said, suddenly yanking the steering wheel down, setting the truck up on two wheels. The back window of Bobo's Range Rover exploded and I covered my head with my hands and ducked.

We were on Lincoln Boulevard, driving north toward Santa Monica. In the sideview mirror, the Cherokee was bearing down on us, driving erratically. Two beefy arms were hanging out the passenger window, wielding a shotgun.

Bobo gave his truck gas and swerved out of the right hand lane and around two cars stopped at a red light. He blew through the light as gunfire pinged off his truck. Behind us, the Cherokee did the same. The chase was on.

It was early Sunday morning and the streets were fairly quiet, but Lincoln is a major thoroughfare and traffic was all around us. Bobo veered off on the 90, a short stretch of freeway that connects to the 405, and hauled ass.

It was harder for the shooter to get in firing range at the speeds we were going and for the moment, the shooting stopped. But we weren't going to lose them out here so as abruptly as Bobo had caromed onto the freeway, he swung the big truck off, hitting the ramp at National Boulevard so hard the truck bounced to the entire range of its shocks and seemed to fly through the air. When we slammed to the pavement, the bumper scraped the curb and sparks flew behind us.

"Somebody wants you dead, girl," said Bobo, who seemed the calm center of the chaos.

"How do you know they don't want you dead?"

" 'Cause most of those jokers are smart enough to know that going after Bobo is like having a death wish."

"That's such a good reason," I said, grabbing for the door handle as Bobo made another series of quick turns.

We raced onward through the deserted streets of west Los Angeles. Bobo knew the city better and the Range Rover had the bigger engine. It was only a matter of time before we put enough space between us and them. We finally lost them down a side street, where he cut the lights and came to a stop.

"You know what a rear window costs for this thing?" he said. "I'd like to find those fuckers and make them pay for it."

"Why don't we?" I said.

"Why don't we what?"

"Find them."

Bobo actually smiled and I knew then why he used it so sparingly. It was a great smile, bright and beautiful and blinding. With a smile like that, nobody would take him seriously as a dangerous man.

He started slowly backtracking toward where we'd last seen the Cherokee. I pulled my Walther out of my overnight bag and checked the magazine. The hunter was about to become the hunted.

forty-five

It took us ten minutes of circling before we found the Cherokee. We had some unexpected help.

While we were searching for them, they were looking for us, using the roof-mounted spots to illuminate the road. It made them visible from San Diego.

I could make out two guys in the truck, the gun-toting passenger and the driver. The odds were in our favor.

Bobo still had his lights off as he slowly nudged the Range Rover up behind them, keeping a safe distance. He followed the Cherokee down a dark street, and when it stopped at an intersection, he let his truck roll backward a foot or two and then in one sudden fierce movement, kicked it into gear, ramming the Cherokee hard enough to throw the two guys up against the window.

We jumped out of Bobo's truck and snuck up to the front of the Cherokee; I took the passenger, Bobo the drivers' side. We didn't need to be so careful.

Both guys were stunned badly and I could see blood stains and a big crooked fissure on the windshield. The driver was unconscious.

I stuck my Walther in the thick of the passenger's neck. Like the driver, he was big, with dark, brown skin. They both wore black bandanas on their heads. I reached inside and ripped the shotgun out of his hands.

They barely knew what hit them.

"Didn't your Mama teach you to wear your seatbelt?" I had the glove compartment open; I was rooting around for the registration. "It's against the law you know."

The passenger lifted up his head and groggily turned toward me. He saw the gun and started shaking.

"Don't shoot," he said, his voice accented British.

"What the fuck are you shooting at us for?"

"Fuck you," he said.

The glove compartment was full of papers and junk and it was difficult trying to go through it with one hand while the other was holding a gun to somebody's head. So I yanked the contents out and pulled my full hand out of the car so I could see. To my surprise, there was a fat stack of bills.

"Bobo, here," I said, tossing the cash over the truck to the driver's side, where Bobo caught it. "That ought to cover the damage to your truck."

The passenger stared daggers back at me. He was out of it, but the driver got the worst of it. He was still in dreamland.

I poked the Walther in his ear and he winced, but he still stayed silent. I did it a little harder and he yelled.

"You don't know who you're messing with," he said.

"You don't know who you're messing with," I said back. "Bobo, you hear that accent? What d'you make of it?"

Bobo reached inside the truck for the driver, picking up his head by his hair and taking a closer look at his face.

"Definitely Africans," he said. "My guess: Nigerians."

I smacked the passenger in the ear again. It was now bleeding.

"You're going to tell me who you're working for or I'm gonna make sure my voice is the last thing that ear ever hears. Understand?"

"Fuck you," he mumbled.

We weren't getting anywhere. Plus, it was getting close to daybreak. So Bobo went back to the truck and got a roll of duct tape and we tied both guys up. Bobo grabbed the car keys and dropped them down the sewer.

"You can't leave us here," the passenger said.

"You can't shoot at people either," I said, throwing the shotgun into Bobo's back seat. "But if you want to lodge a complaint, tell the cops. They'll be along in a couple of hours."

Bobo pointed his Range Rover back to Santa Monica, but we weren't headed directly back to my place. The more I thought about it, the more I wanted to make one more trip back to Jiggy's.

We parked in the same lot that Brooks had used the night we'd gotten into the brawl. The welt on my face had all but disappeared, but a small bruise had lingered.

Even though it's illegal to serve alcohol after 2 a.m. in Los Angeles, it doesn't mean nobody does it. You just have to know where to find the right place. Jiggy's was one of those places. It was a badly kept secret that you could buy a drink there well into the wee hours of the morning.

It was a little bit past 4:30 when Bobo and I walked through the main door. There were about a half-dozen people drinking at the bar. Not one of them looked up when we walked in.

I waited until Georgie was in my face before shoving the Walther under his chin.

"Where's Lunde?" I said.

"Gone," he said.

"Good. I want to talk to that waitress, what's her name, Margo?"

"Sure," he said. "If Lunde ever finds out . . ."

"He won't," I said. "I'm not gonna tell him. Bobo here isn't gonna tell him and I know you're not. So let's just be quick about this, for all our sakes. Okay?"

"Yeah, okay," he said. I noticed he had a bandage on his left ear. "She's in the back."

Margo was sitting at the bar, drinking coffee and reading an old *Hollywood Reporter*.

"Hey, you're the woman who got kicked . . ." She saw Georgie's predicament and decided it was best not to finish her thought. "Don't hurt him."

"Nobody's gonna get hurt," I said. "I just wanted to ask you a couple of questions."

"Me? About what?"

"That night you saw Eddie arguing with that man," I said. "Was that Eddie's only guest that night?"

She shrugged. "I dunno. You can check the ledger though. They have to sign in."

"That's right," I said to no one in particular. "Where's the ledger?"

"In Harry's office," she said, then: "I guess you want me to go get it."

"My friend Bobo will go with you," I said.

She came back with a computer printout. I sat her and Georgie at one of the tables and Bobo kept an eye on them while I scanned for Eddie's name.

His guests were mostly people I expected: Jim, Marcy, a couple of local ballplayers, Marty Bergstein. But there was one I didn't know: David Bradley. The time and the date put him in Jiggy's just hours before Eddie's murder.

"You can keep that," Margo said. "It's a copy."

"Thanks," I said. "You know who David Bradley is?"

She shook her head. I was about to stick the list in my

pocket, when something about the names made me stop. I checked it again.

"Hey Bobo," I said. "Take a look at this list."

"What about it?"

"Anything strike you as unusual?"

He shook his head, but then he was the wrong person to ask.

"Gimme your phone," I said, and dialed Andrea's number. I waited until her machine picked up.

"Andrea, if you're there, pick up," I said. "It's important. Andrea . . ."

"Yeah," she said from deep in sleepdom. "The world better be ending."

"I need your help. Are you up?"

"I am now," she said, her voice thick with sleep.

"Good." I read her the list of names. "What do those names have in common?"

"Is this a friggin' crossword?" she said. "At 5 o'clock in the morning?"

"No," I said. "This is important. Life or death. Listen. Tell me what they have in common."

"Fuck. Read it again."

I read from the ledger again, slowly this time.

"I know," she said finally. "They've all been recent Marcy's Mucks."

"Marcy's Mucks?"

"Marcy Cooke has this feature on TV that she calls Marcy's Mucks where she dishes the latest gossip. I watch it every day."

"I knew I could count on you, Andrea," I said. "Go back to bed."

Now I had a connection to Marcy. And I had another possible suspect. Things were looking up. It was strange to see how many roads were leading back to Jiggy's.

It was the last place Eddie had been seen alive. Watkins was a member. Brooks and I had gotten thrown out and now Marcy seemed to be using the list as fodder for her gossip show.

We left the club as we had found it. Bobo had put a pretty good scare into Georgie. He wouldn't say anything to his boss. Nor would Margo. According to her, old Harry Lunde was a lech and a half.

It was still dark when we got back to my place and even Bobo yawned and stretched when we got inside and threw our stuff on the kitchen floor.

I sat on the couch and turned on the TV, but it was dominated mostly by religious programming and early news shows. I wasn't interested in any of it.

Bobo took off his jacket. His T-shirt was a quote from a two-woman band called the Indigo Girls and it seemed fitting: "You'll never fly as the crow flies, so get used to a country mile."

It's a great line about how most of the time we have to take the long way around, even if that's the most direct route. But I knew the song and its meaning was broader

It was called "Watershed," and it was about that moment where you stand at the crossroads. The instant most of us spend our whole lives waiting for, both hoping and dreading. We often miss it because what we expect is some earth shattering event when in reality we might experience many over our lifetime. They're just smaller then we think.

I felt in some ways like I was standing on one of my own watersheds, looking down that country road and watching the crows flying by overhead. I wanted to be with them, but knew I never would.

Bobo sat down on the couch next to me and stretched. He had small bags under his mismatched eyes — and his blue one was starting to move independently of the other as was its tendency when he was tired.

He reached over and squeezed my thigh. Another one of his gestures that was small and yet carried so many layers of meaning, we couldn't explain it to anyone else.

I put my hand on his and we sat there in the room as the graceful light of a new day gradually engulfed the room. Then silently as morning came, we both drifted off to sleep, our hands still touching.

forty-six

In my dreams I was lying on a four-poster bed with a hole in my chest where my heart used to be. I could hear but I couldn't speak. People were coming to me for help and I knew what to do, but couldn't tell them.

Finally, I raised myself up and stepped off the bed, but there was no floor and I screamed as I started to fall. The dream shook me awake and it was a moment before I realized where I was.

I was on the couch, underneath a blanket, lying with my head on Bobo's chest. As soon as I moved, he opened his eyes.

"Problem?" he said.

"Bad dream," I said, feeling the cotton in my mouth and a crick in my neck. I got up to stretch. I was sore from the awkward position of leaning against Bobo.

It was well past noon and I had to look at the calendar in the kitchen to remember that it was Sunday. What a difference a week makes.

I juiced up the coffee pot and grabbed the Sunday *New York Times* and tossed the local paper to Bobo. I went into the bathroom to take a bath. Everything else would have to wait for now.

I'd been soaking in the tub for nearly an hour when Bobo knocked on the door and opened it without waiting for me to answer.

"Don't I get any privacy?"

"Nothing I haven't seen before," he winked at me.

"What's up?" I said, gathering some of the bubbles so it covered more of me.

"Been reading about this guy, John Dennis Moore."

"The guy who copped to Greeley's murder?"

"Yeah," he said. "They got a story on it in the *Times*."

"He died of cancer, before they could stick a needle in him, right?"

"Here's something funny. He sent out letters to every one of his victims," said Bobo, holding up the *LA Times*. "There are one, two, three . . . there are seven families listed but only six letters were sent. Seven murders and he remembers all but one?"

"What are you saying?" I said, sitting up in the tub, vainly crossing my arms over my chest. "That he didn't kill Bud Greeley? Why cop to a murder you didn't commit?"

"Now there's a good question."

"Jesus, Bobo," I said. "If that's true then you're saying Eddie really did kill Greeley."

"That's one scenario."

The thought made my heart skip faster, but the more I considered it, the more my excitement faded.

"Even if Eddie wasn't dead, it still wouldn't matter," I said.

"Maybe so," he said. "But he might have a lot of trouble keeping clients."

"That's true," I said.

"Food for thought," he said. "Now get outta there before you turn into a prune."

I went into my office, which used to be the second bedroom, and turned on the computer. I can find almost anyone in three days, but I wanted to talk to David Bradley before anyone else got wind of him.

It's easy to locate someone fast on the Internet, though sometimes the less you know from the start, the more money it will cost you. I didn't know anything about Bradley; there were too many David and D. Bradleys in the phone book to start calling them all.

I sometimes do work for an Internet outfit out of Chicago that helps adopted children search out their parents and vice versa. It's run by an old friend, Patricia Robinson, that I got to know when we were both beat writers for a small paper outside San Francisco.

She was adopted and wanted to search out her real parents for health reasons. She found there were hardly any resources, so she quit journalism and started her own company.

I e-mailed her Bradley's name and asked her to call me as soon as she found him. This one was going to be tough even for her. If I was lucky, I'd get my answer in a matter of hours. If not, it could be days, and by then it might be too late.

I warmed up something Sam had brought during my week in bed. It looked and smelled like lasagna, but with Sam you just never know.

Then I called Lorraine to check on Emily. Lorraine has a smooth voice, like Bobo's, deep and musical like there's a chorus behind it.

"Didn't expect to hear from you," she said and something stirred in my gut, something foul.

"Why not?" I asked. "Where's Emily?"

"They came for her a couple of hours ago," she said.

"Who came?" I asked, feeling the panic swell inside me.

"The police," she said. "They said they had to put her in protective custody. I thought you knew."

"Oh no," I said and my heart sank. Then a crazy thought crept into my head. The kind of idea that comes out of nowhere, that has no logic and makes no sense and yet some deep, down instinct tells you that you are right.

"Are you sure they were cops?"

"One had ID but I don't remember his name. But he acted like a policeman," she said, her firm voice shaky. I could tell she felt my panic. "The other man did most of the talking. He was very polite. African, I think. I thought he was the social worker or something."

"Did I do something wrong?" she said to my silence.

"It's alright," I said, but it wasn't alright. Emily was gone and the guys who shot at us last night had her.

forty-seven

Whoever those guys were, it had something to do with Sherrie and Gary.

I dug out Gary's Lakers duffel. I poured the contents out onto my kitchen counter. There was nothing very remarkable about the money except that there was a lot of it. I didn't think it was stolen, not from a legitimate business anyway.

The numbers weren't in sequence and when I searched the Internet, I couldn't find any recently reported robberies involving so much cash.

The serial numbers on the gun had been burned off. I still might be able to trace it, but it would take time and I had a feeling that time wasn't what I had a lot of.

Bobo came in, showered and changed, wearing a new T-shirt, "Don't assume your freedoms are assured." I guess he just liked to let his clothes do his talking for him.

"Don't worry," he said.

"How did they find her?" I asked him, sitting down and grabbing the duffel to move it out of my way. But when I picked it up, I felt something solid on one end, like pieces of cardboard.

"Gimme your knife," I said.

I flicked open his utility knife and cut the side of the bag. It was a hidden pocket. Inside were about a dozen white plastic cards, with numbers across the front and a magnetic strip on the back.

"Merry Christmas," I said.

Bobo picked one up. "Fake credit cards?"

"I think they're masters, what they use to print other cards with," I said, grabbing the phone book and paging through it for a number. "More important, I think we have something to bargain with."

I thought about the broken window at the foster home. And Emily's ransacked room. It all fit; somebody wanted this bag back.

I dialed the Chevron on PCH and had to go through three very slow teenagers before I got Gary on the phone.

"Don't hang up," I said. "If you do, you won't get your Lakers' bag back."

"Who the fuck is this?"

"That's not important," I said. "What is important is that I have your bag and everything that's in it. And when I say everything, I mean everything."

I heard him say "Fuck" under his breath. I was sure he was having heart palpitations. I could practically feel the sweat rolling down his neck.

"I know that voice." "That voice." "You're that fucking maniac private detective."

That's twice in two days I'd been called a maniac. I was beginning to feel like one.

"You win the prize, Gary," I said.

"You don't know who you're dealing with," he said, getting his balance back. "These people are mean motherfuckers."

"I'm meaner," I said. "Especially when somebody kidnaps a little girl."

"What? They got Emily?" he said.

"You mean you don't know? You're one dumb shit."

"We gotta get their stuff back," he said. "They won't stop at Emily. We'll need toothpicks to pick up all the pieces."

"Who are 'they,' Gary?"

"I can't tell you."

"Listen to me very carefully," I said, using as much menace as I could muster. "It's either me or them. Cause if you don't help me and anything happens to Emily, I swear to God I will hunt you down and make you wish they found you first."

"Shit, shit, shit," he said. "Shit."

"I need a full sentence Gary. Tell me what we're gonna do."

"What do you want," he said, and the dejection in his voice was part relief, part understanding that his days as a free man were over.

"The five W's," I said. "Who, what, where, when and why."

"You're not gonna like it," he said.

"I don't have a choice," I said. "And neither do you."

Gary was breathing hard into the phone, almost obscuring the sounds of traffic on PCH and the more distant crash of the surf.

"The guy I'm working for," he said, "his name is T J. T J Oswama."

forty-eight

An hour later, we were sitting on a bench in the Ocean
Avenue Park on the bluffs high above PCH, waiting for Gary
Barnhill to show his sorry ass self.

It was late afternoon and the Santa Anas were in full throttle,
pushing around the weekend debris left by tourists and home-
less people and everyone else who didn't know how to use a
trash can.

The sky was bright and blue and wide and you could see
clearly for miles in every direction. I leaned back on the bench
and lifted my chin to the wind.

I knew why Gary had been scared. He'd be crazy not to be.
Everyone was afraid of Tjungie Oswama, a.k.a. T J a.k.a. Teflon Tjungie.

He is one of a handful of notorious gangsters running one
of the new organized crime syndicates that are born on foreign
shores yet thrive right here in Los Angeles.

Mobsters don't just come from Italy anymore. They come
from Russia, the Middle East, Asia and in this case, Nigeria.

The Nigerians are known for being proficient heroin smug-
glers. In recent years I'd read they'd been using a variety of
credit card fraud schemes to finance their operation of the so-
called Golden Crescent heroin trail.

The trail begins in Afghani opium fields, passes through
Turkish refineries and wholesale hubs in Italy until it reaches
users, mostly in needle parks in Western Europe. While the

Russians are considered the most brutal of the new international syndicates, the Nigerians had a reputation for leaving opponents in small pieces.

And Oswama, who had established a foothold in the LA crime world, didn't do anything to dispel this. He was a flamboyant criminal who thought of himself as a latter day Al Capone.

He was hands on, showing the kind of arrogance that was going to one day nail the son of the bitch. But so far, he had managed to skate by and the FBI had dubbed him Teflon Tjungie.

Like many things that spin wildly out of control, Gary started small. He and Sherrie would rip off credit cards and ATM cards, use them once or sell them on the street.

He got hooked up with Oswama's crew and eventually they started using Gary as a courier. He would deliver cards to a house in Santa Monica Canyon, where they would be reconfigured, then he would take a new bunch of cards and distribute them.

Only Sherrie found out and snatched his Lakers bag. And Oswama wanted it back. And now he had Emily. Now it was personal.

"We should call your boyfriend," said Bobo. "I don't want to go in without backup."

"That's my plan," I said. "But I want to make sure Emily is safe first. And I want them to pay for killing Sherrie."

"You sure they killed her?"

"Aren't you?"

"I don't know," he said. "If Oswama wanted someone dead, he wouldn't make it look like an accident."

I was thinking about that when Gary appeared. He was walking slowly, a slight roll to his gait, and it reminded me of some addicts I know. He had on a black, sleeveless Marilyn Manson shirt, dirty blue jeans and a red bandana tied around his wrist. He was smoking a Marlboro and had a heavy chain hooked to one of the loops on his jeans that jingled when he walked.

Gary sat down on the bench, eyeing Bobo as if any minute he was going to pull out his .44 and blow his head off.

"I hope you brought more than him," he said, sucking in half the cigarette in one breath. His way of hiding his fear.

"Don't you worry about that," I said. "Is everything set up?"

"Yeah," he said. "I called and said I got the bag back."

"And?"

"I'm supposed to meet them," he checked his watch, "in twenty."

"And?"

"Fuck. And, I'm bringing some friends along," he said. "To ensure my daughter's safety. They didn't like that part. I had to do some fast-talking."

"Lucky for us you're such a charmer," I said.

"Where's the bag?"

"Right here," I said, pulling the newly repaired bag out from under the bench and then yanking it out of his reach. "For now, I'm holding on to it."

"You ready?" Bobo said to Gary and the kid nodded.

"Let's do it," I said, getting up and looking out across the Pacific. The sky and ocean both seemed so vast and so endless. It was easy to believe they went on forever. But I knew it was an illusion. Everything comes to an end, eventually.

forty-nine

They wanted to make the exchange at the Santa Monica Pier. It seemed a natural choice. It was very public and you could see someone coming from any direction.

Nine out of ten times, I would have picked it too. But everything I knew about Oswama made the pier the absolute worst place. If something went wrong, his boys would go down shooting and take as many bystanders as they could. I didn't want a massacre on my hands.

So we convinced them to meet us at the mouth of the Sullivan Canyon Trail. It had everything the pier had except people. And Bobo drove up early to make sure we'd be alone. I don't know what he did, but when we got up there five minutes before the meet, the place was completely desolate.

Bobo parked the Range Rover at the opening to the trail, sideways so we could use it for cover. If we had to, we could split on foot. I knew every bump and crevice of these trails and Bobo knew them even better.

But I didn't want to take any chances. I called Brooks on the drive up and told him what was going on. I told him he had to stay back. A girl's life was at stake.

He wasn't happy about it. But he wasn't all that pissed either. Just the mention of Oswama's name got him excited.

Maybe this was the day Teflon Tjungie went down.

Right on schedule, two Mercedes M-3 SUV's came into view and stopped about fifteen feet from Bobo's truck. Four men got out of the first truck. They had deep complexions and two were dressed in army fatigues, one was wearing a Hugo Boss suit and the fourth was in a black Nike sweatsuit with a driver's cap turned backward on his head. The two guys in fatigues had Uzi's and Nike was brandishing a Glock .9-mm. The suit appeared to be unarmed.

He was the one who stepped forward and held his hands up. It was Oswama.

"It's our lucky day," I whispered to Bobo.

He just smiled at me. The kind of smile that isn't a happy one.

Gary started to move, but I stopped him.

"Sorry kid, but this is my gig, now."

He didn't seem to mind. I stood up and came out from around the Ranch Rover. I had the Lakers bag in one hand and I tossed it a couple of feet in front of me. Far enough so they could see it, but not so far that I couldn't get to it before they did.

"Where is Gary?" he said, his voice some kind of a mix of American, African and English accents.

"I'm the negotiator," I said. "I showed you mine. Now you show me yours."

"A woman?" he said. "I am amused."

He smiled as if he was smarter than me and everyone else on the planet. I guess it took that kind of arrogance to make it as a mob boss. That and nerve and a lot of firepower.

"Where's the girl?" I said, ignoring him.

"She's safe," he said, the smile pasted on his face. It was an easy smile, lots of white teeth in the center of ebony skin. It made him look like a small boy and I wondered how old he was.

"I want to see her, now," I said. "Please don't make the mistake of thinking that I am as weak as Gary. You would be wise not to underestimate me."

He stood his ground, but the smile faded a few watts. "Yes, well, as you will," he said and motioned with one hand toward the second truck. The passenger from last night stepped out of the truck, dragging Emily who was bound and gagged and trying to kick out of his grasp. His biceps were bulging with the effort to keep her still.

This seemed funny to Oswama.

"Having trouble with the child?" he said.

This made Emily fight even more and the man reached for his weapon and clocked her over the head. She stopped moving. I stepped forward.

As soon as I moved, Oswama's bodyguards pointed their weapons in my direction. I couldn't see but I knew Bobo was behind me, a .44 in each hand.

"Enough," Oswama said, and his boys lowered their weapons.

"If he strikes her again," I said, "all bets are off. Do you understand?"

"You make a brave noise when you are obviously outnumbered," he said.

"Think what you like," I said. "But remember that looks can be deceiving."

"You're bluffing."

"Can't we stop this chatter and make the exchange," I said.

"Very well," he said. "Washington, bring the girl. Gently."

The man who he called Washington half-dragged, half-carried Emily toward me. I vowed to myself that I would hurt him for what he'd done to her. As he approached, Bobo came out from behind the truck, pointing one of his guns directly at him.

Washington stopped.

"What is the meaning of this?" said Oswama.

"We just want to make sure he doesn't try anything stupid."

"You're dead no matter what," Washington said, but Oswama waved him to silence.

Washington brought Emily to within five feet of me and Oswama told him to stop. Bobo was aiming at his temple but his gaze was directed at me. He had a welt the size of a bread box on his forehead.

"Toss the bag to me," Oswama said. "Carefully." I picked up the Lakers bag and flung it at Oswama's feet. At the same time, I moved toward Washington. He saw it, but I was faster and he was weighed down by an semiconscious ten-year-old.

I was on him in a flash, using the hard part of my elbow on the soft cartilage of his nose. Bobo had both his guns trained on Oswama and his bodyguards; they could only watch.

Washington went for his nose and I grabbed Emily, dragging her away and calling for Gary who rushed out from behind the truck and cradled her in his arms. It was the first time I'd seen him act anything remotely like a human being.

I reached for Washington's gun, but he recovered and knocked it with force from my hand. We both watched it spin out of our reach. He was bleeding pretty badly from his nose, but his rage was driving him and he charged at me, yelling like a soldier going into battle.

He tackled me to the ground and started punching me. I managed to deflect most of the blows with my forearms, but one caught me in the temple and my head started to throb.

His anger was making him flail wildly and it left him open. I kneed him hard in the groin and he toppled off of me. Then I jumped on him and we rolled around in the dirt, trading shots, wrestling for the upper hand.

He was stronger than me, but his emotions were wearing him out and I was a better fighter. Bobo had taught me well. Finally, I separated myself from him, grabbed his gun and pointed it between his eyes.

We were both dirty, bruised and bloodied and breathing hard. He stopped, staring at the gun that was mere inches from his face.

"Don't," he said.

I didn't say anything. I just kept the gun pointed and cocked.

"You have disgraced him in front of his own people," said Oswama. "Kill him. You would be doing him a favor."

There was a flicker in his eyes, a part of him that believed I would shoot him, and I knew why. Because he saw it in my eyes; he saw that in my heart of hearts, I wanted to kill him.

"What kind of man beats on innocent children?" I said.

I pointed the gun at him and started to put pressure on the trigger, feeling the round fall into the chamber.

His eyes got wide and fear registered in their depths. I looked at Bobo but his face told me nothing. Then suddenly, almost imperceptibly, I swore he shook his head. It was so small a gesture, I wasn't sure it happened at all.

I looked back at Washington, my hand steady on the trigger. A trickle of sweat and blood running down the side of my head.

Then we heard sirens. They were loud and getting louder. Brooks.

"This is for Emily," I said to Washington and I twitched my hand. He brought his hands to his face and I laid off the trigger, flipped the gun like Buffalo Bill and cracked him on the side of the head with it.

I stood up and the world seemed to dull around me suddenly, like a slow-motion movie. I watched him fall to the dirt and behind the Nigerians police cars, red lights flashing, came as if out of nowhere.

In the middle of it all, I found Oswama and for a second, we locked eyes. He pointed at me as if I'd just fed him the ball for a score and turned on that high-voltage grin.

Then he dragged his finger across his throat.

fifty

Emily had a pretty bad headache, but for the most part, she was no worse for wear. Thanks to me and Bobo, Brooks had the notorious Oswama in custody and I was hoping this would keep Watkins off both our backs for a while.

Gary got arrested too, but there was a chance he might catch a break if he testified against the Nigerians. He might be the same loser he was before this whole thing started, but when the dust cleared, Bobo and I found him leaning against the Range Rover, cradling Emily in his arms and crying like a baby. Human beings could be found in all sorts of strange places.

Brooks was smart enough to let the Captain in on the arrest so he could be at the scene to gush to reporters. Watkins even shook my hand, though he didn't go near me while the cameras were running. Progress was progress, even in tiny increments.

An hour later, me, Bobo, Watkins and Brooks and a handful of lab technicians and cops were the only people left at the scene. I was surprised the Captain was still around.

"We need to talk," he said to me, and I knew the honeymoon was over before it had even started.

The arrests closed the books on a lot of things, but there was still Eddie Cooke's murder, and so far the only suspect they had was my lawyer and my friend.

"What about?" I said.

"The lieutenant might fall for your crap," he said. "But I don't."

"You're building up a case against an innocent man," I said, "and I'm close to proving it."

"Give it up, Moses. Gray's our man. I know it and you know it."

"No I don't," I said, thinking how Watkins and I seemed to always find ourselves in mini-standoffs. Maybe we should arm wrestle or something. "I think I might be able to provide another suspect, maybe two."

"What is this? Dealer's choice?"

"I'm onto a lead," I said. "It might be nothing, it might prove I'm right. Hell, it might prove I'm wrong, too. Just give me a couple days to run it down."

"And if it doesn't pan out, you'll let this go?"

"Scout's honor," I said.

"You've got twenty-four hours," he said and glared at me like a drill sergeant until I had to drop my gaze. I gave him his small victory, but kept my fingers crossed.

fifty-one

It wasn't until early Monday morning that the call came in from Chicago. I awoke from a dead sleep, my head half on my pillow and half on my Walther. Bobo was convinced the Nigerians hadn't been responsible for Sherrie's death. We all agreed I'd been the target.

So he slept on the couch in the living room and I slept with my firearm.

"Zen, girl," said Patricia. "It's been too long."

"I know, I know," I said, trying to shake the sleep out of my head. "But these cases. I've been busy."

"Don't I know it. I've been watching you on CNN," she laughed.

"I'm trying to cut back on that," I said. "Tell me, what have you got?"

"I'm sorry it took so long," she said. "But you didn't give us much to go on."

"You found my guy?"

"Well, now that's a matter of debate," she said.

"What do you mean? Either you found him or you didn't." I was wide awake now. The morning sun was streaming into the window, but so were the winds.

"The only David Bradley we found fitting that description lives in West Covina with his mother and teaches mechanics at some trade school called CT Tech, in the City of Industry," she said.

"I always said you're the best."

"Wait, there's more," she said. "David Bradley was reported missing more than a week ago."

"What?" I said, my heart sinking. Not another one. "Who reported him missing?"

"His mother," she said.

"This is just great," I said.

"Actually, there's still more," she said.

"More? Like what?"

"It's why we had so much trouble finding the guy," she said. "David Bradley isn't his real name."

"What is it?"

"This is gonna blow your mind, Zen," she said. "His real name is David Bradley Moore."

"Moore? Moore. Why does that sound familiar?"

"His brother is John Dennis Moore; he died on death row for killing . . ."

I dropped the phone before she could finish. I didn't know if you could actually go 60 seconds without breathing, but I'm sure that's exactly what I did.

It was a moment until I heard her yelling for me from the phone on the floor. I picked it up.

"You okay, Zen?" she said.

"I'm fine. You're sure about this, right?"

"Absolutely," she said. "His mother is still living in Sylmar or something. Here's her address. You can go out and ask her yourself."

I hung up the phone, jumped out of bed and raced into the living room where Bobo was watching TV. He had one of my cigars to his lips and he was holding a lit match to one end.

When I saw him, I froze. It's funny sometimes what jogs your memory and how an event of even a week ago can fade into the recesses of your brain so far it's nearly impossible to retrieve. Until one thing, in its own context completely meaningless, jolts the revelation from your head like an earthquake.

And then, in a nanosecond, everything that had been so confusing, so bewildering, so hard to figure out comes into focus and suddenly you're seeing the world through new eyes. One tiny thing. Like a lit match.

fifty-two

It took most of the rest of the day to confirm my suspicions.
There was a lot to do in a short time but I was a new woman.
For the first time in more than a week, I felt like I was ahead
of the game.

By the time Marcy Cooke's day was over, I had most of the
story figured out. It was time to play it out and hope the rest
would fall into place.

The first thing I had to do was get to Marcy Cooke. Her
house was a fortress and getting in to see her at the TV station
was problematic as well. Time to get creative.

I parked my Alfa in an underground lot near Marcy's
office and walked the half dozen blocks through the late, arid
afternoon.

I got to the building, went into the lobby and caught the
elevator. But instead of going up, I went downstairs to the
garage. Predictably, the only people watching the lot were a
bunch of bored parking attendants.

Nobody saw me break into Marcy's fancy Jaguar XJS. Her
locks are electronic and I used a tiny gadget with a computer
chip in it that's programmed for just such a thing. I climbed
into the back and squeezed myself down into the ample space
between the genuine leather seats and the feathery soft carpet.

Everybody in LA gets their car windows tinted. Every few
years, they seem to get darker and darker. Marcy's windows
were tinted well beyond what was legal but it was to my ad-

vantage. There was no way in a dimly lit garage that you could see inside. I shifted around until I got comfortable and then I waited.

A half-hour later, the noise of the attendant opening the drivers' side door startled me out of a nap. But he didn't even notice I was there.

He pulled the car out and held the door as Marcy got in and she squealed her wheels as she hauled ass out of the garage. From my vantage point, I could see buildings and palm trees and streetlights whiz by as Marcy pushed the Jag over the speed limit.

I waited until I was sure she was out of heavy traffic and heading up one of the canyons before I sat up and leaned against the luxurious backseat. We were on Laurel Canyon stopped at a traffic light.

"Hello Marcy," I said and she let out a scream and clutched her chest. But she recovered so fast, it was frightening.

"Get the hell out of my car or I'll call the police." She grabbed at her cell phone, but I reached over and snatched it out of her hand.

"I don't think you want to do that," I said. "Not until you hear me out."

"You've broken into my car," she screamed at me and then someone blew a horn. The light had turned green.

"Green means go," I said, but she didn't budge. Well, if she wanted to play that game. I pulled out my Walther and showed it to her.

"I'm a desperate woman, Marcy," I said. "Drive."

And finally she did.

After a few minutes of climbing up through the canyons, I told her to pull off on a side street and stop the car.

"What do you want from me?" she said after she parked the

Jag along a crowded row of stacked houses that rose up toward the view at the top of the mountain. "Are you kidnapping me?"

"No," I said.

"Well, I'm going home and you can't stop me," she said.

"I spoke with your insurance company today," I said. I was watching her face in the rearview mirror and I could see her expression change. "They're cutting you a pretty big check at the end of the week."

"That's an invasion of my privacy and it's none of your business."

"And what you did to Jim Gray isn't invading anyone's privacy," I said.

"You should talk," she said. "You were a journalist. What glee you must have felt in bringing Eddie down."

"I didn't get any joy from it," I said, "and what I did and what you do have nothing in common. I was trying to uncover corruption and greed. You use information to destroy people. I know you were blackmailing Jim."

"You can't prove that," she said.

"Maybe not," I said. "But I'm gonna try."

"You're so predictable," she said. "A regular Don Quixote. It's so pathetic."

"It's fortuitous that Eddie died before you got divorced," I said. "That way you get to keep all his money and there's that nice, fat insurance check too. Twenty mil. Who would've thought Eddie's miserable life was worth that much?"

She laughed at this, but hers was a baneful, biting, horrible laugh. I felt again the evil in this woman. "God works in mysterious ways," she said.

"What do you want?" she practically screamed this at me. "I know you're not going to shoot me. You're not that kind of person. You're too weak."

"You know, someone said that to me just the other day," I said. "Very similar situation. They called my bluff too. One of these days, I'm gonna have to pull the trigger."

She had turned her head around so she could face me and it somehow contorted her perfectly-tuned looks.

"Tell me what you want," she said through her teeth.

"I want you to take me to see someone," I said.

"Who?" she said.

I sat back in the seat again. The sweet smell of leather in my nostrils reminded me somehow of baseball. Outside the Santa Anas were stirring and evening was drawing itself over the late afternoon. When I spoke, I measured my words, slowly, evenly. I wanted her to hear every one of them very clearly. And truth be told, I wanted to savor the moment.

"I want you to take me to see Eddie," I said.

fifty-three

The first clue Eddie wasn't the dead guy in the Donnell house actually occurred to me without my realizing it. I had asked Bobo to find out why the cops could only identify the body by the dental records.

Fingerprints would be the first method used and when Eddie was arrested on the murder charge, he was fingerprinted. Once your prints are in the system, they stay there. Period.

But I wasn't really sure he was actually alive until I saw Bobo lighting one of my Partagas *robustos*. In the aftermath of finding the corpse and then the freeway adventure with Sherrie and everything else that followed both those events, I'd forgotten that I'd taken a key piece of evidence off the body.

When I searched the dead man, I found a matchbook that had an ad on it for C'T' Tech. When I found out David Bradley worked at the same school and had been missing, the pieces started to come together.

It wasn't until I had Brooks check Bradley's dental records, that we found the real identity of the corpse. And that's when I knew for certain Eddie Cooke was still alive.

It was Lennon who was the reason the cops hadn't found out sooner. Brooks discovered he had falsified the forensics report. But nobody had seen Lennon since he'd been suspended. Why he would go to such lengths to hide Eddie's identity was still a mystery.

I still didn't know why Bradley was killed or even who killed him, though Eddie was the chief suspect. I had gone out to see Bradley's mother, but she was in the far stages of Alzheimer's and could only sit in her easy chair and stare blankly into space. Maybe some memories are best locked away forever.

Her neighbors told me she was a quiet, yet distant woman who raised both her boys on her own, most of the time barely getting by. One of them told me David had come into some money about a year ago and was paying for round-the-clock care for his mother.

Brooks was searching Bradley's bank records, but so far nothing unusual had come up. The only thing we had that connected him with Eddie was their meeting at Jiggy's a few hours before Bradley was killed. I knew in my gut Eddie and probably Marcy had something to do with his death. I was here in the backseat of Marcy's Jaguar to find out how.

Marcy had turned back to look out the windshield, her hands resting lightly on the steering wheel. I could see I'd punctured her veneer.

"I don't know what you're talking about," she said, but she'd lost her bravado. "Get out of my car. Now."

I didn't move. This was my play and I was determined to win the hand.

"If I get out of this car," I said, "I'm gonna start talking."

"You know nothing," she said. "No one will believe the ravings of a private detective of questionable morals."

"That's very funny," I said. "You lecturing me about morality. I'd laugh if it wasn't so pathetic. What about you spying on the tony clientele at Jiggy's? I saw the ledger. Every name on that list has been skewered by you."

"You can't prove a thing."

"Maybe, maybe not," I said. "But I can make a big noise if I want to. It's up to you, Marcy."

"What proof do I have you won't talk anyway?" she said.

"None," I said. "Except I don't like the spotlight. And besides, Eddie's going down with a bang. You'll just be an afterthought. You might even survive the fall."

She thought about this for a minute and gave me the answer by turning the ignition key. She pulled the Jag back onto the road, made a U-turn and headed back out to Laurel Canyon.

We didn't speak again during the drive, which took almost an hour. Part of the reason was crossing town during evening rush-hour. Marcy drove west on Sunset, following the crowded, winding road through Beverly Hills, Westwood, Brentwood and the Palisades all the way to its terminus at PCH. Then she headed north on the Coast Highway before turning up Topanga Canyon.

Halfway up Topanga, she veered up a steep side road, around a couple of drastic bends and down and up a series of even steeper and narrower streets before coming to a stop outside a wrought iron gate that was supported by a ten foot high stone wall.

"He's in there," she said.

"We don't have all day," I said. "Let's go."

"I'm not going with you," she said, handing me a small remote. "It's your funeral. The code is 6387."

I didn't want to argue with her. Besides, this was between me and Eddie. Marcy would only complicate things.

I got out of the car and tried the security code. The gate swung open and I walked inside. It took me 15 minutes to walk up the long driveway and when I got to the front door, it was open.

I let myself in.

The house was enormous. Made of stone and brick with the woods as background, it reminded me of the country homes of New England.

Inside, it was pure California. The foyer opened in to a grand main hall of polished Italian marble dominated by a spiral staircase that wound its way up to the second floor.

From the hall, you could see into the living room and out to the deck, and an enormous swimming pool. Beyond that was a good stretch of land sloping downward, giving a spectacular view of the Pacific Ocean.

It was difficult to see in the dusk, but I thought I saw a figure standing out on the deck amid the yard spots that shone onto the surface of the pool. As my eyes adjusted to the changing light, I saw that it was Eddie Cooke, standing there, watching me, and wielding a military issue flame thrower.

I held my ground and Eddie realized I was staring at his weapon. He gently laid it on one of the lounge chairs, unstrapping the power pack from his back and putting it on the ground next to him.

"It was the perfect plan," he said.

I walked out to the deck, slowly, never taking my eyes off of Eddie. He looked much older than the last time I'd seen him. Notoriety does that to a person.

He was wearing a smoking jacket with satin lapels over a polo shirt, khakis and loafers with no socks.

Seeing him up close after thinking that he was dead, was unsettling. I wanted to get out of there as soon as possible.

"So you found me out," he said. "How disappointing."

"For you," I said.

"Yes, well my luck hasn't been so good lately," he said. "I assume you already know about my money difficulties."

Through my research, I'd found that Eddie and Marcy were over-extended. They'd made some investments that didn't pan out and they were into the IRS for more money than I'd made in the last five years.

"You were so close to settling with the city," I said. "That civil suit was a slam dunk. And what about all your new clients?"

"So you're not the great all-knowing detective after all," he said.

I knew I had missed something. I knew it had to do with John Dennis Moore but I didn't know what the connection was. It was there in front of me, but I just couldn't put my finger on it.

"Let me help," he said. "When is a sure-thing wrongful prosecution suit suddenly not a sure thing anymore?"

"When the plaintiff is found guilty," I said. "But John Dennis Moore confessed to the . . ."

I realized then the clue Jim had dropped into my lap. He knew I'd think his confession was bogus. I didn't see it at the time, but he was trying to help me.

"You paid off Moore to take the rap for you," I said, the words pouring out of me as fast as the ideas came to me. "He was already guilty of six murders. What was one more? He was dying anyway. That way, you win the civil suit, you get to be an agent again. Everything works out."

"It was so perfect," he said. "So beautifully perfect."

"But they got greedy, didn't they?" I said. "Bradley came to you for more money?"

"And more after that," he said. "They were bleeding us dry. His mother had some disease and he didn't want to put her in a home. It was touching really, but I had to do something."

"Bradley was the same height, same weight," I said. "But you needed someone to take the fall."

"And I needed to disappear, Marcy could collect the money and six months later we'd be laughing about it in Monte Carlo or Belize. It didn't matter. New names, new identities."

"But why blackmail Jim?"

"That was the best part," he said. "Marcy found out about Jim's past by mistake. I knew he was your lawyer. We used him to get to you. You were, what do they call it in the movies? Ah, the patsy."

"It was a set up. You wanted me framed for your phony murder? Seems pretty risky."

"Not when you have help on the inside," he said.

"Hands up," said a familiar voice from behind me. It was Vince Lennon. I reached for the sky and turned to see him walking toward me, a slight limp where he'd been shot.

Suddenly Lennon's motivations were clear.

"Drop the gun," Eddie said.

I let the Walther fall to the pavement, then kicked it away from me.

"You did all this to get me?" I said to Lennon. "Do you hate me that much?"

"It's not personal," he said. "It's people like you I don't like. You're so righteous, you make me sick. You skirt the law for your own purposes and call it justice. Give me a break."

"You weren't a bad cop when you reined in that chip on your shoulder," I said. "Why throw it away?"

"Money makes the world go 'round," said Eddie. "Enough chit chat. Let's talk about me."

"Okay," I said. "You really did kill Bud Greeley,"

"The traitor deserved it." He was putting the flame thrower back over his shoulder.

"What are you going to do with me?" I said.

"Kill you of course," he said.

"Let me have the pleasure," said Lennon.

"Fire," said Eddie and I sucked in a breath and hit the deck. I heard someone groan, but it wasn't me.

I turned to see Marcy, holding a gun over Lennon who was lying on his stomach, writhing. There was a hole in his back where Marcy had just shot him.

"Thanks for your assistance," she said to him and shot him twice more, aiming and hitting his head. I climbed slowly back to my feet. Eddie flipped the switch on the flame thrower. I heard a whoosh as the weapon juiced up.

"Two bodies, male and female," he said. "By the time they ID the bodies, or what's left of them, we'll be so far off the radar they'll never find us."

He shot a burst of flame at the ivy that was crawling up his house and it instantly caught fire. He did the same to a spot on his yard. Ten days of Santa Anas had dried everything out and the fire began to spread with frightening speed.

He pointed the weapon at me.

"Isn't payback wonderful?" he yelled at his wife. She was still standing over Lennon, her gun tucked under her arm and a small compact to her face. She was applying lipstick.

fifty-four

There was no place to run. Even Carl Lewis couldn't get far enough away from a flame thrower in the time it took for someone to point it and pull the trigger.

"I was doing my job, Eddie," I said. "It was never personal."

"It was always personal," he said. "That's the part people like you never get. It was personal between me and Bud and it was never anything but that with me and you. At least I have the balls to admit it.

"You just hide behind the First Amendment and all that crap about justice," he screamed this at me, but somehow it came out measured, like he was in complete control of everything even though both of us knew he wasn't. "Capitalism is a rough sport. I play it to win. People should know what they're getting into before they ante up."

"Murder isn't supposed to be part of it," I said. "You're supposed to play fair."

"Fair my ass," he said. "Nobody plays fair. It's like the fucking Roadruner. He plays by the rules and the coyote has him for lunch. Beep. Beep. Game over."

"You're nuts, Eddie," I said, but he just laughed.

"Like this is a fucking revelation? C'mon, Zen, aren't you going to beg for your life?" he said. "Don't ruin my moment."

He pointed the gun at me and laughed and I watched his hand rest on the trigger.

"Revenge is a dish best served hot," he said, cackling like the madman he had become. A roaring flame burst out of the barrel at me.

I took two steps and rolled, grabbing my Walther off the deck and throwing myself head first into the swimming pool. I felt the flame singe the hairs on my arm seconds before I hit the water and the quick, sudden pain made me drop my gun. I watched it drop to the bottom of the pool amid a kaleidoscope of bubbles and fire, which was reflecting off the blue like a watery hell. I stayed under the protection of the pool as long as I could while Eddie sent waves of fire at me. Marcy was at the edge of the pool, emptying her gun.

Only when my chest was aching from lack of air, did I break the surface again. The entire deck was engulfed in flames and it was spreading into the yard and toward the trees, left dry by the recent weather. Soon the Santa Anas would catch the flames and if the wind was blowing in the wrong direction, half of Topanga would be on fire within hours.

I looked around for Eddie. He was running around like a wild man, setting fire to everything in sight. The house was burning. If I stayed in the water, I'd die of smoke inhalation. Already, I could feel it scorching my throat and my remaining lung.

I needed to get the Walther. I took another deep breath and swam to the bottom, grabbing the Walther and letting out my breath before I reached the surface. I broke the plane of the water coughing up water and breathing in smoke.

Another bullet whizzed by me and I knew I had to move. Fast. I had to get the hell out of here. I looked for a break in the flames and quickly pulled myself out of the water, rolling through a wall of fire using my wet clothes as a shield.

I couldn't go back toward the house. Eddie was there and the flames were now coming out of the roof. And suddenly, I heard an enormous explosion and a fireball flew skyward.

I sprinted toward the end of the yard, hopping over patches of fire and holding my hand over my mouth, to keep from sucking in the thick smoke that was all around me. I stopped at the edge and looked down.

It was dark, but I could see it was a good forty feet of rough terrain, rocks, small shrubs and other trees to the hard pavement of PCH. One wrong step and I was roadkill.

I looked back at the house, now engulfed in flames, and then saw Eddie, rushing toward me. Behind him, Marcy was firing toward us. I grabbed a tree branch and swung out over the slope, found a foothold and started to scamper down.

Above me I heard someone call my name. It was Eddie. His face was black with soot and part of his clothes were burned. He had a new weapon, a high-powered rifle with a sight. I was only about fifteen feet below him. At that distance, with that gun, even in the dark he could blow my head into a million tiny pieces.

I got as flat as I could against the ground and pulled my Walther out again. I wasn't sure it would work after getting soaked so I quickly pulled out the magazine, shook it dry and slammed it back in.

Eddie was aiming the rifle at me. Behind him the fires were getting higher and higher. It was as if he was standing in the very center of hell. The smoke was drifting toward me and in my exertion I was taking in too much of it.

My chest and throat were burning, and my breath was coming in fitful spurts. I could feel myself fading and only a near fall kept me from passing out.

A shot flew by my head and then another, even closer. I

wasn't going to make it like this. I stopped, aimed the Walther and fired. The third or fourth shot, winged Eddie on the shoulder and he stepped back in pain and shock.

Then he recovered and aimed again, but before he could pull the trigger, an explosion rocked the mountain and behind him flames shot up, engulfing his entire body in seconds. He tumbled off the cliff and I could hear his screams even after he hit the rocks below and went silent.

Then Marcy appeared. Her clothes were burning and she was screaming, but no sound was coming out. One of my feet slipped and when I looked back up again, she was gone.

But the flames were pushing onward, rushing over the side of the mountain down the slope at me. I hurried to beat them. Almost two-thirds of the way down, I lost my footing and plummeted to the ground. I remember hitting the soft dirt of the roadside. And then nothing.

fifty-five

I woke up in the hospital two days later. Everyone was around me. Sam, Bobo and Brooks. Dr. Sherman was staring down at me as if I was a specimen under one of her microscopes.

We had a conversation that I don't remember, but I'm told she didn't have to try hard to convince me to have that bullet removed from my chest. I said something about it being bad luck.

It doesn't sound like me, but there you are.

I suffered a few bumps and bruises and some pretty major smoke inhalation, but I came out of what was being called the great Topanga fire in pretty good shape.

The picturesque canyon, which includes bike trails, hiking spots and pristine areas of virtually untouched wilderness, wasn't so lucky. Ten days after Eddie started the fire, it was still burning.

I had stayed off my feet for a week after my operation, mostly because I didn't much feel like going anywhere or doing anything. Emily came by to say good-bye. She was headed to Minnesota to attend Billy Gray's school. It was being renamed after Jim.

Gary was staying in LA to testify against the Nigerians, but he hoped to join his daughter when everything was said and done. He was going to have to change his name, he told me; might as well change his life, too.

Jim's father drew his last breath while I was still in the hospital recovering from my fall. His family's secrets would be buried along with him. Billy wanted to come forward, but in the end we all talked him out of it. What would be the point?

Bobo had gone back to Minnesota and using notes he stole from Marcy's house, we started to piece together the rest of the story.

Nobody had ever missed Joe Conrad, a drunk who picked fights for fun and was bound to eventually lose one of them. Billy's role in his death might never be known, but there are nights, he says, when the broken memories come back to haunt him. He will have them always. Believe me, I know.

Billy had rebuilt his life, found something meaningful in it and was spending his days helping children to avoid the mistakes he had made when he was young. If that's not rehabilitation, then the concept doesn't exist.

Jiggy's was now under new management. It turns out that the Cookes were silent partners with Lunde. Marcy was using her access to get inside dope on the celebrities who hung out there. Eddie was using Lennon for muscle. Everybody was using everybody else.

It was Eddie who had my fuse box rigged, causing Sherrie's death.

I'll never know why Sherrie was there on my back porch that night. But whether she meant to or not, she had saved my life. It was too late for it to mean anything to her, but it made me feel better when I thought about it like that.

As for Noodles the wonder dog, well he was in the one place nobody thought to look: Marcy Cooke's house. He was never missing in the first place. It was all part of the set up. I'd found Eddie's first murder victim, he thought it was somehow symbolic that I be there for the second one. Noodles was just bait.

But with Eddie and Marcy believed dead, Noodles was heading back to Minnesota with Emily. They'd already become fast friends.

Brooks had asked me out on another date but I hadn't decided whether to say yes. I still might. I'm thinking about it.

I was lying on my couch, trying to make it through the crossword and listening to a melancholy Dave Alvin album on the stereo.

It was Sunday, exactly five weeks since the day I'd met Sherrie and I was still carrying around the wounds, both physical and emotional.

Eddie Cooke and Vince Lennon had showed me a kind of hate I'd rarely ever experienced. That it was directed at me made it even more disturbing.

I wasn't naïve. The world is a scary place, full of evil and random violence and you had to make your way with care. But I knew there was love and forgiveness, too and it was all around me.

I wanted to believe in the power of those things, that goodness was somewhere within all of us. I wanted to believe in redemption, that the devil could be cast aside, even here in the City of Angels.